INTO THE STORM

Also By Ray Gleason

The Gaius Marius Chronical

De Re Gabiniana – The Gabinian Affair
De Re Helvetiana – The Helvetian Affair
De Re Suabiana – The Swabian Affair
De Re Strigis – The Vampire Affair
De Re Belgica I, Boudica – The Belgian Affair 1: Boudica

The Gaius Marius Mysteries

Vindicta A Sanguine – Blood Vengeance

Also

A Grunt Speaks: A Devil's Dictionary of Vietnam Infantry Terms,
2nd Edition
The Violent Season

INTO THE STORM

RAY GLEASON

Copyright

Dedication

In Memory of
All of Us
Brothers and Sisters, Who Served
And Especially
Our 58,220 Brothers and Sisters
Who Gave All

Ayant perdu ses meilleurs amis dans l'effroyable lutte
Having lost his best friends in the horrible struggle
Apollinaire, "La Jolie Rousse"

Contents

1

The Bay, Part I

The boy sat on a sandy bluff overlooking a broad bay on the Hudson River. To his right, greenish-brown translucent waves broke on a rocky breakwater below the open, stark plain where the New York Central railroad yards hissed and steamed. Across the bay to the north, buildings poked out of rocky, wooded headlands like broken teeth marking the village of Groton-on-Hudson. Over his left shoulder, the north side of a wooded peninsula reached out into the river like an embracing arm curving back into the bay which it created. To the west, the blue-grey hills of the river's western shore shimmered as the cool river currents mingled with the sweltering airs of a New York August.

The boy sat well back, out of sight, in the shade of one of the many red maples that grew along the bluffs looking down on the river. He nestled on top of a carpet of the dead, brown leaves, remnants of departed summers. The shrill tones of summer cicadas were almost deafening as he inhaled the fragrances of decaying leaves, damp earth, and moss. Behind him, a patch of dense forest separated the river from a collection of bungalows on a hill known as Groton Point Park, where the boy spent his summers with his grandmother.

The woods were a place of magic. When the boy entered them, he was transported back to the forests of the Northern Adirondacks in the lands of the mighty Iroquois confederation. His T-shirt became a buckskin blouse, his dungarees fringed leather trousers, his Hi-Top sneakers moccasins. A long stick became a rifled musket; the short sticks, a hunting knife and a tomahawk. Chingachgook, the boy's Mohegan brother, had shown him all the secret paths of the forest, paths invisible to the eyes of white men, in order to reach unseen the "place of watching" overlooking Lake Champlain near the English fort at Crown Point, where the he now rested.

The boy had left the settlement along a well-traveled path through the forest that ran from the bungalows to the village meeting house where the settlers had their Saturday night parties and showed movies every Tuesday. Instead of continuing along this path, he turned off it as it dipped into a valley and onto an invisible deer path that followed the valley floor to the west.

This was the most dangerous part of the journey, Chingachgook had warned him, because the boy's movements could be seen from the meeting-house path. There were some in the settlement who would reveal these secret paths to the French for gold or furs. Or worse, the Iroquois, who only pretended to be friendly to the settlers, would discover his movements and ambush him in the lower valley.

After a quarter mile, the valley turned to the north; the boy was deep among the trees, safe from detection. From there, the valley descended toward the lake. Here, the walls of the valley pressed closely around the path and the trees blocked the sun. At the bottom of the valley, where the path brushed along the edge of the foul-smelling swamp of oil from the railroad yards, it branched in three directions.

Straight ahead, the path led to a sandy beach along the lake. There, a mad, white-bearded hermit lived in a wooden shack. Chingachgook had told the boy to avoid this man. The Manitou spoke to him. This was dangerous. But should the French and their Algonquin allies come down the lake to attack the settlement, this is the path they would use.

The thick trees and the steep hills surrounding the path would give the boy and Chingachgook a place to hold off the French until the women and children of the settlement could reach the stockade and the militia could be mustered to counterattack and push the French back into the lake.

Another path led east into a hidden, wooded valley. Chingachgook had told the boy that this valley was sacred to the Iroquois, and he should avoid it. Here the Iroquois took their captives and offered their blood to their savage gods.

Once he and Chingachgook had to raid the valley to rescue Alice and Cora, the daughters of the English Colonel at the fort. While they were in the secret valley, Chingachgook had shown him the flat stone where the Iroquois beheaded their captives. The stone was stained black and brown with the blood of hundreds of unfortunate victims. After a desperate fight, they were able to bring the girls out before the Iroquois could sacrifice them.

To the west, a path climbed up and over a sandy, wooded bluff to the place of watching, where the boy now sat, his musket across his legs, peering intently across the waters to the north for any sign of war canoes. If the French appeared, the boy would have time to reach the place of ambush where he would rendezvous with his Mohegan brother, Chingachgook. There they would wait, concealed in the forest, until the French and their Indian allies moved up the path from the beach into their trap.

As the boy sat under the maples, he remembered that it was Friday, the day his uncle and aunt came up from the city. He looked forward to this day all week.

Without thinking, he checked the cuffs of his dungarees for sand. His aunt was a bit fussy at times. She worried too much about dirt in ears, dirt under fingernails, washed hands and face. But, to the boy, she was a glamorous presence—tall, red haired, sophisticated and smart. She only drank cocktails and smoked only while seated like the pictures of stylish, society ladies in *Life* magazine. She was Claudette

Colbert to his uncle's Clark Gable, Nora to his Nick. If she were to fall into the hands of the Iroquois, who considered red-haired women were powerful magic, he would gladly risk the hidden valley single-handed to bring her out.

But that would never happen. Even the savage Iroquois feared his uncle.

He was a New York City plain-clothes policeman, a detective who hunted the cleverest criminals in the city's most dangerous neighborhoods. Even arch-criminals like Flat Top and the Joker feared the boy's uncle.

He was as tall and square-jawed as Dick Tracy, with piercing blue eyes that saw through every trick a criminal could think of. Most of the time, he wore a dark overcoat and a snap-brimmed fedora on the job. But sometimes he wore his police uniform, a navy-blue overcoat with two rows of bright gold buttons, a shiny, square, silver badge, highly polished black shoes with rubber soles, and his night-stick and service revolver strapped to his hip.

To the boy, his uncle had the class of Nick Charles, was as relentless as Phillip Marlowe, and was as clever as Boston Blackie. When he walked a beat in the city, the good people welcomed him, and the criminals fled.

The boy especially looked forward to those Saturday mornings when his uncle drove him into the village the settlers called Harlin for his haircut. He got to sit in the front seat of his uncle's big, green DeSoto. His uncle called his car the "Green Hornet." It had a police radio in the dashboard and a big searchlight next to the driver's window, which the boy knew his uncle used to search out evil throughout the night on the tough city streets.

They would drive together across the rickety, black trestle over the New York Central yards connecting the settlement to the village. His uncle drove with the windows down, his pipe in his mouth, singing "Red Sails in the Sunset," stopping only to point out the tower where the railroad stored its coal for the steam engines that ran upstate, and the roundhouse where the steam engines were repaired. Sometimes, a steam engine passed under the trestle as they drove, engulfing the Green Hornet in smoke and noise.

That used to frighten the boy, but Chingachgook, his Mohegan brother, had told him never to show fear in front of another warrior. And he knew that he could show no fear in front of his uncle so he would be thought worthy of joining him some day on the police force to fight evil in the city.

The boy knew he had to be careful around his uncle. Last summer, before he had proven his courage fighting the French and the Iroquois with Chingachgook, he had gone to the Tuesday night movies at the meeting house in the settlement. That night they showed a monster movie about a reptile-man with big claws, who lived in the murk of a swampy lake, and crept out at night to kill people who strayed too close to his lair.

One day, the monster kidnapped the movie's beautiful heroine. The boy wasn't sure why, but he had seen enough monster movies to understand that this was what evil monsters sometimes did.

Of course, the hero had to rescue her. He had a terrible fight with the monster under water and finally killed him with a speargun. The heroine, who had spent most of her captivity fainting and screaming, seemed strangely sad when the monster died. The boy didn't understand this, but he knew that this was the way heroines in monster movies sometimes behaved.

That night, after the movie, he had to walk through the dark woods to his grandmother's bungalow. Although he saw the monster get killed in the movie, he wasn't sure that was the end of it. And, with the woods, the river, and the swamps all around, the settlement was the perfect place for a swamp monster to hide. Didn't his grandmother always warn him and his older cousin, Janey, not to go out at night because, when criminals escaped from the prison down in Ossining, they would hide in these woods?

When he managed to get home without running into any monsters, he quickly assessed the weaknesses of his grandmother's bungalow against swamp monsters. The boy decided that a swamp monster wouldn't just try to walk through the door. They were much too cunning for that. He'd somehow get into the house with the water.

He examined the kitchen and decided the monster couldn't get in through there. The faucets and drains were much too narrow.

Then the boy remembered the shower that his uncle and father had installed in the bathroom. It drained directly under the house! Worse yet, in order to pee, the boy had to turn his back to the shower whose insides were hidden by a vinyl curtain. So, all the swamp monster had to do was wait until dark, creep into the house through the shower drain, and wait for the boy to go to the bathroom. He'd be a sitting duck!

So, he developed a plan to foil the swamp monster.

At night, when he had to use the bathroom, he'd first turn on the porch light, then he'd inspect the bathroom from a safe distance. If it seemed clear, he'd approach. But before entering, he'd snake his hand in through the door and flip on the bathroom light. He'd then check to make sure there were no monsters visible in the bathroom. Only then would he go in. Then, very carefully, he'd pull back the shower curtain a bit to make sure the shower stall contained no lurking monsters. Only then would he turn his back to the shower stall, march up to the toilet and pee.

This ritual served him well for most of the summer, until one night his uncle, who had been watching this little routine for a couple of days, said to him, "So, I guess you're not going to be a cop when you grow up?"

"Whatta you mean, Unc," the boy responded, "I still want to be a cop!"

"Well," his uncle replied, "You can't be a cop if you're scared of the dark. Cops have to search dark buildings for dangerous criminals with nothing more than a flashlight and a nightstick. But you can't get to the bathroom without turning on every light in the house. Then, you won't even go in until you've checked in the shower. What're you afraid of in the shower? A monster? Can't be a cop if you're afraid of the dark or monsters."

Now the boy knew his uncle was watching him when he went to the bathroom, watching and testing his courage to be a New York City cop. So now he had to march boldly across the porch in the dark. He had to enter the bathroom *before* he turned on the light. And he must never be caught checking out the shower before he went about his business.

All this worked out well for a couple of days until his uncle hid in the shower and, as soon as the boy turned his back, flung open the curtain and snarled exactly like a hungry swamp monster.

Even his aunt would have thought it funny, had the boy not peed all over the bathroom.

But now the boy was a warrior in his own right. With his Mohegan brother, Chingachgook, he had fought the wily French from Canada. He had defeated the fierce Iroquois. He wasn't even afraid to go into the woods by himself when Chingachgook was off on the hunt. In fact, in a strange way, the boy felt comforted surrounded by the wooded hills.

It was his secret place.

A magical place.

His place.

2

Soldiers of Christ

I

On a chilly Sunday morning in early spring, the students of Our Lady of Lourdes elementary school in Astoria, a working-class neighborhood on the East River opposite northern Manhattan, were filing into the parish church for the nine o'clock mass.

Each student wore the uniform of the parochial school. The boys, white shirts, blue ties, navy blue pants, black shoes; the girls, white blouses, blue cravats, navy blue jumpers with the school escutcheon emblazoned on the left breast over the heart, navy-blue knee-socks, sensible black shoes, no open toes.

The good sisters of the Sisters of Charity of St. Joseph, in their flowing black robes, starched white collars and headpieces, carefully policed their charges, rosary beads clicking as they made their rounds. Most importantly, the boys and the girls, especially the older ones, had to be kept strictly segregated as they assembled for mass — there could be no tolerance for allowing occasions of sin, especially among the older children. And, when they were assembled so closely together, as they had to be enclosed within the narrow alleyway beside the parish church, there was no telling where their hands were. So, boys to the front, girls to the rear, no mixing allowed.

Attendance was taken — the nine o'clock mass was mandatory for all students of Our Lady of Lourdes elementary school. Each student was examined for proper uniform, shined shoes, clean hands, fingernails, face, ears, haircut and missal.

At ten to nine, the children were filed two by two into the church through a side door to occupy the front pews on the gospel side of the altar which were reserved for the school.

Mickey Dwyer was among the eighth graders with his best friends Johnny Toussaint and Joey Simon or, as Joey was sometimes known around the schoolyard, "Joey the Jew."

Not that Joey was Jewish.

In fact, Joey's grandfather, Giuseppe Benedetto Simonetti, a fervent — at least by Italian standards — Roman Catholic, had immigrated to America from the southern Italian region of Calabria at seventeen years of age, just after America's war with Spain. The elder Simonetti had established himself on Henry Street on the lower east side of Manhattan, literally in the shadow of the Manhattan Bridge. He immediately got himself what he considered good, steady work helping dig the new underground railroad, or "subway" as it was called in America.

Between his twelve-hour shifts digging up the streets of lower Manhattan, Giuseppe took some time to contemplate his situation in his new homeland. Although he understood that America's streets were not paved with gold, he decided that America was in fact a land of endless opportunities for someone who was smart, ambitious, and willing to work hard, as long as one condition was recognized. Assimilation! You had to be white, speak English without an accent, and not be too Catholic.

So, Giuseppe Benedetto Simonetti Senior resolved that he would never again speak his native Calabrian dialect, nor the Italian he had learned in school. He would learn to speak English without an accent.

And, all his children, should God be so kind to him, would finish at least eight years of school in the wonderful, free, public schools that America provided for all of its citizens.

As a sign of his resolve to be completely American, Giuseppe Benedetto Simonetti renamed himself Joseph Benedict Simon.

The one thing the newly minted Joseph Benedict Simon would not compromise on was his faith in the Roman Catholic Church, which in his opinion offered the only path to eternal salvation, although sometimes it got in the way of his being hired for the better jobs.

The only flaw in Joseph Benedict Simon's plan for complete and seamless assimilation into the American dream, except for the Catholic issue, was that the name "Simon" sounded Jewish to many New Yorkers. In fact, when Joseph Benedict Simon the Third started the first grade in the parochial school of Our Lady of Lourdes parish in Astoria, and the teaching sister, Sister Maria Paulina, who had, like Joseph the Third's grandfather and father, grown up cheek and jowl with Jewish immigrants from Russia and Poland along Hester Street on New York's lower east side, read his name, "Joseph Simon," while taking attendance, she immediately blurted out, "Is that a Jewish name?"

To give the good sister her credit, she imagined that Joey's presence in her classroom was the result of the miracle of conversion and baptism which would save poor Joey's Jewish soul from the fires of eternal damnation. However, her announcing this assumption in front of the entire first grade class of Our Lady of Lourdes School became the crucible for Joey's survival in the Darwinian soup that was schoolyard and the neighborhood for many years to come, since, in the schoolyard, any flaw, any seam, any difference, no matter how slight or how tenuous, was exploited in the ruthless competition for survival and dominance.

At first, Joseph the Third had to put up with the mocking cry, "Is that a Jewish name?" from his classmates. And this was quickly picked up by the older, bigger boys.

Eventually, due to the efficient ecology of natural selection operating in the schoolyard, which abhors the use of wasted syllables and is forever in search of a good alliteration, the cry quickly evolved into the moniker, "Joey the Jew."

At first, Joey had to take it, being a first grader and one of the smallest kids in the schoolyard. He couldn't go to the nuns with it. That was "ratting," the worst crime imaginable to any kid trying to survive in the schoolyard. And he couldn't make the kids stop. Most of them were a lot bigger and certainly nastier than Joey had yet had a chance to become.

Once, when a seventh grader, a renowned and infamous schoolyard bully known as "Nugy" O'Reilly due to his practice of smashing smaller kids on the top of their skulls with his knuckles, called him "Joey the Jew," he ran home in tears and, in his terror and despair, made the egregious mistake of telling his mother.

Mrs. Angie Simon, whose formal, Catholic-school name had been Angelina Madelena Giudice, came from a family that had, within living memory, immigrated from a small village near Palermo. She herself had been born in the small back bedroom of a fourth-floor walk-up apartment off Delancey Street where she had lived with her parents, grandparents, brothers, sisters and an uncle or two, depending on who was working at any moment or who didn't want to be found for any reason.

Angelina Madelena Giudice was no stranger to the laws of the schoolyard, having cut her teeth in Transfiguration parish on Mott Street back in the days of the Great Depression when, as she told her children, "things were hard."

Angelina Madelena knew there were a couple immutable decrees for surviving in the neighborhood. First, never rat on anyone, especially to the cops, but certainly not to the nuns or priests. Second, never be a punk, a coward, or you'd never have respect and you'd be everybody's punk. Finally, for girls, never be a *puttana*, or you'll shame your family, never have honor, and never find a husband.

Angelina Madelena remembered well how she had learned that last lesson.

When she was in the seventh grade, one of the nuns doing her daily neighborhood patrol for sinners and delinquents caught her and her girlfriend smoking in one of the playgrounds under the Manhattan bridge. Of course, the nun frog-marched her home and told her mother.

When the nun left to take her girlfriend to meet her doom, Angelina Madelena's mother slapped her across the face. "*Sulu na puttana fuma fora di casa unni tutti la ponnu vidiri!* Only a whore smokes outside the house where everybody can see her." she shouted in little Angelina's face, "*Vuliti ca tutti ntô vicinatu pensunu ca si na puttana? Vuliti fari vergognari a to patri e a to famigghia?* Do you want everybody in the neighborhood to think you're a whore? Do you want to shame your father and your family?"

From this, Angelina Madelena understood that it was alright to smoke, just not outside where anybody could see it. To this day, Angelina Madelena only smoked in her own kitchen. Never outside on the street, never in front of her father-in-law, Papa Joe, who lived with them, and never in front of her children.

So, when a weeping little Joey the Third burst into her kitchen, she had to quickly hide the Lucky Strike she had only half finished while getting her husband's dinner ready for his imminent return from work.

"What's the matter with you," she asked her son, blowing a stream of white smoke up toward the ceiling, "You hurt?"

"No, Mama," wept little Joey the Third, "A big kid at school called me a Jew."

"A Jew?" exclaimed Angelina Madelena Simon.

Now she was confused. Why would anyone call her son *n'ebbreu*, a Jew?

Certainly, Mrs. Simon knew what Jews were. When she was growing up, they lived mostly around Hester Street. Her people never had any problems with Jews, unlike those damned Irish who were always drunk and always starting fights. The Jews kept to their neighborhood; the Sicilians kept to theirs.

She knew the priests said that all the Jews were going to hell for killing Jesus. But that was priest business, not street business. Besides, her neighbor on the first floor, Mrs. Goldstein, was Jewish and such a nice lady, always kind to little Joey. Mrs. Simon could not understand why God would want to send such a nice lady to hell. But that was priest business.

On the street, there were Jewish neighborhoods and Sicilians neighborhoods. There was Jewish business and there was Sicilian business. They never mixed. Typical of America. One country, many neighborhoods. Everybody kept to themselves, or there was trouble.

"Why'd this boy call you a Jew?" Mrs. Simon asked her oldest son.

"I don't know, Mama, I don't know! They do it all the time," Joey sniffled.

Now Mrs. Simon knew she had a problem on her hands. She just wasn't sure what.

"Who is this kid?" she demanded.

"Just a kid, Mama, just a kid," little Joey answered.

Good, Angelina Madelena Giudice of Delancey Street thought, he's not *nfurmaturi*, a rat.

"So, why're you coming home with this?" she demanded.

"He's big, Mama! He could beat me up," Joey sobbed!

Madonn', thought Angelina Madelena, he's a punk, *nu scantulinu!*

She remembered, once in the Transfiguration schoolyard, when she was in the fourth grade, one of the eighth-grade girls, who was at least twice her size, had called her *Angelina la Bambina*, Angelina the Baby, for no better reason than to impress her girlfriends. The bigger girl got to say this only once before Angelina Madelena had her on the ground and was pummeling some sense into her.

When the nun broke it up, she asked both girls who started it. Neither girl would break the schoolyard code; neither would speak.

Since Angelina Madelena seemed to be the aggressor, she was frog-marched into the school and given a few strokes with a leather belt. Angelina Madelena took her beating without making a sound. She knew even the nun respected her for not snitching, for standing up for herself, and for taking her beating without so much as a whimper.

This was the respect, *rispettu*, that every kid in the schoolyard had to earn and had to have. Without respect, you were nothing! So, Angelina kept her mouth shut, took her beating, and got respect for it. That's the way things worked in the schoolyard and in the neighborhood.

"Did anyone else hear him say this thing to you?" she quizzed her son.

"All the kids were there! They laughed when he said it!" Joey sobbed.

"So, you let this ... this punk say this thing to you in front of the whole neighborhood! And then you ran away crying?" exclaimed Mrs. Simon.

Without thinking, she grabbed her cigarette from the ash tray hidden behind the bread box on top of the ice box and took a deep drag.

Joey was amazed. His mama was smoking right in front of him. He knew she smoked, but never right out in the open like this!

She bent down into his face and lowered her voice so Papa Joe, her father-in-law, wouldn't hear her, "*Si chistu lu risolvi, pirdisti l'unuri. Nuddu ti rispettarà mai.* If you take care of this, you have lost your honor. No one will ever respect you."

Joey now knew he was doomed!

He should have thought this through before getting his Sicilian mother involved in a schoolyard fight. Not only was she standing right in front of him smoking a cigarette, but she was talking to him in Sicilian, using the magic words *anuri* and *rispittari*.

Using Sicilian in his family was like the priests using Latin in the mass. It was a sacred, magical, and binding language. The language of the old country. The voice of their ancestors. The sound of *obbligatu*.

But *anuri*!

Joey wasn't absolutely sure what that entailed, but he knew that when his Sicilian grandfather and uncles used the word, it was in a hushed voice, accompanied by solemn nods, like praying in the church before God.

Joey was now bound by *anuri*, the Sicilian language, and his mother's cigarette to go back to that school and kick Nugy O'Reilly's ass or die in the attempt.

Even at that young age Joey was sensible and had no inclinations to suicide.

He left the apartment, apparently on a mission to regain his *anuri*, but instead hid out for a couple of hours down the block at the apartment of Mickey Dwyer, his best friend. Later, on his way back home, he scraped his knuckles on the side of a building and told his Mama that he had done the deed.

Her terse response, "Good! Serves the punk right! Now wash your hands for dinner! You got blood."

Initially, Joey's only viable strategy for dealing with the "Joey the Jew" problem, was to ignore it. Never respond. Never let them know they're getting to you. Hopefully they'll get bored with it and go find a new victim. Unfortunately for Joey, having a "Jew" in the parish was too much a novelty to be ignored or forgotten.

Soon, the problem leaked from the schoolyard and permeated the neighborhood. Joey was safe on his own block on Crescent Street where he and Mickey lived. But anytime he had to leave that area of sanctuary, going to the deli to buy bread and milk for his mama, or going to the candy store to get his papa's newspapers and cigarettes, or walking to school, he was "Joey the Jew" to any kid who could make it stick.

This continued for some time with varying degrees of intensity and viciousness. Some kids actually believed Joey was Jewish. What a Jewish kid was doing attending a Catholic school in Astoria never seemed to cross their minds. But Our Lady of Lourdes school was not known for the scholarship of its charges.

In the fifth grade, two things happened to Joey the Third.

The first, he had a growing spurt and, almost overnight, the skinny little runt that Mickey Dwyer had known since the first grade, was over five feet tall and a good twenty pounds heavier.

Second, Joey the Third decided that he wasn't going to put up with this shit anymore. His new policy about the "Joey the Jew" issue was, if any kid said it to him — no matter how big, how tough, how well connected around the neighborhood — he would punch him in the face.

The implementation of this new policy was neither smooth nor flawless.

At first, Joey had to put up with a fair share of ass-kickings from the bigger kids. And, Mickey Dwyer, as Joey's best friend, had to back his play. So, he suffered his fair share of damage too. But Joey declared he would rather take a beating than have to put up with this shit any more.

Joey soon noticed that despite losing a lot of his "Joey the Jew" fights, the harassment lessoned and finally stopped, as the word went around the parish that, if you opened your mouth to this guy, he was going to come at you. You might beat him, but you were going to know you were in a fight! So, as is the eternal code of bullies, they went to find easier victims.

So ended the era of "Joey the Jew."

At least for the most part. Joey would tolerate some teasing from the kids he trusted, and Mick Dwyer always had his back in the bad old days.

So, when Joey showed up for assembly that Sunday morning, Mick greeted him saying, "Joey! What are you doing here? I didn't know Jews had to go to mass!"

Joey just smiled and said, "Keep it down, Mick! I'm undercover. I heard at the synagogue that Catholic girls are easy ... especially the Irish ones."

II

By the time they had gotten to the eighth grade, Joey and Mick were no longer a duo, there was a third member of their entourage, Johnny Toussaint, or as he was sometimes called, Johnny Two Saints or Johnny T.

Johnny wasn't one of the original gang. He had suddenly appeared among them in the fall of their sixth-grade year.

Now, having to integrate oneself into a group where the factions have already formed is difficult at best, but in Our Lady of Lourdes schoolyard, there was no place to hide. Without a gang, without someone to watch your back, Johnny had as much chance for long-term survival as a canary in a room full of starving cats.

Johnny T's second problem was he was dark in a sea of pale Irish faces — even darker than the southern Italians and Sicilians. So, he stood out which, when you got no one to back you up, was never a good thing in Our Lady of Lourdes schoolyard.

Then, there was the English problem — Johnny didn't speak it very well — in fact, he didn't speak it at all.

Cast adrift in a sea of first, second and even third generation immigrant kids, speaking unaccented English — unaccented, that is, to a working-class New Yorker's standard—was a necessary pedigree. Even the Irish kids right off the boat lost their brogues by the second grade. But Johnny T didn't just speak accented English; he really didn't speak anything much resembling English at all.

The final blow came his first day in the sixth grade at roll call.

In Parochial school, the good sisters insist on using "formal" Catholic names, not street names. So, Joey Simon was "Joseph Simon," because Joseph was a saint and the foster father of our Lord, Jesus Christ. Mickey Dwyer was "Michael Dwyer," because Michael was an Archangel, beloved by God.

So, the entire sixth-grade class quickly learned that Johnny T's formal, Catholic, nun-name, pronounced according to the good sister's south-end Boston accent, sounded like "Jean Mary Baptist Two Saint."

This was seemingly the final nail in Johnny's coffin. Not only was he a boy with two girl's names, but he was also named "Two Saint."

Then, as if matters couldn't possibly have been made worse, the nun announced that Johnny and his family came from a place in the Caribbean called Haiti.

Now, the sixth-grade scholars of Our Lady of Lourdes elementary school, despite having studied geography since the fourth grade, had only a dim understanding about the Caribbean and had no idea about a place called Haiti. Some of them knew that at one time, and maybe still, the Caribbean had been infested with pirates. But Johnny "Girl Names," who was kind of dark, skinny, and runty, didn't look like no pirate to them.

Some of them knew that the Caribbean was a place where rich people went on vacation. But Johnny "Two Saint" obviously wasn't rich; rich people didn't live in the parish. And they certainly didn't send their kids to Our Lady of Lourdes parochial school.

What they did know was the Puerto Ricans, who were moving into the upper west side of Manhattan by the thousands, came from somewhere in the Caribbean. And, the Cubans, who were buying up houses and apartment buildings all over Corona, were from somewhere in the Caribbean. They also knew that both Puerto Ricans and Cubans tended to be dark ... some were actually Negroes ... they had strange sounding names, and they didn't speak English very well, if at all. They had heard their fathers and uncles refer to these people as "spics."

Therefore, by the inescapable logic of the Our Lady of Lourdes schoolyard, the new kid, the outsider, was at least a spic, maybe a nigger, as their fathers and uncles also said.

All this took less than an hour to process and spread throughout the school. Johnny T didn't have a snowball's chance in hell of making it through his first week in the schoolyard.

Except for Mickey Dwyer, and by necessary association, his best friend, Joey "the Jew" Simon, intervening.

III

One of Mickey Dwyer's secrets was that he had a French grandfather.

Not that Mickey was in any way ashamed of his grandfather, or his French heritage, but Mickey had learned way back in the first grade that you didn't volunteer information like that around the schoolyard. There was no way of telling how it might rear up and bite you in the ass. Mickey was perfectly comfortable being just another mick in a sea of micks and wops, instead of being "Mickey the Frog," or "French Boy."

Not only did Mickey Dwyer have a French grandfather, he had M. Auguste Frederich Hussmann as a grandfather.

Auguste had immigrated to the United States just after the turn of the century, while his beloved, native Alsace was still occupied by Bismarck's and the Kaiser's Germanic barbarians, *les salles boches*. To his eternal shame, on Auguste's immigration record in Ellis Island, the American officials insisted on writing "German" as his nationality, despite Auguste Hussmann's insistence that he was *de France*.

When the United States declared war on Germany in 1917, M. Auguste Frederich Hussmann rushed down to the Marine Corps recruiting office in lower Manhattan to volunteer to defend *sa patrie*, not necessarily the United States, and strike a blow against *les salles boches*, who had been oppressing his people, not necessarily the Americans.

Yet again, to Auguste's shame, when having to deal with American bureaucracy, he discovered that, although his diminutive body just barely satisfied the minimum height requirement, he did not meet the minimum weight requirement to become a United States Marine.

Swearing never again to be defeated by the Germans, or by American officialdom, Auguste went to a near-by fruit vendor and bought all the bananas the man had. Then, he took the bananas with him to a bar a block away from the recruiting station, where, to the landlord's displeasure and horror, he ate them all and drank as much water as his tiny body could hold.

He then waddled back into the recruiting station.

This time he made the minimum weight requirement by three ounces. The first thing Auguste Frederich Hussmann did as a newly minted United States Marine was to throw up a gout of bananas and water on a shocked Marine recruiting sergeant.

Auguste Hussmann believed that all that was good and all that was worthwhile in civilization was expressed in French culture. Despite that, he did not object when his youngest daughter, whom he had named Jeanne Marie, though everyone in the neighborhood called her Joanie, got engaged to an Irish American serviceman named Dwyer coming home from the second German war in Europe.

Always a practical man, a most French virtue, Auguste was worried about his eighteen-year-old daughter and the way she was carrying on since her high school graduation. In the closing days of World War II, while the French and their allies were bombing Germany into the stone age, much to Auguste's delight, his youngest daughter was spending her time going to USO dances, hanging out in the service canteens, and, he suspected, a few bars, where she was collecting an impressive collection of hickies and autographed portraits of sailors and soldiers from practically every branch of the US armed services, "To My Dearest Joanie... All My Love..."

To Auguste's mind, marriage and family was needed to settle the girl down before the inevitable scandal. And the Irish, despite having no real culture or cuisine to speak of, were at least Catholics, though a bit too serious about it for French tastes, but Catholics none the less. Besides, his new son-in-law had fought alongside his beloved French to defeat Germany, a pedigree Auguste Frederich Hussmann could live with.

When Auguste's first grandson was born, blessedly a good ten months after the wedding, he was for some obscure and tasteless reason named after his Irish grandfather, Michael Aloysius Dwyer. Despite that, Auguste decided to give the child the most precious gift he could, the French language.

Auguste taught, coached, read to and conversed with his little Michel in French every chance he could. When other boys in the neighborhood were getting Captain Video space cadet uniforms and Hopalong Cassidy cap-guns for their birthdays, Michel Dwyer was getting copies of *Le Petit Prince*, and *Histoire de Babar, Le Petit Elephant* and Dumas' *Les Trois Mousquetaires*. Auguste, or "Pop" as Mickey called him, would visit his daughter's home and read to his Michel from the classics of French literary culture every chance he got.

Although Mickey learned to understand the words well enough, he didn't understand what most of this stuff meant. But Mickey did recognize the beauty of the poetry, especially the tragedy of Apollinaire, severely wounded in the Great War and his dying *cri de coeur* to his beautiful, red-headed lover, *la jolie rousse*. He simply didn't understand a thing about the eternal struggle between order and chaos.

Mickey especially loved the intimacy of sitting with his Pop on winter evenings and listening to the music of Pop's beloved French language. Decades of chain-smoking unfiltered cigarettes and drinking glass after glass of the sweet white wines of his native Alsace finally caught up with Auguste Frederich Hussmann in the spring of Mickey's fifth grade year, not long after his confirmation, which Pop was too ill to attend, Mickey was devastated. All that was French in Mickey was his Pop and all that was his Pop was French.

And so, on that fall day at the beginning of his sixth-grade year, when Mickey heard the name "Jean Marie Baptiste Toussaint," and, despite the nun's Southy Boston pronunciation, he instantly recognized it as a French name, and Mickey was instinctively drawn to the new boy.

Johnny T's differences — his darkness, his inability to speak English, his coming from some unknown and exotic place called Haiti — were rendered totally irrelevant. He was French! He was one of Pop's people. Therefore, he was one of Mickey's people.

IV

When morning classes let out for lunch on that first day of sixth-grade, Mickey spotted Johnny T standing on the corner where the sisters released the kids outside the school, looking a bit confused and disoriented.

Before the circling schoolyard sharks could descend and begin ripping Johnny T to shreds, Mickey walked up to him, offered his hand and said, "*Bonjour, Jean. Je m'appele Michel. Bienvenue à l'école.* Hello, Jean. My name is Michael! Welcome to the school!"

Johnny T's face instantly passed from shock to delight. Then, he flooded Mickey with a torrent of French that Mickey only half understood.

Mickey pulled Joey over to him and said, "*C'est mon ami,* Joey Simon. This is my friend, Joey Simon."

Joey had no idea what Mickey was talking about. In fact, he was a bit surprised by his friend, whom he thought he knew, speaking Puerto Rican. But he recognized his name and figured it was an introduction. So, he stuck his hand out and shook Johnny T's hand. If the spic was good enough for Mickey, Joey concluded, he's good enough for me.

Besides, if all the "Joey the Jew" shit that Joey had had to put up with didn't make him tolerant of differences, it at least taught him the dangers of being different and being isolated in the schoolyard. He didn't like it much when he was the target of the mocking and bullying, so he wasn't going to sit back and let anyone else go through that shit.

Now the other kids were absolutely amazed by what they were seeing.

They knew what a handshake meant — recognition... acceptance... a pact... and here were Mickey Dwyer and Joey Simon shaking hands with the spic. In fact, no one imagined that Mickey Dwyer, as Irish as Murphy's jackass, could speak Puerto Rican. Worse, Dwyer was a greatly respected "founding member" of the sixth-grade faction. He had been with them since the first grade. And, here he was, out of the blue, talking Puerto Rican and accepting this spic into their fellowship.

Despite any misgivings the schoolyard crowd might have about all these revelations, they now understood that to fuck with the spic was to fuck with Mickey Dwyer, and to fuck with Mickey Dwyer was to fuck with Joey Simon. And too many of them remembered the "Joey the Jew" beatings they had taken to want to try that again anytime soon.

So, if not accepted into the schoolyard, from that day forward Johnny T was left alone.

Mickey and Joey's first challenge was to transform Jean Marie Baptiste Toussaint into an American. First, Johnny got a crash course in New York English.

"Johnny, don't say '*n'est-ce pas*'," Mickey told him, "Say 'or what.' Like, 'you gonna pay me the money you owe me, or what!'"

Then, there was how to dress around the neighborhood. At school, because of the uniforms, dress wasn't a problem. But the first Saturday morning that Johnny T showed up on Mickey and Joey's block, they almost shit a brick. He was wearing a straw hat with a green hatband and thought it looked pretty svelte, for God's sake. Nothing says 'please kick my ass' in Astoria more than walking around with a panama hat on your head.

Some cultural issues weren't much of a problem, like baseball. Johnny T lived and breathed baseball. Even better, he loved the Dodgers.

Since the Dodgers used to play in Brooklyn before they broke everybody's heart and moved to the west coast in '57, like the goddamn Giants, and since Astoria was a working-class neighborhood, most of the kids were still either Dodger or Giant fans, like their fathers. The Yankees were still playing in New York, not that anyone in the neighborhood gave a shit. If you wanted to be a Yankee fan, move to Forest Hills or the Bronx with the rest of those white-collar, republican stiffs.

Johnny was a hell of a baseball player. Not much bat, but good leather, a dependable middle infielder with a lot of speed on the bases. There were still a few cultural burps, like the time Johnny took a called third strike that he thought was off the plate. He turned around and called the ump a *"maudit salaud!"* The ump had no idea what Johnny said, so he didn't even throw him out.

When Johnny got back to the bench, Mickey leaned over and whispered, "Johnny, *pas 'maudit salaud'... la prochaine fois dis* 'son of a bitch'. Johnny, not *'maudit salaud'* ... the next time say, 'you blind, you son of a bitch'"

The lesson took. The next time Johnny didn't like a call, he succeeded in getting his point across in good New York, working-class English and getting his ass thrown out of the game to boot.

Soon, in the schoolyard and in the neighborhood, everybody knew that Mickey, Joey, and Johnny were a team. Like the three musketeers from one of Mickey's favorite stories, you fucked with one, you fucked with all three.

They each had a role in the group.

Mickey was the *consigliore*, the reasonable one. If you had to negotiate your way around or out of a problem, he's the one you talked to.

Joey was the enforcer. If negotiations failed, Joey stepped in to settle things.

Johnny T was the clown. He loved to crack jokes, have a good time. But everybody knew not to piss him off. If Johnny T got on your ass, you practically had to kill him to get him off it. And that wasn't going to happen as long as Mickey and Joey had his back.

The guys around the neighborhood referred to them as "the Mick, the Spic and the Wop," but of course not to their face.

This made life good for the three musketeers, because now nobody ever fucked with them. They didn't try to run the schoolyard. With Mickey's easy-going, live-and-let-live attitude and Joey's experience being Jewish, they just weren't interested. It was live and let live as far as they were concerned.

But whoever was trying to run the schoolyard, or run the park where they played ball, or run various parts of the neighborhood, like the Crescent Street Kings or the Steinway Saints, knew better than to fuck with them.

Live and let live was a good policy when you were dealing with the Mick, the Spic and the Wop.

V

By that spring Sunday morning, they were at the top of their game. They were eighth graders, the biggest kids in the schoolyard. School would be over in a couple of months, and they would graduate and escape.

They all had made it into Catholic high schools.

Not being known for their scholarship, they had not been accepted into the new, elite diocesan high school in Astoria, *Mater Dei*. But they avoided shaming themselves, and their families, by being judged irrevocably stupid by the Catholic education system and being relegated to that anteroom of hell, the local public high school, Bryant.

So, next fall, the three musketeers would split up as they traveled into the city to three separate Catholic high schools that thought the souls of these barely C-level scholars were worth saving.

As they got ready to file into the church with the rest of their class, the line of girls drew parallel with the line of boys. Mickey knew he shouldn't be looking around — the nuns might catch him, or even worse, Joey — but he couldn't help but look for Lori among the girls.

Lori, or Loretta Margaret McShea, as she was known to the good sisters of Our Lady of Lourdes parochial school, and her family had moved into the ground floor of a row house on Mickey's block on Crescent Street about four years ago. The family came over from a place in Ireland called Cavan. Lori was the oldest of six McShea children, four girls and two boys, by Irish standards a modest-sized family.

When they first moved into the neighborhood, they all sounded like they were auditioning for bit parts with Barry Fitzgerald in *The Quiet Man*. But, after a while in Our Lady of Lourdes' schoolyard, they all were perfectly fluent in New York English. Lori was a year behind Mickey in school, a seventh grader this year.

Mickey had never had any interest in girls. But, for the last few months, something seemed to be changing. Gradually, he began to realize that he thought he might think otherwise. He wasn't interested in what girls did; that was all pretty silly and useless stuff as far as he was concerned. But he was becoming interested in girls themselves. Why? He didn't have a clue; because they were girls, he guessed. He never gave it much thought.

But whatever was going on, it was probably sinful and should be suppressed, because it felt so ... so ... strangely delightful and fascinating.

Mickey didn't want to suppress it, especially with Lori, even if it did endanger the salvation of his immortal soul. For him, Lori was a blond-haired, blue-eyed ray of sunshine in his shadowy world of predators and power in the schoolyard, the playgrounds and the streets of the neighborhood. She was smart, friendly, and Mickey even found himself hanging out with her on her stoop, but only when Joey and Johnny T weren't around.

Now, when he saw her, something seemed to happen inside him, something he didn't quite understand. But he knew he was fascinated by it, strangely elated, attracted by it, and frightened by it, too. He felt happy and strangely excited by just seeing her.

This made absolutely no sense to Mickey, but here he was on a Sunday morning trying to catch a glimpse of Lori on his way into mass. Mickey suspected that somehow this was not the best way to prepare himself to receive Holy Communion, the spotless white body of the sacrificial lamb, but he didn't want to miss the chance of catching a glimpse of her. He just couldn't.

Then he spotted her!

She was a few yards behind him in the girls' line.

How could he have missed her?

She was wearing a bright, pink ribbon in her short blonde hair. Not exactly part of the required school uniform, but Lori was a good student and a respectful girl, so the nuns cut her a break on the ribbon ... bright pink... *un cordon rose...* floating in a sea of white and navy blue ... the rose of dawn... *"la rose du monde, the rose of the world"* ... the rose of her smiling lips.

Suddenly the words of a poem that his Pop used to read to him came flooding back. Apollinaire following a beautiful woman through Amsterdam, a woman he had seen on the street. He stood outside her house hoping for another glimpse of her ... *"mes doigts jetèrent des baisers*, my fingers threw kisses".

"It took you long enough," whispered Joey in his ear, "How the nuns didn't spot you I'll never know."

"What are you talking about," Mickey hissed back, jerking his head forward.

"What am I talking about?" Joey whispered, "If that girl back there with the ribbon were cream, you'd be a cat the way you're lapping it up. You were looking so hard you almost walked into a wall. Who is that? Isn't that one of the McShea girls from down the block? You got a thing for Lori McShea?"

"No ... no ... I don't ..." Mickey stammered.

"Michael Dwyer! Joseph Simon!" their teacher, Sister Agnes Immaculata, hissed at them, "Talking in line, being disrespectful, right before you enter into the presence of the Blessed Sacrament! I'll talk to you two right after mass!"

After they passed Sister Agnes, Joey hissed into Mickey's ear, "So, Mickey Dwyer's got a thing for Lori McShea! Will miracles never cease, Lord, will miracles never cease?"

VI

"*Lectio sancti Evangelii secundum Lucam*, A Reading of the Gospel According to Luke," the priest intoned.

"*Gloria tibi, Domine*, Glory to You, Oh Lord!" his two altar boys responded.

Standing on the left-hand side of the altar with his back to the congregation, Father James Brendan Peters read that Sunday's gospel in Latin finishing with the ejaculation, "*Verbum Domini*, The Word of the Lord."

His two altar boys parroted, "*Laus tibi, Christe*, Praise to You, Oh Christ!"

Fr. Peters slowly and gravely descended the altar steps and walked toward the pulpit to deliver his Sunday sermon. As he walked, hands folded and head bowed in seeming meditation, he heard the thunder echoing off the stone walls of the church as over a hundred of the faithful took their seats after standing to hear the words of Christ read in a language that none of them understood. Fr. Peters then climbed the three stairs up into the pulpit and assumed his position hovering some five feet over the heads of his flock.

As his teachers in the seminary had taught him many years ago, he remained silent and still, waiting for the congregation to settle down. He rested his hands on the pulpit's marble rail and stared out over the heads of the assembled people focusing on the stained-glass windows above the choir loft in the back of the church. The morning sun was flooding through the clerestory windows illuminating the gothic cavern that was Our lady of Lourdes Church in glowing pastels, pinks, greens, yellows. Fr. Peters gazed into the eyes of St. Cecilia, who had stared down at the church for decades from her stained-glass window between the pipes of the church's massive organ.

As Fr Peters intended, the faithful presumed their priest was communing with some higher power hovering somewhere behind them, over their heads. Finally, when he was satisfied that even the children of the parochial school in the front pews had stopped fidgeting, he began.

"My brothers and sisters! And my children in Christ! I take as the text for my sermon St. Paul's Letter to the Ephesians, Chapter Six, Verse Twelve, 'For our wrestling is not against flesh and blood; but against principalities and power, against the rulers of the world of this darkness, against the spirits of wickedness in the high places.'"

"Our wrestling is with our underwear all twisted up our crack," Joey Simon whispered to Mickey Dwyer sitting next to him in the second pew practically under Fr. Peter's substantial nose. Mickey did his best to keep a straight, and solemn, face.

"Certainly, as good Catholics, we must struggle everyday against sin, especially against those pernicious sins of the flesh which seek to condemn our souls to the eternal fires of damnation.

"But, as St. Paul teaches, personal sin is not the only danger facing us, our church, and our nation in these troubled and troubling times. For, as St. Paul reminds us, 'the rulers of the world of this darkness,' the forces of worldly evil in the form of world communism, threaten our spiritual existence as in no time in our history."

"Communism is the blackest and most absolute evil afflicting humanity today! Why? First and foremost, it's atheistic. It denies the existence of God! And it despises Christianity! In every land and in every nation that this evil has infected, it has tried to destroy the Holy Church."

"Hear that, Johnny? I knew you Cubans were commies," whispered Joey.

"Can it," Johnny T hissed back, "He's going to hear you."

"Communism also hates our American way of life! The communists want to destroy our freedom of choice, to destroy our freedom of expression, and to destroy our ability to worship our God in this very church. Communism would forbid even these innocent children sitting here before me from praying to God and learning their catechism in school. Communism seeks to turn all Americans into its Godless, mindless, silent slaves!"

"No church! No more catechism drills," hissed Joey out of the side of his mouth! "This communism shit can't be all bad."

"Shut up!" Mickey hissed back, "You'll get us in even more shit with the nun."

"Today our country and our church are engaged in a great battle against the evils of world communism. Some call it a "cold war." But I tell you it is a real war nonetheless! And, at stake is the very salvation of our country and of our souls!"

"Already, since the end of the last great war in which many of our young American boys sacrificed their lives to destroy the hideous and fanatical fascism of Germany and Japan, the greedy jaws of communism have devoured Eastern Europe. There, it has destroyed churches, murdered priests and nuns, and enslaved the people of God in Poland, in East Germany, in Yugoslavia, and in Czechoslovakia."

"Now, Communism has reared its hideous head in Asia, devouring China and Mongolia. There it has destroyed our Catholic missions and murdered our Catholic missionaries."

"In Western Europe, Communism is attacking the still-free Catholic nations. In France and in Italy and in Greece, the very birthplace of democracy, courageous men and women of faith and of conscience are battling this communist plague in the streets and in the halls of government."

"In Asia, communism sent its Godless hordes into South Korea where, some ten short years ago, our American boys again were called upon to sacrifice themselves to push this red menace back into the hellish wastes of its own creation.

"And yet again, since the defeat and destruction of our French allies, communist gangs rule in Indochina, thirsting for the day when they can spread their poison into the fabled lands of Cambodia, Siam and Burma."

"And, my dear brothers and sisters, when these lands finally fall and are locked in the atheistic shackles of communist chains, how long will America be able to withstand this evil on its own."

"Most recently, communism has overthrown the democratic, Catholic government of Cuba and has established a communist, government, puppets of Soviet Russia, a mere ninety miles from our shores. Already, thousands of our fellow Catholics are fleeing the totalitarian torments of Castro and arriving among us with stories of the torture, rape, and murder of the faithful of Christ.

Let us now pause in silence and offer up a prayer for the suffering of our fellow Catholics on the island of Cuba and pray that God will give strength and wisdom to our President, John Fitzgerald Kennedy, to defend us from this communist onslaught."

"Hey, Johnny, Cuba, that's your old neighborhood?" hissed Joey.

"I'm from Haiti. Cuba's different," Johnny hissed back.

"But why should we fear what is happening in Cuba when the communists are already among us? They have disguised themselves as our friends, our neighbors, our co-workers. They have infiltrated our newspapers, our radio, on our television, our movies and, most sadly, our very government on which we depend to defend us from this terrible scourge. Our secular leaders, men of faith and conscience, constantly struggle to root out the communist rot affecting all aspects of our society."

"Do not fear, my brothers and sisters! As powerful and as menacing as communism appears to us today, it shall be defeated! It shall pass away! For, as Christ, our Savior, has promised us, at the end of time, when He comes again in glory, all things and all peoples of this earth will be subject to Him, and to Him alone. He will judge the living and the dead, and the faithful of our Catholic church will join with Him in the Communion of His Saints. All evil that denies Christ and persecutes his faithful on this earth shall be separated from his flock and condemned to an eternity of torment in the everlasting flames of hell! We shall be a church triumphant!"

"But, until that glorious day, when Christ, our Redeemer, returns, we, his faithful, must struggle with all our might, and with all our hearts, and with all our resolve, against this evil that besets the church. We must be Soldiers of Christ in the war against this black evil which is communism."

"We'll probably still be sitting here listening to him until 'that glorious day'," muttered Joey.

"Will you stop! He's looking right at us," whispered Mickey.

"As good Catholics, we must take arms against this evil. We must fight this communist scourge through our prayers and through our contributions to Holy Church.

But we must also fight this red menace through our actions. Support the efforts to root out communism in our society. Support our president in his efforts to root communism out of Cuba. Support him in his efforts to stop the expansion of communism in Western Europe and in Asia."

"He just blew through the ten-minute mark," hissed Joey out of the side of his mouth keeping his head straight and his eyes on Fr. Peters.

"Some of us are called to take up arms against communism, as members of our armed forces. These brave Catholic boys, these Soldiers of Christ, must confront communism directly on the battlefields of this world, as they did in Korea. And, as they must do in the future war to halt the expansion of this Godless plague to the free lands of the earth.

"My cousin Rocco was in Korea ... an MP ... said it was colder than a nun's heart," whispered Joey.

Mickey just shushed him out of the side of his mouth.

"And remember what our savior said in the Fifteenth Chapter of the Gospel of St. John, his most beloved disciple, "Greater love than this no man hath, that a man lay down his life for his friends. You are my friends, if you do the things that I command you. I will not now call you servants: for the servant knoweth not what his lord doth. But I have called you friends."

"So, I say to you, any Catholic who sacrifices his life in this war against communism, Jesus, our Lord, will call him friend and welcome him into the Kingdom of Heaven. The sufferings of these Soldiers of Christ on this earth will purge them of all sin and imperfection. If they should die in this holy struggle, they shall rise up as purified spirits and take their places in the glory of our Lord along with Saint Michael and all the Lord's beloved warrior angels, who defeated Satan and cast that serpent down into the fires of hell for all eternity."

"As Saint Paul writes in his letter to the Ephesians, 'In all things taking the shield of faith, wherewith you may be able to extinguish all the fiery darts of the most wicked one. And take unto you the helmet of salvation, and the sword of the Spirit which is the word of God.'"

"I call upon you, my brothers in Christ, as good Catholics and as good Americans, to become Soldiers of Christ! Take up the arms of righteousness to redeem the lands enslaved by communism as Christ took up his cross to redeem us from the deadly sin of Adam. Fight against this curse of communism with all your strength! Root it out! Destroy it wherever it manifests itself! Fight, sacrifice, and even be willing to give your lives for your enslaved brethren as Christ, our Savior, gave his life for you on Calvary's Mount when you were enslaved by sin.

Soldiers of Christ! Bring forth the day of the Triumph of Holy Church in the glory of Christ Jesus, Our Lord."

"*In nomine Patris, et Filii, et Spiritus Sancti*, In the Name of the Father, and of the Son, and of the holy Spirit."

"Amen!" echoed the congregation.

"Thank God that's finally over," whispered Joey, coming to his feet for the *Credo*, "I thought he'd keep us here 'til lunch."

VII

Father Peters came into the church from the sacristy still dressed in his alb and cincture. He gestured to one of the nuns.

"You're Sister Agnes, are you not? You have the eighth grade at the school," he asked?

"Yes, Father," she responded.

"Sister, two of your boys, they were sitting in the second pew next to that negro boy, they were talking and carrying on during my entire sermon!"

Sister Agnes' face reddened. "Oh ... that is probably Joseph Simon and Michael Dwyer. We have more trouble with those two ..."

"I want you to speak to them, Sister. Deal with them. They were most disrespectful. And, with Jesus right there on the altar in front of them! What have you been teaching these young hooligans for the last eight years?"

Sister Agnes' face was now burning. "I shall take care of them, Father. Oh, yes, I shall!"

VIII

An hour later, Joey Simon and Mickey Dwyer finally emerged from the church onto Crescent Street.

Under the close supervision of Sister Agnes Immaculata, they had spent an hour on their knees, on an unpadded kneeler in the side chapel, praying all fifteen decades of the Rosary, five decades for each of three, the "Joyous" the "Sorrowful" and the "Glorious" mysteries, a hundred fifty Hail Mary's, fifteen Our Father's, one Apostles Creed and an Act of Contrition thrown in for good measure.

Before releasing them, Sister Agnes had made both boys promise to go to confession the very next Saturday afternoon and confess to Fr. Peters that they had disrespected the Blessed Sacrament, the Mass, and him by talking and carrying on during his sermon. So, the boys could look forward all week to another thorough tongue lashing and another hour or so on their knees begging God for forgiveness.

The good news, as far as the boys were concerned, was that they didn't have to take a beating from the nun. Sister Agnes rarely raised her hand to her students, but she had other more subtle ways of getting her point across, as the boys' aching knees bore witness. Now, if they could figure some way of explaining to their parents why they were over an hour late getting back from church, they were home free.

"I never saw old Aggie Mac so pissed off! Her face was so red I thought she was going to explode," said Joey.

"Christ! How am I going to explain this one to my ma," responded Mickey, "I was supposed to bring the rolls home from the bakery for my old man's coffee."

"Just tell her you were over my house," said Joey, "I'm sure as hell going to tell my mom I was over yours. They never check anymore."

"I just wish you wouldn't pull that shit in church, Joe!" said Mickey. "We only got a couple more months of this shit and we're sprung."

"That's a fine way to show your gratitude," sniffed Joey, pretending to be insulted.

"Gratitude! What the fuck are you talking about? Gratitude! For what? I just got reamed out by Aggie Mac, my knees hurt so bad I may never be able to walk right, and I got more of this shit to look forward to Saturday!"

"Ah, my child," quipped Joey, "Had the good sister not kept you after church, you would have sought out the fair-haired and lovely Lori McShea right after mass. Then, right after having received the sinless and immaculate body of Christ, you would have filled your perverted and twisted guy-mind with sinful and lecherous thoughts. And, as the good sisters have often taught us, even to think such dirty things is in itself a mortal sin. So, this morning, I have saved my best friend's soul from an eternity in hell. Or, at least from a bad case of blue ball."

"You've got one twisted mind, Father Joe," answered Mick, "One really twisted mind."

"Come, my dear fellow soldier of Christ," said Joey, grandly gesturing down Crescent Street, "There is no time for girls when we must dedicate ourselves even unto death to the holy crusade against the curse of Godless communism."

"Rosemonde"

Michael A. Dwyer
St. Agnes High School

September 30, 1964
French 4 Translation Exercise

"Rosemonde"
by Guillaume Apollinaire

Standing a while on the steps
Of the house the lady entered
She whom I had followed
For two happy hours in Amsterdam
My fingers threw kisses
But the canal was deserted
The embankment too and no one saw
How my kisses found her
The one to whom I had devoted my life
That day for more than two hours
I christened her Rosemonde
Hoping to be able to recall
How her mouth blossomed in Holland
Then slowly I withdrew
To seek out the Rose of the World

3

A Duel in the Sun

Pat Green has one more batter to face. At least that's what he hopes. If he can get this guy out, his school, the St. Xavier Academy for Boys, wins the game and wins back the Bishop's Cup.

It doesn't matter that their regular season had been mediocre at best ... why not just call it what it is ... their season sucked. They have a seven and sixteen record and this is their last game.

But any season they beat their arch-rivals, St. Agnes High School, is a good season.

Besides, this is Pat's last game in high school. He's going to Fordham in the fall, the Engineering Program. Still, he'd like to end his high school baseball career on a high note, a win over St. Agnes and the Bishop's Cup.

Traditionally, there always has been bad blood between the schools ... why not just call it what it is ... the schools hate each other.

The St. Francis Xavier Academy for Boys is a Jesuit school on the upper west-side of Manhattan that's strictly college prep; a student must have at least a B average just to get in. Tuition's high, fifty dollars a month, and mandatory. Most of its grads go on to college, hopefully, to a good Catholic University like St. John's in Queens or Fordham up in the Bronx. Even a "public" college like NYU or Columbia would do in a pinch.

Every year, one or two of their more gifted boys actually achieve Irish-Catholic, academic nirvana and is accepted to Notre Dame, way out in some distant and mysterious place west of New Jersey, called South Bend, Indiana. Such a wondrous occurrence is always mentioned by Father Rector during his graduation remarks.

Of course, there is always the fond hope that one, or maybe two, should Jesus be so kind, of St. Xavier's graduates will decide to enter the priesthood, and go on to the seminary, preferably a Jesuit one.

In order to nurture the vocations of the chosen few, and good academics for the rest of the boys because the good fathers know that teenage girls make teenage boys stupid, the school does not encourage their charges to socialize with members of the opposite sex. Being caught in a "public display of affection" with a girl within two blocks of the school gets a student a week of detention. Of course, there are no school dances, and during the summer, the boys are encouraged to avoid mixed company, as well as other occasions of sin, and to attend mass every morning.

St. Agnes is more of a"working class" institution. It's a Marist Brothers school in mid-town near Grand Central whose goal is to give any Catholic boy, who desires it, a good, Catholic education despite any disadvantages, financially and academically.

Their goals are as modest as the clay with which they work. The good brothers prepare their students to go on to one of the better jobs open to Catholics in New York City: the cops, fire department, sanitation, the subway, the buses, the trades or, for a lucky few, a white-collar with the city. In recent years, some of St. Agnes' more promising grads actually got jobs with the phone company as messengers and frame men, demonstrating how liberal the city had become since the war.

The school happily takes boys whose academic disabilities prevent them from getting into any of the better Catholic schools, even the recently arrived Puerto Ricans from the West Side and the Cubans from over in Corona, good traditional, Catholic cultures both, whose conduct and English are, shall we say, challenging. Tuition is nominally set at twenty-five a month, or whatever a family can afford.

The good brothers of St. Agnes have no delusions concerning the academic and social potential of their graduates. They assume that their boys' most hopeful contribution to the future of Holy Mother Church is the begetting and nurturing of the next generation of Catholics. This, of course, requires an early marriage with a good Catholic girl, before the boys can become distracted by the alluring wiles of sinfully infecund and extra-marital sexuality with some non-Catholic or even worse, non-Christian.

In order to facilitate this holy mission, the school organizes frequent mixers with the Catholic girls' schools around the diocese, even going as far afield at times as the Diocese of Brooklyn, just across the river. A student can of course bring a date, as long as the girl is Catholic and is in good standing at some high school, even a public one; calls have been known to be made concerning this. Of course, these dances are carefully chaperoned and the behavior of the children carefully scrutinized by the brothers of St. Agnes and the teaching sisters of the guest school.

Although the good brothers look forward to the next generation of Catholics, there's no hurry to get it started. Slow dancing too closely merits a warning; a second offense means being thrown out of the dance, boy and girl separately of course, and one week of detention for the boy. Being caught making out with a girl on school premises is good for four weeks of the "Big D" and being banned from dances for a semester.

So, the boys of St. Agnes consider the boys of St. Xavier a bunch of spoiled, lace-curtain pansies, while the boys at St. Xavier consider St. Agnes boys a bunch of ignorant, shanty-Irish losers.

That is the polite way of expressing the rivalry. If one were to ask one of the boys what they thought about their opposite numbers, out of the hearing of any of the Marist brothers or Jesuit priests of course, the most common answer heard would be, "They're a bunch of assholes!"

To exacerbate the situation, sometime back in the early forties, some Marists and Jesuits got together, probably over a sacramental bottle or two of twelve-year-old Irish, good Catholic stuff, not that Prot swill from the north. After a prodigious sharing out of the water of life amongst themselves, and a long, heated argument over which major-league baseball team truly represented the spirit of New York and Irish Catholicism, the Yankees, Giants or even the lowly Brooklyn Dodgers, they came up with the grand idea for an annual baseball competition between the two schools.

Although most ideas are "grand" only after a few belts of the gargle, the Archbishop of New York, Francis Joseph Cardinal Spellman himself, may His Excellency be loved for as long as he lives and live as long as he's loved, liked the idea so much that he donated a large sterling-silver cup, which forever after would be called the "Bishop's Cup."

The winner of each year's game was awarded the cup at their graduation ceremony in June by the Cardinal himself, may His Excellency be loved for as long as he lives and live as long as he's loved, and got to display it in the center of their trophy cabinet.

It was also rumored, at least among the boys, that the Cardinal himself, may His Excellency be loved for as long as he lives and live as long as he's loved, gave the faculty of the winning school enough of the sacramental, twelve-year-old Irish, good Catholic stuff, not that Prot swill from the north, to fill the cup to the brim.

Up the Republic!

So, boys, priests and brothers all took the game seriously.

On the day of the game, all classes were of course cancelled. The entire congregation of each school, students and faculty, even the alumni, attended a special mass at nine a.m., St. Xavier in its auditorium, St Agnes in the parish church next to the school.

There, each school asked Jesus, the Blessed Virgin, and all the saints, especially Saints Patrick and Michael the Archangel, to intercede for them, to give them victory, and to smite their cross-town, cross-cultural rivals, who on that day were no better than a bunch of snotty-nosed, shifty-eyed Prots and heretics.

After mass, faculty, students and alumni *en masse* got on the subway, the Eastside IRT for St. Agnes, the Independent Line for St. Xavier, and travelled to a ball field up in the Bronx for the annual game between the two Manhattan schools. The Bishop's Cup itself was carried up by the previous year's winner, and prominently displayed behind home plate on a table, covered in rich, shining, red fabric, bordered in gold, for that year's winners to take back to their school in triumph after the game.

The crowd, after a few nips of the holy water of life from silver flasks on the St. Xavier side, and pint bottles in brown paper bags on the St. Agnes side, got quite vociferously involved in the game. Even a few fights were known to break out, now and again. But, with a crowd full of cops, firemen, city politicians, and clergy, the fights never lasted long or amounted to much of anything more than some mussed hair, a rug or two askew, a torn shirt or an occasional bloody nose.

After all, the day was for the boys, baseball, and the greater glory of God.

On this particular fine New York City morning in late May, with the illustrious Bishop's Cup, the pride of the school, and a couple of fifths of fine, twelve-year-old Irish at stake, the good Catholic stuff, Pat Green toes the dirt in front of the pitching rubber trying to fill in a small ditch.

Part of the trouble with playing their games on a city field is that the Parks Department provides little to no grounds maintenance. The kids who play here, when there's no high school games scheduled, just tear the field up and leave it that way. The pitcher's mound and the right-handed batter's box always take the worst beating. When this game started, the batter's box was so badly dug up that a right-handed batter almost needed a ladder to climb out of the hole and get up the first base line.

With his spikes, Pat toes in enough dirt into the fissure in front of the pitching rubber so that he won't break an ankle trying to throw a pitch. Since there's a man on second and he's pitching from the stretch, it isn't that big a deal. But it annoys him, and at this point of the game, he doesn't need any distractions.

They should be out of it, he grumbles to himself.

They came into the last inning up two to one. Their starter, Pat's classmate, Guy Franks, still looked strong and he was facing the eight, nine and lead-off hitters. He should have had at least two outs before St. Agnes could send any serious lumber to the plate. That was the theory, anyway.

But the wheels began to wobble when the lead-off man walked on what Guy thought was a strike three. From Pat's position at shortstop, the pitch looked like it broke right across the middle of the plate. But the umpire called it a ball and gave the batter first base.

Unfortunately, for someone who lived and died on his curve ball, Guy had a bad habit of losing it when he didn't like a call. After that one, he stood on the back of the mount mumbling and cussing out toward the outfield.

The wheels really began to shudder when Guy went 0 and 3 to the number nine hitter. This was a guy to whom he should just throw fastballs over the plate and dare him to hit it.

The first pitch was a high fastball, a little inside. The batter over-acted, stumbling back out of the batter's box, and the St. Agnes bench started giving Guy shit about the dust off.

Guy's second pitch was a curveball, his bread and butter. It froze the batter, who was still thinking about the chin music he had just seen, and the ball looked like it broke right over the plate. Blue missed it again and called it a ball. Ball two.

Then, Guy started popping off at the home-plate umpire, never a good idea with the guy who decides whether your pitches are balls or strikes.

Since the ump didn't seem to know how to call a curve, Guy's next pitch was another fast ball. Again, the pitch seemed belt high and well on the inside part of the plate. Again, the ump called it a ball. Ball three.

With that call, Guy came off the mount toward the plate.

Father O'Dea, their coach, came running onto the field to intercept Guy, while calling for time.

Pat was running toward second from his position at short in case the runner tried to advance in the confusion.

Petey McKenna, their catcher, was running toward the mound, ball in hand, trying to stay between Guy and the umpire, and keep an eye on the runner, all at the same time.

The St. Agnes base runner got caught up in the drama and was standing flat footed about six feet off the bag.

Petey spotted it and fired the ball to Tony, their first baseman covering the bag, who tagged the runner.

The first out!

But, no!

The infield umpire called "no play" because time was out, although no umpire had called it.

The wheels were now completely off the cart for the Xavier nine.

Fr. O'Dea got things settled down and Guy back to the mound. Then, he called Pat over to the rubber.

When Pat got there, Fr. O'Dea handed him the ball and said, "Get me three outs and we can go home," and retreated back to the bench with Guy in tow.

Coach sent one of their sophomore JV players out to take second, and the second baseman, a junior in his first varsity season named Jack McKinnis, moved over to take Pat's spot at short.

In his own mind, Pat wasn't a pitcher. He didn't like to pitch, but the team was thin on pitching that year.

They had three starters, barely. There was Guy, and another senior, Steve Badlissi. Both guys threw a lot of junk, because they couldn't sneak their fastballs past a little league hitter. When they were getting the call with the curveball, and the hitters started moving up in the box looking for it, even their fastballs were effective.

That's when they could get the call with the curve.

When they couldn't, it was a long day for St. Xavier, usually ending when the slaughter rule was mercifully called in the fifth inning.

St. Xavier had another starter, a big strong polish kid from St. Stanislaus parish in Queens, a sophomore named Stanley Kolodziejski, whom everybody called "Alphabet."

Alphabet didn't pitch. He just reared back and threw. The result was a baseball hurdling towards the plate at over eighty miles an hour. Most batters just watched the pitches zip across the plate, took the strike, and thanked God for sparing them.

The problem was Alphabet could only keep this up for three, maybe four innings. Then a combination of the better hitters getting his timing and his arm running out of gas ended his day.

Alphabet wasn't available. He had pitched two days ago, a 13–2 loss to St. Thomas Aquinas, who scored most of their runs in the fourth inning ending the game in five, so he was in right field hoping he didn't have to make any throws with his sore arm.

Steve was available, but Fr. O'Dea didn't want to take a chance with him and his junk pitches. This umpire didn't seem to like curve balls all of a sudden.

So, Steve stayed on third and Fr. O'Dea gave the ball to Pat with a runner on first, a 3-0 count on the hitter, a one-run lead, the last inning, three outs to get and the Bishop's Cup shining in the sun behind the backstop.

Pat took the ball and filled in the mound so he could throw a pitch without falling off the pitching rubber. He put his right foot against the front of the rubber and looked in for the sign.

Petey dropped one finger, fast ball, right down the middle. What else on a 3-0 count to a weak hitter, who was taking all the way.

Pat came to the set position ... got his grip, two fingers across the seams ... checked the runner on first ... looked back at the plate ... broke his hands ... slide step toward the plate ... picked up the catcher's mitt ... arm reached back ... shoulder, hips, hand exploded through the release point ... follow through ... see the ball into the catcher's mitt.

The ball popped into Petey's mitt with an explosion of dust.

No swing!

The batter took it, looking for the walk.

Pat got the call. Strike one.

Pat took the ball from his catcher.

He stood behind the rubber and rubbed the ball up.

Count, 3-1 ... no outs ... runner on first ... go back ... do it again ... same pitch ... don't put the winning run on base ... don't put the tying run in scoring position ... he's still taking ... can't give up the walk.

Pat glanced at short ... saw Jack give the new second baseman the sign for who covers on the steal.

Come backer to me ... look to second, Pat thought.

He got back on the mound, put his right foot against the front of the rubber, and looked in for the sign.

His catcher dropped one finger. Another fast ball down the middle.

Pat came to the set position ... got his grip on the ball ... checked the runner.

Before he broke his hands, he said out loud, clearly so the batter could hear him, "Here it comes again."

He saw something register in the batter's eye ... "I was going to take the pitch, but ..."

Pat broke his hands ... stepped toward the plate ... picked up the catcher's mitt ... delivered the pitch.

The batter's concentration was broken.

He swung ... timing off ... little late ... bottomed the ball... pop up ... right side ... foul territory ... too far for the catcher.

Pat pointed at the ball... yelling, for the first baseman "Tony! Tony! Tony!".

Tony looked up ... spotted the ball ... back-pedaled up the line.

Pat moved to cover the bag ... the runner retreated.

Tony caught it ... immediately looked for the runner ... saw him still on the bag.

Tony ran the ball back into the infield.

Good man, Pat thought, don't throw unless you have to.

Tony tossed the ball over to Pat.

First out ... pop foul on 3 and 1... that's why you're hitting ninth, rube, Pat thought, as the St. Agnes batter retreated back to the bench.

Get ready for the next batter ... their lead off guy!

Forget and Focus, Pat thought.

That's how Fr. O'Dea taught the game, "Forget and Focus." Don't let the last play, good or bad, affect the next. Forget it. Focus on the next pitch, the next play.

We caught a break, Pat knew, now forget about it. Focus on the next hitter ... the next pitch.

Pat watched from the back of the mound as the next hitter took a couple of practice swings.

Pat had seen this guy hit three times today. A Puerto Rican kid, named Cruz. Had some speed on the bases. He liked to go deep into the count ... would take the walk if it was there.

I need a ground ball, Pat thought. *Left side's stronger than the right ... first time up he walked on five pitches ... we nailed him trying to steal second ... second time, he lined a hit into left on an inside fast ball around the letters ... got to third on a base hit ... died there ... third time, flew out to left on the same pitch ... maybe a little higher ... likes to pull ... likes the inside pitch ... little up in the zone.*

The batter was in the box, ready.

Blue gave the signal to pitch.

Pat put his right foot against the rubber, looked in for the sign.

Petey dropped one finger, fast ball, outside.

Good ... Petey's been paying attention ... fast ball, outer half ... low.

Pat came set ... got his grip across the seams ... checked the runner on first ... broke his hands ... slide step toward the plate ... picked up the target ... through the release point ... follow through ...

Ball's hit the catcher's mitt ... batter took it.

The umpire stabbed his right hand in the air, strike one called!

That should get the bat off your shoulder, Señor, Pat thought.

Pat took the ball back from his catcher. He walked behind the mound, rubbing it up.

What next? Still need the grounder ... double play, game's over ... focus ... just get the out ... don't let the game play out too far out in your head ... that's how you get burned ... focus on your next pitch.

Cruz was back in the box.

The umpire dropped his hand calling for the pitch.

Pat took the rubber ... looked in for his sign.

He saw Petey look down at the batter's feet. Lead foot's a bit closer to the plate than the trail foot.

He's looking outside.

Petey dropped one finger ... fast ball ... patted his left thigh, inside.

Pat nodded and came set ... got his grip ... checked the runner on first ... no lead ... looked toward the batter ... broke his hands ... the ball came through the release point... sailed right under the batter's hands, inside part of the plate.

It froze him.

Blue called another strike.

Cruz didn't like the call. He stomped out of the batter's box ... his mouth was going ... kicked up some dirt.

The umpire watched the demonstration, daring him to challenge the call.

Petey flipped the ball back to Pat.

0-2 count ... way ahead on the count ... still one out ... runner on first ... could use a ground ball ... trust the defense ... give him the same pitch ... he won't take it again ... too close ... he'll ground it to short.

The batter was back in the box. He was still talking to himself ... bat going back and forth furiously ... lost his focus.

I own your ass, Señor.

Blue signaled time in.

Pat put his right foot on the rubber, looked in for the sign.

The catcher dropped one finger, fast ball, pats his right thigh, outside.

Pat saw the batter's feet squared ... he's looking inside.

Pat shook off the sign.

Petey looked down at the batter's feet, then at the way his hands holding the bat were white-knuckled ... holding the bat too tight ... slow through the zone ... won't get around on the inside pitch ... then patted his left thigh ... come inside.

Pat nodded.

He came set ... got his grip ... checked the runner ... looked back ... broke his hands ... delivered the pitch.

Cruz swung.

Ground ball ... skipped past the mound on Pat's right side... just beyond his reach ... heading for short.

Pat broke for the third base line, watching the play.

Jack was in position ... square to the ball ... glove down.

The ball hit something on the infield dirt ... it skipped ... its trajectory rose ... it seemed to pick up speed ... Jack rose out of his crouch adjusting to the ball's path ... the ball bounced off the heel of his glove ... hit him in the chest ... fell to the ground in front of him ... he picked it up ... looked toward second... no play ... threw to first.

From the third base line, Pat thought the runner was through the bag ... safe.

The infield umpire yelled, "Out!"

Cruz turned ... a look of anguish and disbelief on his face.

The St. Agnes' bench erupted.

Cruz jumped up and down on the base path ... slammed his helmet down on the infield dirt.

The runner on second looked confused.

Pat screamed for the ball pointing at the runner

The St. Agnes coach ran out onto the field

The first baseman finally woke up ... he ran the ball into the infield, eyes on the base runner at second d... the runner retreated back to the bag.

The two umpires, Cruz and the St. Agnes coach were in a tight knot of waving arms at first base.

Pat and most of his infield stood behind the mound and watched the show. They knew the call was not going to get reversed. Too much ego involved for the umpires.

Two down and one to go.

As far as Pat was concerned that was a giveback from Guy's earlier strike out being called a walk.

It's just baseball.

What goes around, comes around.

That's the way the game works. Got to forget it. Get it out of your mind. Stay focused. Play through it.

The St. Agnes coach was really raising hell with the umpires.

Good! Now their wheels are wobbling ... go ahead... piss off the umpires ... just keep it up ... that's got to be worth a couple of close pitches called strikes.

Respect the game, that's what Fr. O'Dea taught them, respect the game. She gives and she takes as she sees fit. Sometimes she hands you a break. When that happens, just take it and keep your mouth shut. But don't expect another. That's not how she works. She gives and she takes. Bad call puts a guy on first. Bad call keeps a guy off first.

Baseball's a fickle bitch.

Mick Dwyer watched the play from the on-deck circle.

It was a bull-shit call. Julio was across the bag when the ball got there. So instead of runners on first and second, one out, I got a runner on second, two out, he thinks.

Pitcher's got decent speed. Throws all fast balls. No breaking stuff. Good control. He's fast through his motion, hand break to release point. Smooth. Nothing jerky. Very predictable.

I got his timing.

I need to get my motion started when he breaks his hands ... get my front foot down early ... release point's pretty visible ... nothing tricky ... I should see the ball okay.

Mick approaches the plate but stays out of the batter's box.

I can hit this guy ... I just need one pitch, that's all ... runner on second ... I want to hit behind him... I'm looking for something on the outer half, between the knees and belt ... line it into right field ... that should score the guy from second ... tie the game ... just need that one pitch ... I can hit this guy.

The ump puts his mask on and Mick steps into the box.

He raises his right hand for time while he digs in a bit.

He goes through his check. He bends his knees, shakes his shoulders, makes sure his body is loose, weight equally balanced.

He holds his bat up before his eyes, sees the label. Hands loose ... hold it like an egg ... knuckles aligned ... label facing him.

Two very loose practice swings. He pulls the bat back ... his weight's still balanced ... body loose.

He gets into the zone ... he hears nothing ... sees nothing... nothing exists except the pitcher and the ball.

Got to see the release point ... pick up the ball.

I'm looking outside ... belt high.

The pitcher goes set.

Mick focuses on the pitcher's hands.

The pitcher looks away back at the runner on second, then suddenly steps off the rubber ...

Blue calls time.

Mick tumbles out of the zone.

Pat sees the argument at first finally break up. Entertainment's over ... time to get back to playing ball. The infield resume their positions.

Pat stands behind the mound rubbing the ball.

Two out ... runner on second ... just get this out ... concentrate on the batter.

This is their number two hitter ... Mick something ... their left fielder ... makes good contact ... disciplined ... not a hacker.

First time up, he waited, ignored the curve balls, and got a base hit to right on an outside fast ball with two strikes.

Did the same thing his second at bat ... almost scored Cruz from first.

Third time, Pat had Jack at second base shift three steps into the hole and three steps toward the outfield and they barely got him on a low, sinking liner.

He likes the ball a little outside ... that's where he's looking ... put it behind the runner ... get it into right field ... game's tied ... Alphabet's nursing a sore arm ... don't give him that pitch ... two outs and first base's open ... show him nothing too good ... nothing he wants ... don't want to walk him ... bring up their number three guy ... lot of power ... just end it here ... just don't give him the outside pitch.

Pat comes to the front of the mound, digs up the dirt a bit with his toe.

The batter steps into the box.

Pat steps on the rubber, looks in for the sign.

Petey drops one finger, hits his left thigh.

That's right, Pat agrees, *nothing to the right side.*

Pat comes set, gets his grip on the ball, checks the runner on second.

He doesn't like what he sees.

Short and second aren't pinching ... not keeping the runner close.

He steps off the rubber and calls time.

Pat calls his infield and catcher over behind the mound.

When they're assembled, he goes over the play he wants. "Short and second, pinch the runner ... Jack... you know the play ... keep the runner close to the bag ... maybe we can stop him at third on a base hit. When I go set, I want both of you no more than ten feet off the bag, behind the runner ... make noise... talk to him ... slap your mitts ... distract him. After I get my sign, I'll look right at him for a couple of seconds ... try to freeze him. When I turn back toward the plate, watch me. If I drop my chin, I'm coming to the bag ... right-handed hitter so second base takes the throw behind the runner. If I don't drop my chin, I'm going home. Both of you get into position when I break my hands. Got it?"

Everyone nods and agrees they got it.

Then Pat reminds them, "There's two out. Get the batter and we're out of it. Play's to first on the ground ball. Ignore the runner on second."

Again, everybody nods.

We'll soon find out, we practice this damned play enough.

The meeting breaks up and Pat goes back to the mound.

The batter's back in the box and blue calls time in.

Pat puts his right foot on the rubber and looks in for the sign. Same thing. Inside fastball.

He comes set ... gets his grip ... checks the runner on second. He looks back at the batter. He doesn't drop his chin. He's just about to break his hands and go into his motion.

Suddenly, the St. Agnes coach calls for time.

Mick Dwyer stands alongside the batter's box and watches the defense discuss what they want to do about the runner.

His mind wanders off to the dance at school that night. Lori Mc-Shea agreed to go with him. They'd been kind of dating since last summer ... an awkward double date to the World's Fair with Joey and Theresa ... he didn't dare put his arm around her as they watched the lights from the New York State tower ... he's amazed she still talked to him after that ... since then, a few movies ... coffee at a diner under the el ... nothing fancy ... a dance, though... that meant dress-up ... and dancing.

The defensive meeting finally breaks up, and the pitcher walks back to the mound.

Mick gets his head back in the game and steps back in. For him, nothing's changed.

I still want to hit behind the runner... I'm looking for something on the outer half.

The ump calls time in.

Mick raises his right hand while he digs in.

He goes through his ritual, knees ... body loose ... weight balanced ... hands loose ... a couple loose practice swings ... bat back ... weight still balanced ... get into the zone ... see the pitcher ... looking outside ... belt high ... see the ball.

The pitcher goes set.

Mick watches his hands.

The pitcher looks back at the runner on second. He looks back to the plate ... then Mick hears his coach call time.

Blue calls time, and Mick steps back out of the box.

He sees one of his teammates run out on the field with a helmet on and replace the runner on second, a little more speed to get around third and score the tying run ... fuck with the pitcher's mind a bit ... disrupt his timing ... his rhythm.

Coach explains the replacement to the umpire, who notes it on his score card. Then the umpire yells over to the St. Xavier bench, "Seven for fifteen."

Mick waits a few minutes for things to settle ... somehow in his mind there's the image of him and Lori at the top of the New York State Pavilion ... looking out over Flushing Meadows ... he wants to put his arm around her ... he chickens out ... he just stands there next to her ... he feels like a dork.

Then it's back to work.

Mick gets back in the box.

The ump gives the signal to play ball.

Mick digs in. He goes through his check, knees ... body ... weight ... hands ... practice swings ... bat back ... weight again ... into the zone ... see the pitcher ... looking outside ... belt high ... see the ball.

The pitcher goes set.

Mick watches his hands.

The pitcher looks back at the runner on second.

He looks back at Mick.

He breaks his hands.

Mick puts his body in motion.

He swings his hands and weight onto his back leg ... he steps toward the pitcher with his front foot ... he keeps his hands back ... front foot down... ready to hit ... sees the release point ... picks up the ball right out of the pitcher's hand ... fast ball ... going inside ... don't want it.

He relaxes.

The ball passes him inside ... hits the catcher's mitt.

Blue calls it a strike.

Strike one.

Mick steps out of the box.

I didn't want that one had ground ball written all over it ... third out.

He thinks for a second.

That's the third time in a row he's thrown that pitch ... he's getting the call ... I can't let him have it ... he's not so fast that I can't get around on him inside ... next pitch ... look inside, adjust outside.

Pat takes the ball from his catcher.

He walks behind the mound and stands there rubbing it up.

Got the call on that pitch again ... ahead on the count ... 0 and 1 ... this guy's too good a hitter not to adjust. What did coach say about pitching ... position and timing ... constantly change the zone and the speed ... keep the batter guessing ... off balance ... same arm motion, different speed ... that will fool a batter.

Pat had learned that if he changed his grip on the ball, positioned it farther back into his hand, he could take some speed off his fast ball without changing his arm motion ... a change-up, Coach called it. He had worked with the pitch all season, and he trusted it ... he could throw it pretty much where he wanted.

Okay ... same place ... different speed ... foul ball ... or a grounder to third ... or ... he'll see it coming and put it into orbit.

Pat comes to the front of the mound ... toes the rubber ... looks in for the sign.

Petey, the catcher, checks the batter's feet ... checks his hands ... no tells.

You're a crafty one, you are.

He gets his sign ... fast ball, in.

Pat brushes his front leg with his mitt ... change up.

Petey acknowledges ... gets into position ... raises his crouch with a runner on and a slow pitch coming.

Don't tip it, Petey, don't tip it ... the runner could get third.

He comes set ... gets a fast ball grip on the ball then lets his fingertips slide up a bit.

He looks back to check the runner ... he's dancing around off the bag ... faking moves toward third ... talking some shit.

Gotta shut that down.

He turns to look at the batter, adjusts his grip on the ball, then drops his chin in an exaggerated nod.

Mick gets back into the box.

The ump gives the signal.

Mick goes through his check ... gets into the zone ... see the pitcher ... look inside ... adjust out ... see the ball.

The pitcher comes set.

Mick watches his hands.

The pitcher looks back at the runner on second.

He looks back then he seems to nod slowly right at Mick.

What the fuck?

Suddenly, Mick sees the second baseman cut in behind the bag ... the pitcher breaks off the rubber ... spins around.

Mick quickly backs out of the box yelling, "Back! Back! Back!"

The runner freezes for a second ... the pitcher throws to the bag ... the runner seems to twist his body around, diving toward the base ... second baseman's in position for the tag ... ball and runner seem to arrive at the same time ... an explosion of brown dust at the bag ... hand goes in ... tag goes down!

"Safe! Safe! Safe!" the infield umpire yells, running in on the play, arms straight out.

In the momentary confusion, Mick gets the attention of the third base coach. "Pick off sign's when the pitcher nods", he whispers.

"Got it," affirms the coach.

Mick goes back to the on-deck circle waiting for the defense to untangle itself.

He watches the runner standing on the bag, dusting his chest and the front of his pants off with both hands.

Keep your head outta your ass ... you got lucky that time.

Again, his mind wanders back to Lori. They actually had their first kiss at Christmas ... it was an innocent, little thing when they exchanged presents in her family's front room ... their lips touched ... lingered for a second ... then parted ... her little brother caught them ... started dancing around and singing, "Lori and Mickey sittin' in a tree, K-I-S-S-I-N-G."

Then, Mick sees the pitcher with the ball again.

He walks over to the batter's box.

I've seen one fuckin' pitch and I feel like I've been up here half the day.

Mick gets back into the box. He goes through his ritual ... gets into the zone ... look inside ... adjust out... see the ball.

The pitcher goes set.

Mick watches his hands.

The pitcher looks back at the runner on second. He looks back toward the plate ... no nod...

He's coming to the plate.

The pitcher breaks his hands ... starts his motion.

Mick rocks his weight and hands back ... steps toward the mound ... foot down ... hands back ... he feels a slight pull across his chest ... ready to hit ... sees the ball ... he's going inside again ... fastball.

Mick triggers his swing... hips then hands ... the bat's moving through the zone ... something's wrong ... he gets it all but contact's late ... the ball screams into the Xavier bench ... foul ... players and spectators duck and scramble.

Mick recovers from his swing.

Changed speeds on me, ... a change-up. This guy's got a better head than I thought. This is turning into a real battle.

Pat watches from the back of the mound as one of the bench jockeys chases the foul.

He thinks about his acceptance letter from Fordham ... it finally arrived last week ... the engineering program ... it was late ... he didn't think he'd get in ... it's so competitive ... Fr. Rector told him not to worry ...

He's going to Fordham in the fall!

Blue tosses the ball out to him...

o and 2 ... let's end this now ... he's got to chase anything close ... something out of the strike zone, but close... maybe he'll bite.

Pat gets back on the mound, toes the rubber, looks in for the sign.

Petey signals fast ball, up.

Good idea; Pat nods.

He goes set ... checks the runner ... turns back to the batter.

This is it ... end it here.

He breaks his hands ... sways back... his entire body explodes toward the plate ... last pitch ... release point's perfect ... right over the plate ... just over the letters...

Petey has to rise slightly out of his crouch to get to the pitch.

The batter doesn't flinch ... he's not biting...

The umpire sees the catcher's motion.

"Ball," he calls.

One and Two.

The batter backs out and the ball comes back to Pat.

He backs off the mound, rubbing the ball.

This son of a bitch has ice water for blood taking a pitch like that ... he didn't even twitch.

Okay, still up on the count, one and two. He's still got to swing at anything close. He's not going to let the umpire take the bat out of his hands with a called third strike ... not with the tying run in scoring position.

He likes it outside. Okay ... that's what he'll see. Outside ... low and just off the plate.

Pat gets back on the mound, on the rubber. He looks in for the sign.

Petey again signals fast ball, up.

Pat shakes him off. Just tried that ... he didn't bite.

Pat dangles his mitt to his left side, the first base side, and shakes it.

Petey nods ... signals fast ball, outside.

Pat nods ... he goes set ... checks the runner ... turns back to the batter.

The first baseman sees the sign ... he cheats a couple of steps toward the line.

The right fielder follows his move sliding to his left.

Pat sees the movement.

Don't tip it! Don't tip it!

He breaks his hands ... sways back ... comes forward ... pitch looks good ... little outside ... little low.

Bite, Pat's mind screams, bite!

Mick's in position to hit ... weight and hands back ... front foot down.

He detects movement on the right side of the infield... getting ready for something ... he's coming outside.

He picks the ball up out of the pitcher's hand ... he's coming out-side ... fastball ... looks off the plate ... too close to take ... too close ... fight it off!

Mick throws his bat out at the pitch.

He hears a slight click as the ball ricochets off the top of the bat. The ball careens down the first base line, foul. Too far for the first baseman to make a play. He grandstands it anyway diving across the line at the ball. He stirs up some dust but doesn't come close.

Mick backs out of the box.

Fuck! That was close ... too close ... just got a piece ... lucked out on that one!

Pat watches some kid running down the first base line returning the foul ball.

Fordham! I'm going to Fordham in the fall ... first in my family to go to college ... mom said they could get a loan for the tuition from the Savings and Loan down the block ... two grand a year ... Pat had difficulty even imagining that much money.

He takes the ball from the umpire and backs off the mound rub-bing the ball up.

That's two good pitches that asshole's ruined!

Okay ... okay ... forget about it ... get focused ... got to show him something he isn't expecting ... got to fool him ... how?

I got that drop pitch ... I'm pretty good with it.

No ... if it dives and gets past Petey, the runner's on third ... maybe scores.

A curve? Steve showed me a curve ... threw it a few times in warm up ... just a little more pressure with the middle finger ... aim just inside his shoulder ... it should drop in ... he's looking fastball.

Pat gets back on the mound and looks in for the sign.

Petey calls for another fastball, in.

Pat shakes him off, rolls his mitt at him ... go through the signs.

The catcher drops two fingers, curve ball.

Pat nods ... he can see Petey's eyes widen a bit behind his mask.

Mick watches the pitcher get his sign, shake it off, roll his glove, then nod.

What's this?

Is he off the fastball?

The pitcher goes into his motion.

Mick gets in position to hit ... weight and hands back ... front foot down.

He picks the ball up out of the pitcher's hand.

It seems to pop up a bit ... not a fastball?

It looks inside ... a bit high.

He relaxes a bit ... let's up... it's out of the zone.

Shit!

Spin!

Red dot!

Breaking pitch!

Get it back... get it back... don't freeze!

Mick watches the ball dropping down into the zone ... his bat's finally moving ... he sees the ball get behind him ... then he feels contact.

It's not solid ... where's the ball?

He takes a few steps up the line toward first.

The catcher's looking back.

The home plate umpire is yelling "Foul... foul!"

The ball hits the backstop and falls.

Mick comes back down the line.

He picks his bat up by the barrel and hits the handle knob on the plate. He hears a solid thunk. It's not cracked.

Good! My favorite bat … don't want to lose it now … bad sign … bad luck.

So, this son of a bitch has a curve ball.

He had to roll the signs to get it … not a pitch he's comfortable with … don't expect to see it again … back to the fastball.

I think.

Pat rubs the ball up behind the mound.

How can I get one by this guy?

Fordham … two grand …

No … get back into the game.

Going at this the wrong way … Got eight other guys with me here … Don't need a strike out … trust the defense … that's what coach says … trust the defense … he's got two strikes … he's got to swing at anything close … make him hit my pitch … nothing too good … put it in play … a pitch he can't do anything with … nothing he can drive … he likes it outside … he bit on the outside fastball out of the zone … okay … let's see what he can do with it this time.

Pat calls time out.

His catcher and infield meet him behind the mound.

"I'm going outside, fastball!" he tells them. "Tony, you and Bobby cheat a step or two into the hole. Don't let the ground ball get through … smother it … I got the bag. If there's no play at first, look home. That runner's just stupid enough to try to stretch it and be a hero."

Everybody nods.

"And, Tony," Pat continues, "Tell Alphabet to cheat into the gap. I don't think this guy can push a line drive up the line. He'll pop it into right or send it into the gap. Okay? Let's get 'er done!"

Pat watches as his defense return to their positions.

As he climbs up onto the mound, somehow he knows that this is going to be the last pitch of the game.

Mick watches the infield meeting from beside the batter's box. They're getting ready to pull something, he knows. What?

He has a plan for tonight ... he isn't sure he's got the nerve ... he's going to kiss Lori ... a real kiss ... when he takes her home after the dance ... on their way to the subway ... right under the clock in Grand Central ... a real kiss this time ... if he's got the nerve.

He notices the slight shift on the right side of the infield. He sees the first baseman positioning the right fielder.

They're setting up this pitch ... they expect me to go the opposite way ... got to be another curve ... or a fastball outside ... I'm down one and two on the count ... two out ... got to swing at anything close ... okay, asshole ... serve it up and let's see what you got.

Mick steps into the box.

The pitcher looks in, goes set, and looks back at the runner on second.

Catcher already has the pitch, Mick knows.

The pitcher turns, looks, breaks his hands and goes into his motion.

Mick's ready ... weight and hands back ... front foot down.

He picks up the ball ... no pop ... no spin ... fast ball... little outside ... little low ... too close to take.

Mick triggers his swing ... hands and bat come through the zone ... contact ... solid ... a bit back in the zone ... the ball sails out over the infield, just to the right of the first baseman.

Mick's out of the box and up the line ... the ball's headed toward the gap... little high... a little too far right ... Mick sees the right fielder digging hard ... center's nowhere close.

The white ball arcs across the blue sky and begins to fall...

4

Meeting Engagement

Pat Green had a problem.

A woman problem.

It wasn't so much that the woman was the problem as it was he didn't know what to do *about* the woman.

That was the problem.

So, he decided to seek the counsel of his more "worldly" friend, Jimsey Leary.

He and Jimsey had been classmates in high school, St. Xavier's Academy down in Manhattan, and now they found themselves together in their first semester at Fordham.

Pat was in the engineering program, but Jimsey hadn't declared a major yet. He was "dabbling," as he put it, sampling from the cornucopia of intellectual delights with classes in literature, art appreciation, political science, and Eastern philosophies. As long as no term paper was required, Jimsey was interested.

To be perfectly honest, Jimsey Leary wasn't really Jimsey Leary at all. He was James Patrick O'Leary, Jr., of Kingsbridge Road in the Bronx. But, in his senior year of high school, he decided that he needed a new "handle," something less "ethnic," less "bourgeois," and more

65

"jazzy," "beat" and "with it" than "James Patrick O'Leary, Junior." So, he re-christened himself Jimsey Leary.

He would have grown a goatee, but the Jesuits didn't allow that; worn a black turtleneck, but the school required a white shirt, dark tie, and sports jacket; smoked black cigarettes in class, but again, the *Rule Book for Students* declared, "No smoking within two blocks of the building."

Jimsey did start showing up at school wearing a black beret and dark sunglasses. About this, the school had no specific prohibition, as long as he removed the hat when entering the building and took off the glasses in class. But Jimsey soon tired of getting his ass kicked by the jocks and hoods. The hat and glasses went south, but "Jimsey" remained, undefeated, unbowed.

When Jimsey arrived at Fordham that September, he arrived with the goatee and with his six-foot, hundred-forty-pound frame dressed in somber-colored clothing, black turtle necks, tight jeans, the beret, dark glasses and sandals; and there was always a long, black cigarette hanging out of the side of his mouth.

Fordham did have a dress code for the students, but the free-thinking faculty over in the liberal arts building, where Jimsey spent most of his time, considered themselves above enforcing the fascist dictates of the Jesuitical administration, so he pretty much got away with it.

Of course, behind his back, Jimsey was known around campus as "Maynard G. Krebs."

Jimsey was much more "worldly" than Pat, especially when it came to women. Pat had not dated in high school; it wasn't encouraged. He spent most of his time studying to get good grades so he could get into an engineering program. He didn't go to dances in high school; there were none.

Pat's entire high school sexual development was listening to Jimsey's tales of his lurid and exiting exploits down in Greenwich Village.

Pat learned from Jimsey that a guy could get served in the bars; no one ever asked for proof. There were jazz clubs in the smoke-filled basements of brownstones on Christopher Street, where the musicians handed out reefer like it was candy. There were college girls, Jewish girls from NYU, who had their own apartments and didn't have all that Catholic-girl guilt about sex. They thought nothing of picking a guy up, especially Catholic guys because somehow that didn't count in their religion, taking him up to their pad and, as Jimsey put it, "knocking his balls out of the park."

Pat actually went down to the Village with Jimsey one Friday night in his senior year, but it must have been an off night. They got kicked out of a couple of bars for being underage. They couldn't even get into a jazz club. And, the college girls, Jewish or otherwise, wouldn't have anything to do with them.

Jimsey told him it had to be because it was Friday, the Jewish Sunday. The girls couldn't go out; it was one of their religious things. Saturday nights were a lot hotter. Then, the NYU girls, and even their shiksa girlfriends, were all over you. It was probably a lot of built-up sexual energy and frustration from being locked up on Friday.

Jimsey obviously had analyzed the situation and understood these things.

So, it was to Jimsey that Pat went with his woman problem.

He found his friend having lunch in the small cafeteria in the basement of the nursing school that he haunted in order to scope out the nursing students.

"Women rank in order of hotness," Jimsey once lectured Pat in high school, "First, divorced women, because they're used to getting it all the time; second, flight attendants, because of their wild lifestyle; and third, nurses, because they look at guys' peckers at work all day, and it gets them hot."

So, by hanging out in the nurses' cafeteria, Jimsey thought he was just getting ahead of the game. When these girls saw their first pecker, Jimsey wanted to be around to console them.

"So, tell cousin Jimsey what's your problem," he told Pat.

They were of course not cousins. Jimsey had picked the expression up from a popular disc-jockey on WABC and thought it was cool.

"Well ..." Pat started, "... there's this girl..."

"Ah," Jimsey rhapsodized, "How many sad and lurid tales have started off with the words, 'There's this girl'. Tell me, my son, tell me how I can help you with your *Crise du Coeur*."

Jimsey speaking in tongues was never a good sign. Pat needed him to be focused.

"Could you return to the planet long enough for me to tell you?" Pat asked.

Jimsey nodded, slowly and benevolently.

"Well, there's this girl ... her name's Judy Kelly ..." Pat attempted.

"Ah, you know the sweet, young damsel's name ... that's always a good start." Jimsey said.

"Focus, will you!" Pat demanded. "Her name's Judy Kelly. We share two classes, Intro to Lit and Calc ..."

"Oh! A woman who studies calculus," Jimsey warned, "Never a good sign ... never a good sign ..."

"Yeah, well that's not the problem," Pat interrupted, "Besides, I think she's struggling a bit in Calc ... but here's the deal ... this girl's a goddess ... an absolute goddess ... I think I want to go out with her, but how do I talk to her? What do I say?"

At this point in his life, Pat Green had not shared a classroom with a member of the opposite sex since the eighth grade when he was thirteen-years old. And in college he discovered that a few things had changed since then.

His memory of awkward, skinny, stringy-haired girls dressed in shapeless Catholic-school jumpers had been abruptly shattered by the image of Judy Kelly, a well-developed, auburn-haired, beauty in lipstick, eye-shadow and skirts that never quite made it over her knees when she sat in a desk less than six feet from him in two of his classes.

The Jesuits of St. Xavier Academy had done nothing to prepare him for this moment except convince him that every time he so much as thought about Judy Kelly, he was committing a horrible sin and endangering his immortal soul.

He never even consciously realized that it was she who had chosen to sit near him, and this had to mean something important.

No! He couldn't think. He couldn't function. He couldn't keep his eyes off her.

He found her very act of breathing fascinating, the way she filled her stylish white blouses that moved in and out ... in and out... as she took each breath causing a condition in him that any first-year nursing student sitting in that cafeteria at that moment would immediately, and correctly, diagnose as hyper-ventilation.

"Ah, yes ..." Jimsey was saying, "The old trick of breaking the ice ... getting the fair damsel's attention in a positive and constructive manner ... an age-old problem ... an age-old problem to be sure."

Of course, Jimsey Leary, the arbiter of seduction, also did not pick up on the fact that Judy Kelly was in fact pursuing Pat, not the other way around.

In Jimsey's world, there are only seducers. A seductress, even a discrete coquette, would scare the crap out of him, rendering him speechless, which was quite a feat with Jimsey Leary.

"Jimsey, I can do without the history lesson," Pat was saying, "And don't say 'if we don't learn from history, we're doomed to repeat it ...' I have no history! I want to create some! What can I do?"

"Hmm ..." Jimsey said, a sound he made when he wanted his audience to believe he was being introspective, "You say you share two classes with this damsel?"

"Yeah, Calc and Lit," Pat agreed.

"Okay ... forget Calc ... math is not romantic ..." Jimsey mused, "Let's think about Lit ... what are you covering?"

"*Beowulf*," Pat answered.

"*Beowulf*!" Jimsey exclaimed. "You mean with the monsters, the blood and the torn off arms ... no ... that's no good ... can't work with that. I was hoping for a sonnet or one of the Rossetti's ... something! But *Beowulf*!"

"Okay," Pat agreed wondering where this was going.

"Okay... now ... let me think," Jimsey was being introspective again. "Does your Lit professor use a lot of big words ... you know ... stuff that sounds like it should be Greek or Latin?"

"Oh yeah!" Pat agreed. "All the time."

"Then that's it!" Jimsey declared.

"That's what?" Pat said, confused.

"Just wait until the pompous, tweed jacket throws out one of those ten-dollar words, lean over to the lovely Miss Kelly, ask her what it means, and you're in!" concluded Jimsey Leary, master of the soft-sell. "Once you got her talking to you, you got it made!"

Pat thought about it for a second. Since the idea of just asking the lovely Miss Kelly, who had given every sign that she was interested, to coffee after a morning class would never have occurred to a good, Catholic boy like him, this seemed like a great idea.

"I like it," Pat said, "It might just work."

Later, Pat found Jimsey at his accustomed table in the nursing cafeteria, sipping coffee and surreptitiously peering over the top of a paperback copy of Eric Fromm's *Art of Loving* at two young women having lunch at the next table. Pat wondered for a brief second whether his friend attended any classes at all.

Then, he remembered the purpose of this visit.

It was to murder Jimsey Leary.

"You stupid son of a bitch!" Pat hissed, a bit too loud for the mid-afternoon tranquility of the mostly vacant dining hall. "I don't know why I ever listen to you! I've never been so embarrassed in my life..."

"Whoa ... whoa ... mi amigo," Jimsey started, using tongues again.

Then, he noticed that the two comely nursing students he'd been staking out for the last twenty minutes had looked over at them, probably wondering who this loud, uncouth, hooligan with the slide rule attached to his belt could be.

Jimsey responded to Pat while simultaneously giving the two young women his most charming smile, "Whoa ... what happened... tell your cousin Jimsey your tragic tale of woe."

The two young nurses-to-be weren't buying any of Jimsey's beatnik charm and went back to their cottage cheese platters.

"Well, I did what you told me," Pat explained. "I waited until the professor used a word I didn't understand. Instead of looking it up in my dictionary, I leaned over to Judy and asked her what it meant."

"Good ... good ..." Jimsey said, wondering what could possibly have gone wrong. The plan was airtight.

Then he had a thought

"What was the word?" he asked.

"Copulate!" Pat shrieked out of the depths of his despair.

This of course caused the two nursing students to look over again, with somewhat more interest.

Without thinking, Jimsey blurted, "What did she say?"

"Fuck!" Pat bellowed.

Now, the two girls decided that this was indeed interesting.

Pat of course understood *that word*.

But, in all his life, he had never heard *that word* pass the lips of a woman, especially the crimson-red lips of a woman with whom he unconsciously wanted to do exactly that. Of course, as soon as she said it, Pat's face matched her lipstick.

"I was never more friggin' embarrassed in all my friggin' life!"

Pat was actually *fucking upset* but trying to put some distance between himself and that word.

"Not only does she think I'm a complete friggin' idiot, but my face could have lit up Yankee Stadium at midnight!"

"Well ..." Jimsey scrambled, "Did she say anything to you after class."

"Oh sure," Pat said, "I tried to escape, but I couldn't get out of there fast enough. She caught me at the door. She said she was sorry that she embarrassed me ... embarrassed me for God's sake ... that's not the way I wanted this thing to go ... her feeling sorry for me!"

"So, was that it?" Jimsey pressed.

"No," Pat said, "She asked me if I was the same guy from her calc class ... I told her I was ... so she said that I seemed to be getting it ... the calculus, I mean ... I said I did ... so she asked me if I would help her with her calc."

Jimsey was a bit confused by his friend's reaction to this wonderful opportunity that he had just been handed. Then he realized Pat wasn't getting it, not getting it at all.

"When and where is this grand enlightenment into the dark secrets of calculus supposed to take place," Jimsey asked?

"I'm meeting her over at the library at four," Pat said, showing as much excitement about this impending rendezvous with the object of his fantasies as if it were an invitation to watch concrete dry. "She's meeting me on the upper level, behind the stacks."

"The upper level, behind the stacks," Jimsey repeated. "You really are an idiot, aren't you.

Pat didn't know what to say to that. The intended purpose of this encounter was to choke the shit out of Jimsey Leary for setting him up. Now, he was on the defensive.

"What do you mean I'm an idiot?" Pat challenged, his hands itching to feel Jimsey's throat between them.

"The upper level ... behind the stacks," Jimsey repeated slowly. "She didn't invite you to teach her calculus, chump! She invited you up there to make out!"

5

Loyalty

Mick Dwyer hated it when his friend Joey got like this.

It was usually after a few beers and it had been happening more often lately. In the age-old and venerable classification of drinkers, he was becoming a "maudlin drunk," as opposed to a "mean drunk," a "happy drunk," an "amorous drunk," *et cetera*.

In other words, Joey was no fun to drink with and, at times, was a major pain in the ass.

This evening, after an hour or so of drinking beer, and just into the sixth inning of the Mets game, Joey was starting to climb onto his usual and recurring hobbyhorse, "I can't get into the trades!"

Both guys had been best friends since their schoolyard days in Our Lady of Lourdes down on Crescent Street. Although they had gone to different high schools, they had remained close, even double dating a couple of times, before Joey's girlfriend, Theresa Contadino, had dumped him right before prom in his senior year.

Not good timing, but Joey's mother, Angelina, had proclaimed that the little blue-eyed *vacca* was no loss. She wasn't Sicilian. Her family were from the north! They didn't even speak Sicilian and spoke Italian like a bunch of Krauts!

That sentiment did not seem to give Joey much consolation, and he hadn't dated anyone since.

Mick had been "going steady" with his girl, Lori McShea, for just about two years, but he sometimes wondered if going steady was an appropriate state for a guy who was nineteen and almost a year out of high school.

Lori would graduate in less than a month. Mick had just laid down a bundle to rent a white tux, buy a wrist corsage of red roses – "red for passion, white for purity, yellow for friendship" – and pay for his share on a rented limo for her prom at *Mater Dei*.

What's supposed to happen after "going steady, Mick wondered.

He had some ideas, but with Lori planning to start college at Hunter in Manhattan in the Fall, and Mick's planned career in a regulatory stasis, he wasn't quite sure how to navigate such socially and religiously treacherous waters.

Mick's goal was to get on the cops. He had wanted to do that for as long as he could remember. And, although Lori, who was going to study history in college, and maybe teach, supported that, Mick couldn't get on the cops until he was twenty-one and could legally carry a gun in the city.

So, he was kind of floating.

He had a job with the A&P. He had worked there part-time as a box boy, cashier and grocery clerk while he was in high school, a buck and a quarter an hour, minimum wage. After he graduated from high school, they gave him more hours, mostly working the night shift, midnight to eight, in various stores around Queens, cleaning up, taking in deliveries, and stocking shelves.

He liked the work but, since he didn't own a car, getting around to the stores was sometimes a pain in the ass.

Recently, he had been working regularly in a small store on Corona Avenue in Elmhurst. He had to take two trains to get there, the BMT down to Queensboro Plaza then run upstairs to catch the Flushing

IRT out to Junction Boulevard. Then, he had to walk about ten blocks down to the store.

It was a small store and the manager, Ray DiCarlo, was a pretty good guy who said he might make Mick permanent. So, he got almost forty hours a week at a dollar and a quarter an hour, minimum wage.

Mick was also taking some classes at city college, just to fill the time. Nothing too stressful, some classes in French Lit. His grandfather had taught him to speak French when he was a kid, and he had taken French four years in high school because for him it was easy, and usually his only "A." So, he was taking this course in French poetry, Apollinaire, Baudelaire, Éluard, and that bunch.

He was actually enjoying it. He had little trouble with the language itself and loved the class discussions about "meaning" and the "mechanics" of poetry. Mick's professor actually suggested to him that he might consider matriculating as a French language major.

Mick was polite, but for the life of him he couldn't see the point, to say nothing of the money, of spending four years just studying French.

No ... being a cop was much more practical choice.

Strangely, his girlfriend, Lori, seemed to take the professor's side in this issue, even after Mick explained to her that the NYPD was a civil service job. He'd start at sixteen-five with two weeks' vacation, and he could retire on half pay in twenty.

Meanwhile, he was in a bit of a holding pattern until he was old enough to take the civil service test to get on the cops. And, he had to listen to Joey's constant bitching about the war, not being able to get an apprenticeship in the steamfitters, and how Mick was pussy-whipped.

Lately, the tirade began regularly after Joey's fifth or sixth beer, to the point that Mick was lighting candles at church in hopes that his friend would get a construction job, get laid, or both.

Mick and Lori had never done it. The furthest they had ever gone was kissing and making out, to the point where Mick could hardly walk home, which was just up the block from Lori's building. According to the church and their parents, especially Lori's father who had boxed in Dublin as a young man to pick up a few bucks, such things were reserved for when they were married, about which he and Lori sometimes talked.

Mick still vividly remembered the "talking to" Lori's father had given him in his junior year of high school.

He had gone by her house to pick her up for a date. They were taking the subway into the city to see a movie. Lori was dying to see *My Fair Lady*, and Mick thought Audrey Hepburn was kind of hot. He was hoping that with all that singing and romance stuff, Lori wouldn't mind if he put his arm around her as they sat in the theater.

When he got to the door, Mrs. McShea had let him in, sat him down in the kitchen and told him that Lori would be ready in just a few minutes. While Mick sat there, Lori's dad came in and joined him at the kitchen table.

Liam McShea was about five six, a hundred seventy pounds. Although his close-cropped hair was graying at forty, his flinty, blue eyes seemed able to pierce into the deep, murky recesses of a teenage boy's dark and sordid heart.

Mr. McShea worked for the transit authority. Mick wasn't sure what he did, but he feared that Liam McShea spent his days swinging a ten-pound sledge, driving rail spikes into tough wooden ties down in the subway tunnels until his body itself was as strong as tensioned steel, able to snap a sixteen-year old boy in half without as much as catching a breath.

Mr. McShea lit a cigarette without once taking his all-seeing eyes off Mick Dwyer. Then he began, "So, Michael, Loretta tells me you're in high school."

"Yes, sir," Mick responded.

"That's a good t'ing," Mr. McShea continued, "What school?"

"St. Agnes, sir," Mick said.

"Oh ... a Catholic school... that's a good t'ing," Mr. McShea continued, "And where is that?"

"Manhattan, sir," Mick answered, "Mid-town just off of Third Avenue, sir."

"Oh," Mr. McShea said, "Near the big church by the Grand Central, is it?"

"Yes, sir," Mick confessed, "Church is on forty-third, the school's on forty-fourth."

"Yes … Yes… I know the place," Mr. McShea remembered, "I used to go to Novena there when I worked in the area … I remember all the boys from the school sitting in the front pews … what's the name of the pastor … heavy-set … loves to sing …"

"That's Monsignor Dennehy, sir," Mick offered.

"Monsignor now, is it," Mr. McShea continued, "Getting up in the world, is he?"

Mr. McShea took a drag off his cigarette, looked at its burning tip for a few seconds, then got to the real reason for his visit.

"You know, Michael, the relationship between a fader and his daughter is a special one. A fader's responsibility is always to protect his daughter, keep her safe, make her happy. It's very special … very precious."

Mr. McShea paused to take another drag and let his message sink in a bit. Mick felt some sweat building up on his forehead and his upper lip. He wondered why the McSheas kept their kitchen so warm.

"I tell you this, lad," Mr. McShea continued, "I know you're an American, and here in America t'ings are different than we had back in Ireland … expectations … rules you might say. But it is indeed a great privilege to be allowed to take a man's unmarried daughter out of his home unchaperoned. So, by allowing you to take my Loretta into the city, I am placing great trust in your … what's the word now … your good judgment … your prudence … your maturity … are you understanding what I'm sayin' to you, lad?"

Mick nodded dumbly, a trickle of sweat rolled down past his ear and down his cheek.

"That's a good lad," Mr. McShea said! "You won't disappoint me now, will ya?"

Mick was still nodding. The drop of sweat rolled over his chin and plunked on the kitchen table.

"Ah, here she is now," Mr. McShea said getting up from the table. "And what a picture of loveliness y'ar!"

Lori had finally arrived to rescue her boyfriend.

Mick understood clearly that he had been placed on some sort of Irish-Catholic probation. His "courtship" of Lori McShea would be closely scrutinized by God, Holy Mother Church, and Mr. Liam Mc-Shea ... and of the that trinity, the one that worried him the most was Mr. Liam McShea.

Mick imagined that, once he had sprung for the engagement ring and gotten down on one knee, things would loosen up a bit. Even the sternest of priests winked at that, and Lori's da was unlikely to kick his future son-in-law's ass, especially after he had put a diamond on his daughter's finger.

But there was no chance of that happening before he got on the cops, and no wedding ceremony until Lori graduated from Hunter.

So, Mick's timeline was pretty much set ... save up for the ring ... propose in 1969 ... get married in 1970.

It seemed like an eternity.

"You're not listening to me at all are you?" Mick heard Joey saying.

They were sitting at the end of the bar, where it curved around into the wall. It was their spot, kind of dark, kind of private, at least when no one was talking on the pay phone mounted on the wall beside them.

They had found this little place on Twenty-First Avenue, a block north of where the BMT subway ended at Ditmars Boulevard. It was far enough away from their regular stomping grounds down on Crescent Street that they didn't have to run into all the busy bodies from the neighborhood reporting their drinking habits.

Mick remembers one night, walking into a neighbor place for a beer and spotting Mr. McShea sitting at the bar. No way he was ready for that!

So, they had found this nice, little neighborhood place, an "old man's bar," a couple of doors down from Thirty-First Street. On a Friday night, they had some elbow room, a good view of the game on TV, and there was a pizza place two doors down, twenty-five cents a slice. Frank, the bartender, kept their glasses full ... Schaefer on tap ... twenty-five cents a glass ... a buy-back on every fourth ... every third, after Frank understood they were good tippers ... a nice little joint.

Mick was trying to get buzzed and watch the Mets, pretty much in that order.

No one took the Mets seriously.

They were playing the Cubs that night at home. Gardner and Holtzman were locked in a pretty interesting pitchers' duel. Grote had come around to score the Mets only run in the bottom of the fifth, but Santo had parked one in the seats in the sixth to tie it. Mick wondered how the Mets were going to blow this one.

And he couldn't get used to seeing Yogi Berra in a Mets uniform.

That was just wrong!

"The son of a bitch actually questioned my loyalty!" Joey was saying. "Why was I trying to get into the apprentice program when there was a war going on, he told me!"

"What was that, Joey?" Mick asked, tearing himself away from the Mets games and his nightmares of Liam McShea.

"That fuck-head down at the union hall," Joey repeated. "He said I should take care of my 'military obligation' before I tried to get into their fuckin' apprentice program ... fuckin' tin-knockers, for God sakes ... who the fuck do they think they are ... they're no better than the fuckin' plumbers."

"Oh ... that's too bad, Joey," Mick said, half in and half out of the conversation.

It was still Mets, 1, Cubs, 1. Gardner was mowing down the Cubs in the top of the ninth.

"You had to go all the way out to Brooklyn just to hear that shit, eh?" Mick responded.

"Fuckin' A," Joey complained. "An hour sitting in that fuckin' GG local, all the way down to Smith and Ninth. For what? To be told I should be in the fuckin' army? Where'd that asshole come up with that one?"

Since the World Trade Center started going up, there were plenty of construction jobs in the city, but the trade unions owned the jobs. If you weren't in the union, you didn't work. If a construction site hired a scab, the unions shut them down ... usually after the scab had an "accident."

Joey's dad was in the steamfitters' union, where Joey wanted to go. And, normally, having a relative in the union meant you got in.

But the government had screwed the pooch on that.

Uncle Fed was pushing integration these days and had decided that there were not enough blacks and Puerto Ricans in the trades. So, they were threatening to take the unions to court unless they set aside a percentage of their apprenticeship slots for minorities. The unions in turn shut down the apprenticeship programs under the theory that you can't demand thirty percent of nothing.

What the Feds didn't quite understand was, the unions weren't discriminating primarily on race. The unions were run on a patronage system. You had to have a connection, a relative, a friend, or somebody connected, to get in. And, since the trades were predominantly the Irish, Italians and Pollocks, the blacks didn't have a chance, not based solely on their race, although none of the union guys Mick knew were about to embrace the blacks as equals.

It was nepotism, pure and simple. So, the unions basically shut down entry into the trades at the height of the biggest construction boom the city had seen since they built the independent subway system during the Great Depression.

Now it was a matter of who blinked first.

Meanwhile, Joey couldn't get a job in construction.

Mick had experienced his own run-in of sorts with the unions at the A&P. In high school, even a minimum-wage box boy, had to join the union, which took five bucks dues out of his paltry, part-time paycheck every month.

Back then, other than paying money seemingly for the right to work for a buck and a quarter an hour, it didn't bother him much. His old man was union; now he was union. It was the right thing to do.

But now that he was out of school and wanted to work more hours, the union had become a major pain in the ass. It seems that, under the "contract," which Mick had never seen, "part-time employees," which Mick technically was, were not eligible for "over-time pay" at the contract-mandated time-and-a-half and were restricted to working no more than thirty hours in any calendar week.

The company was happy to work Mick as many hours as they could, because they didn't have to pay him overtime, or pay for his benefits, or contribute to his pension. So that no single shop steward could figure out what they were doing, the company moved him around from store to store.

For the life of him, Mick couldn't figure out why the union didn't want him to work. He was paying his dues every month, wasn't he?

The official line was that he was taking overtime pay away from a union member, which made no sense at all to him. Who was he taking money from? If there was a guy with a family who needed it, Mick would gladly step aside. But where was this hypothetical full-timer, who needed the money, versus an additional twelve fifty, pre-tax dollars in Mick's paycheck.

Then, he figured it out.

One Mick Dwyer, working forty hours a week, paid five bucks a week into the union. Two Mick Dwyers, each working twenty hours a week, paid ten bucks a week into the union.

Simple math!

When Mick had explained this to his dad, his old man just said, "Don't be a scab!"

Fortunately, in his new store, Mick had worked out an arrangement to work the extra time without getting into trouble with the union.

It seemed that the full-time night guy there, Leon, had refused to work alone. He said it was too creepy to be alone at night; he heard noises in the store. One morning Ray, the store manager, had come in to open only to discover that Leon hadn't re-stocked any of the shelves because he was afraid to go into the basement to bring up the boxes of groceries.

Ray was fit to be tied. He even threatened to fire Leon. But, Sam, the store shop steward, who ran the produce department during the day, took Leon's part in all this, especially since he and Leon "went way back."

Sam demanded that Ray hire another guy to work nights with Leon. Ray explained that 1) there wasn't enough work to justify a second night guy in so small a store; and 2) his budget couldn't afford another full-time employee with a ten percent night increment.

Enter Mick Dwyer.

Mick had worked there as a box boy and cashier while he was in high school and had a pretty good rapport with both Ray, management, and Sam, union.

So, Mick became Leon's "baby-sitter."

Ray bought off on it because Mick was cheap, no overtime, no night increment. Sam bought off on it because his buddy Leon got to keep his job. Leon bought off on it because now he had company at night and didn't have to lock himself in the men's room when things went bump in the night. Mick bought off on it because he got more hours; he didn't have to move from store to store; and he was only doing about fifteen hours of real work for forty hours pay.

As long as Sam kept his mouth shut, he wasn't officially "scabbing."

His friend Joey was doing okay, too.

When he graduated, his mother, Angie, got him a job working for her brother, Gerry Giudice, or as Mick was used to hearing him called, "Uncle Gerry."

Uncle Gerry owned a big catering place and restaurant over by Astoria Park, that he called *La Roma*, because "Gerry's" didn't sound Italian enough, and *La Roma* didn't sound Sicilian. In fact, with *Mater Dei* High School just up the block from the place, Mick was going to an after-prom party with Lori in one of *La Roma's* reception rooms.

Uncle Gerry had some other business interests and gave Joey a job with the vending machines. Joey went around Queens visiting bars and restaurants filling up the cigarette machines, changing out records in the juke boxes, and squaring away the commissions with the owners.

It was a pretty good job. Joey got to drive one of Uncle Gerry's vans, white and unmarked, that he picked up in a warehouse in Long Island City every morning with his stock. He made at least three times what Mick made an hour, got "a piece" of the vending machine revenues he collected, and had his pick of any of the records he took out of the juke boxes.

It was all pretty much legit. The cigarettes all had their tax stamps. But Joey did tell him a story about the records that Mick only half-believed.

Joey said there was no such thing as a real "hit record." The record companies had to pay off the radio stations and the juke box guys, like Uncle Gerry, to get their stuff played. Mick had heard about the pay-offs to disk jockeys, but this juke box deal was news to him.

Joey assured him it was gospel. Unless the record people paid off his uncle, their records didn't go in any of his juke boxes, and he had hundreds around Queens and Nassau County, a virtual monopoly. If they did pay off, the records *had* to go into the juke boxes. The business owners had no choice, and they knew it.

It was all pretty good, but Joey knew he had the job only because of his mother. Since his grandfather had come from Calabria, not Sicily,

Joey would never be fully trusted, never be fully a part of the *famigghia*. So, Joey wanted to be his own man and get in the trades like his old man.

"Maybe that's what I should do!" Joey was saying. "Join the fuckin' army! Why not! I can't get any work around here!"

This was new, Mick realized! He was watching the Mets center fielder, Cleon Jones, coming to the plate in the bottom of the ninth, when Joey dropped this bombshell.

"The army!" Mick said. "Whatta you outta your fuckin' mind! There's a war goin' on. The fuckin' army!"

"Yeah!" Joey said. "Isn't that what you're supposed to do when there's a war? Go defend your country?"

How much of this was beer and how much of it frustration, Mick wondered.

"That made sense when we were fightin' the Japs and the Krauts, and everybody had to go," Mick countered. "But this is just some bush war off in some Asian piss-hole you can't even find on the map, Joe! Whatta you thinkin'? The Vietnamese are going to invade Long Island?"

"No," Joey continued, getting on a roll. "That asshole in Brooklyn was right! What the fuck am I doin' whinin' about not being able to get into the trades, when our boys are out there dyin' in the jungles? I should join up. Be a paratrooper like my Uncle Frankie in Normandy."

"Joey! Think about what you're sayin' here," Mick argued, totally missing Jones belting a slider up in the zone into the seats to win the game for the Mets, 2-1. "Your Uncle Frankie's buried in Normandy! You never met the guy because of that! It broke your mother's heart, losing her little brother. Now you're talkin' about the same shit. If the army needs you, they'll come and get you. Until that happens, forget about it!"

Mick signaled the bartender for another round. Maybe more beer would wash this crazy army bullshit out of Joey's head.

Frank, the bartender, came over with two fresh glasses of Schaeffer. He looked at Joey and asked, "You Joey Simon?"

"Yeah, what of it," Joey answered.

Mick silently thanked all the angels and saints for this distraction, though he had no idea where it was going.

"Your mother's named Angelina, right? Angie Simon?" Frank persisted.

"Yeah! What the fuck!" Joey challenged. When a mother's name was evoked, the shit better be serious.

"Hey! Nothin' personal," Frank said, holding up his hands. "But you guys tied it on pretty good here last week, right? Friday night?"

"Yeah! We were here," Joey said, "What of it?"

"Well, your mom ... I mean Mrs. Simon called the boss and told him she didn't like him getting you drunk and all ... so the boss told me that if I saw you again, I was to cut you off before you had too much. That's all."

Mick was amazed. Angie's network in this neighborhood was astounding ... the all-seeing eyes of Angie Simon.

"So, you just do what she tells you?" Joey challenged.

"No," Frank said, "I do what my boss tells me. I want to keep this job and, just between you, me and the wall, anyone in this neighborhood better think twice before he crosses the Giudice clan, unless he wants to find his garbage cans through his front windows. So, this is a roader ... on me ... have a good night, boys!"

"Jesus Christ," Joey said, after Frank walked away down the bar, "Can you believe this shit! That's another reason why I got to go in the army! I can't even have a couple of beers in this fuckin' neighborhood without my ma buttin' in, for Christ's sake."

"You're going in the army to get away from your ma?" Mick blurted.

"Fuck no!" Joey countered. "I'm goin' into the army because it's my fuckin' duty as a loyal American ... and I can't get a fuckin' decent job in this town ... and it seems I can't have a few fuckin' beers, either!"

Mick had never seen Joey this wound up ... even back in Our Lady of Lourdes when the kids were calling him "Joey the Jew."

"... but I don't expect I can count on you, Mick," Joey was saying.

"What!" Mick said. "Whatta you mean count on me?"

"The army," Joey said. "I can't count on you to join the army."

"Join the army!" Mick sputtered, realizing too late that this conversation was now totally out of control. "Why the fuck ..."

"No," Joey mused, "Little Miss Lori McShea would never stand for that, would she? How long we been together ... you and me ... ten years or so ... third grade? We always had each other's back ... right? Now what? I'm off to Nam and you and McShea are holdin' hands waving me goodbye ... that's what it's come to ... right, pal?"

"Lori's got nothin' to do with this, Joe," Mick insisted, "The whole army idea's fucked up! You goin' in the army, the paratroopers, and asking them to send you to Nam ... I'm tellin' you ... the whole idea's fucked up ... somethin' will come along, Joe ... you'll see."

"Yeah! You used to be a regular guy, Mick," Joey continued, "Somebody I could depend on ... no matter what, you always had my back ... then you started up with this girl ... now I don't know who the fuck you are..."

Mick had had enough of this. He had to wash these crazy ideas out of Joey's head with some more beer. There was another place down the block. Maybe it was off Angie's radar. He finished his beer and got up off his stool.

"Come on, Joey! Let's go down the block. I'll buy you a few more before we go home." He dropped a buck on the bar for Frank.

"You sure it's alright with Lori?" Joey sang at him as he got up.

"Fuck this shit!" Mick said! He just hoped he could get Joey plastered enough that he didn't remember any of this army shit in the morning.

A Letter Home

J une 16, 1968

Dear Mom & Dad,

I arrived safely yesterday afternoon in Vietnam. I guess that sounds kind of weird ... Ha! Ha!

We landed at a place called Ton Sun Nhut airbase. I'm in what the army calls a "reple deple," a replacement depot, in a place called Long Binh. I think that's somewhere near Saigon.

From what I can see here, the army has converted this part of Vietnam into one huge base. There is nothing here but wooden barracks, barbed wire, bunkers, and sandbags as far as I can see in every direction.

It's unbelievably hot, and there's no shade at all. My arms and the back of my neck got sunburned from just being out one day. The permanent party guys here keep reminding us to drink water and take our salt pills. In fact, they hand the things out like candy at the mess hall.

Get this. At a briefing last night, a sergeant told us that if we get badly sunburned, we could get court martialed ... it's against army regs to "damage army property." That's what the guy said! Well, I should've listened better, because I got sunburn on the back of my neck, my face, and forearms from just being out this morning. The top of my ears is the worst. I'm keeping my sleeves rolled down, but these baseball caps we have to wear are no use at all in the sun. Typical army!

This place is pretty much like army bases back in the states. I thought they'd issue us weapons and ammo right when why got off the plane because they told us back in the states that the VC are everywhere. But this place is just like a regular army base with formations, inspections, work details and everything. I haven't even seen any Vietnamese except for a couple at the airport yesterday.

I did see this Vietnamese girl in the air base terminal when we went through it. She was really pretty. Don't tell Judy I said that. She was wearing a round, conical straw hat and this light blue Vietnamese dress with white pants.

They had me on a work detail all this morning. Typical army stuff ... picking up litter and cigarette butts from around buildings, but most of the time we were just hanging around. The sergeant in charge was just coming back from his R&R leave. He was from the 9th Division down in the Mekong Delta. He called his unit the "Devil Dogs' or something like that. He told us he was "short" meaning he doesn't have much time left before he goes home. He wasn't like the sergeants back in the states, all gung ho and stuff. In fact, after we worked about fifteen - twenty minutes policing stuff up, he got as all together behind a building where there was some shade and told us to keep it quiet and just hang out there for a while.

He wanted to take a nap, but some of the guys wanted him to talk about what it was like. I can't write down what he actually said, but it meant something like "All screwed up."

They say it might be a week before I get orders for a unit. A guy in the mess hall was saying that the worst place to get sent is up in the mountains, the highlands they call it here, because that's where the North Vietnamese Army is. I was kind of surprised at that. Back in the states the VC are all they talk about. This guy in the mess hall was saying the VC are a bunch of push overs compared to the NVA.

I don't know if I believe any of this stuff. Guys are always trying to scare us with their war stories.

Got to go. I only have about five minutes before the next formation.

They told us to wait until we get to our permanent units before we give out a mailing address. Like I said, I should know that in a few days then I'll let you know.

Oh! I almost forgot. We don't have to pay postage when we write home. We just write "Free" on the envelope where the stamp should go.

See you in about 363 days!
Give everybody my love!
Pat

6

Initiation

Private First Class Pat Green was resting against his rucksack on the airstrip with five other replacements for Alpha Company.

In typical "hurry up and wait, then hurry again and wait again" army fashion, Green had spent almost nine days in the battalion's forward supply area, called the "Combat Trains," waiting to go forward to join his unit. There, he was treated like everybody's "gofer." During the day, he pulled work details in the supply sections or KP in the mess section. At night, he pulled sentry duty on the perimeter.

He never imagined that one of the "dangers" he would have to face in Vietnam was dish-pan hands. But he had scrubbed so many greasy, rusty pots and pans with steel wool, hot water, and caustic soap that his hands were red and achy. In fact, one of the mess sergeants thought Green's work so good that he offered to go to the officer in charge of the trains, the battalion XO, and ask if Green could kept back off the line as a cook. Green decided he'd rather be shot than have to scrub another pan, so he declined.

That morning, no sooner had Green gotten back from pulling bunker guard and had crashed into his cot to try to grab a few winks before he had to report for another work detail, then one of the supply sergeants burst into the Alpha Company tent and, as if the tent were on fire, roused the replacements to "pack their shit and get their asses on the deuce parked outside ASAP!"

The truck drove the replacements down to the airstrip, where they were dumped off next to the helicopter pads and told to wait ... which they did for the next hour and a half with no further instruction whatsoever.

A couple of the replacements had dumped their rucksacks and shimmied out of their gear to explore their new surroundings. As far as Green could see, there was nothing interesting to see: a few huge black rubber blivets, which by their sweet-kerosene smell were full of JP4, aviation fuel for the choppers; a water trailer rigged to be choppered out; piles of supplies — cases of C-Rats and 5.56mm ammo waiting to go out to the units in the field; a couple of young Vietnamese girls, children really, selling warm soda and beer at fifty cents a can.

Green decided that if no one was going to fuck with him for the time being, he was going to catch a nap up against his ruck. The army would tell him what to do as soon as they figured it out themselves, which as far as Green could see was never.

Green could feel the letter from his girlfriend, Judy, in his breast pocket of his jungle fatigues. It had caught up with him while he was stuck in the trains. She had written it on some fancy, light-yellow stationery and sprayed it with perfume. This of course did not go unnoticed by the other guys in his tent, so Green got his fair share of shit over it.

He and Judy had been dating for about eighteen months before Green had been drafted. They had met during their first semester at Fordham, had their first "date" in back of the "stacks" in the university library, and began seeing each other exclusively by the end of the fall semester. They had had the summer between their freshman and sophomore years together.

Green tried to teach Judy the fine points of jazz, using his 78rpm LP collection of the classics — Ella, Billie, the Bird, and Anita — and the art of baseball at Shea Stadium.

When he visited her at her parents' house in Port Washington, she tried to teach him the fine points of the social graces — what fork to use for the salad, how to tie a full Windsor knot, and why a beer should be poured into a pilsner glass and not drunk out of the bottle.

They both tried to teach each other the fine art of Catholic "sex with your clothes on" every chance they got.

They never did go "all the way." The closest Green had come to an actual consummation of their make-out sessions was an afternoon that August in her parents' game room, while her folks were out of the house. He actually got Judy's blouse open and was working on the catch to her bra. But Judy lost it and started crying. Green spent the next three days groveling, apologizing, and wondering what sins he had committed.

On Green's last leave before shipping out to Nam, they had talked about sex and marriage. They agreed that they shouldn't do anything until Green got back from Nam. When he did get back and finished engineering school, they would think about marriage.

Judy's letter to him was chatty. She talked about what their friends at school were up to and what a complete jerk her psychology professor was. She said that she was considering transferring from the teachers' program at Fordham to the State University out on the Island. It was a much easier commute for her, and they had a good pre-law program there. Judy was considering becoming a lawyer like her father. She felt that "women needed to escape their stereotypical roles in the workplace of being only housewives, teachers, nurses and babysitters in our society" and "establish themselves in the workplace as equals of men."

Green wasn't sure what all that meant. He was just damned glad that his Judy didn't have to end up in a place like Nam because she was a number in the quota of some draft board.

Judy said her parents had asked about him and what did he think about her going to visit his family while he was away. She didn't say much more about what she was doing at school, or how she was spending her time. She closed with "all her love" and three hugs and three kisses.

As he dozed on the airstrip, he felt the paper of her letter crinkling under his fingertips, and he felt somehow comforted by it, somehow attached to her. He knew he should write her back, but the warmth of the sun and the buzzing of a faraway fly were lulling him into a stupor. He felt himself drifting off.

Suddenly, someone was kicking his boots.

He looked up.

A line of deuces had pulled in and lined up near the chopper pads. One of the supply sergeants was there, kicking his foot.

"Saddle up, rook! Off your ass. The company's in-bound!"

Green got to his feet. He buckled what needed to be buckled, tightened what needed to be tightened, put his steel pot on. Then, he bent down, jerked his rucksack up off the ground, swung it across his shoulders, and almost followed it around and into the ground because it weighed so damned much. Back in base camp, he had asked one of the NCOs what he was authorized to take into the field, and the sergeant just said, "Whatever you can carry." Green suspected he was somehow being set up in some perverse army way.

With only Catholic Youth Organization camping trips and stateside army training to go by, he had packed extra socks, underwear, a transistor radio with extra batteries, a spare set of jungle fatigues, his shaving gear, writing materials, an air mattress, a shoeshine kit, some pictures from back home and his letters, a towel and wash cloth, a can of Brasso, nine C-Ration meals, a tube of Colgate toothpaste, a waterproof bag, some ration-heating tabs, sun glasses, a small camera and three rolls of film and extra batteries, insect repellent, salt tablets, a box of matches wrapped in a plastic bag, sun tan lotion, a flashlight with extra batteries, a tooth brush, three quart-sized canteens filled with water, a mess kit with clean socks stuffed in it so the silverware didn't rattle and the socks stayed dry, a poncho and poncho liner, a GI Bible, some rope, a field sweater, a cigarette lighter, a set of rosary beads, water purification tablets, a folding knife, a roll of toilet paper, a bar of Ivory soap in a plastic soap dish, an extra belt with buckle, a box of Band-Aids, a government pamphlet about Vietnam, two hundred extra rounds of ammunition in cardboard boxes, a rifle cleaning kit with patches and a set of bore brushes, a few packs of Wrigley's Spearmint gum, a paperback copy of Tolkien's *Lord of the Rings*, a large plastic bottle of weapons oil and more patches, a whetstone, a jar of Vaseline, and, just to be safe, some extra batteries.

With his ruck on his back, Green could hardly stand up straight without falling on his ass and going turtle. Added to that was his "basic combat load" of ten magazines of ammo for his M16, protective mask with carrier, bayonet with scabbard, four fragmentation grenades, an entrenching tool in its carrier, a first-aid kit, a smoke grenade and a white phosphorous, "Willy-Pete," grenade, all hanging from various straps and belts on his web gear.

Green could hardly walk at all.

With the other replacements, Green waddled over to the edge of the chopper pad and waited, bent over by the weight of his equipment and using his rifle to support himself. Soon, he could hear the staccato beat of chopper blades echoing off the mountains to the west.

Green looked toward the sound and, against the face of the dark green mountains, his eyes soon detected movement which quickly resolved into a line of what appeared to be six small, black dragonflies flying in a row.

Green heard a pop on the landing zone and saw what appeared to be a smoking, gray-green beer can rolling across the chopper pads. Soon the grenade was hissing out a stream of purple smoke, which rode the light breezes, reaching out toward the mountains.

The dragonflies turned and aligned themselves on the streams of purple smoke.

"They like to land into wind," the sergeant, who had popped the smoke, said to no one in particular. He stood behind the hissing smoke grenade and raised his arms straight over his head like a football ref calling a touchdown.

Green could only see the lead bird as an irregularly shaped black dot in the distance. The rest of the flight was lined up behind it, flying straight in on the smoke.

Soon the dot resolved itself into a small cargo helicopter, an Army UH1, or "slick" as grunts called them. The bird flew straight toward him along the line of purple smoke.

He could see the two pilots sitting in a glass bubble in the front of the slick, their flight helmets and shaded visors making them appear like some alien bug-men in olive-drab coveralls. With purple smoke and brown dust billowing and eddying through its blades, the slick flew across the landing strip straight at the soldier holding his arms in the air. Just as it was about to run him down, the helicopter pulled its nose up and seemed to hover some three feet in the air.

The soldier dropped his arms and pointed to a spot on the ground.

Green spotted another of these strange bug-men sitting in a cubicle on the side of the slick. As the bird descended in a cloud of smoke and dust, he was looking out over a mounted M60 machine gun pointed straight down at the ground and talking into a microphone attached to his bug helmet.

As the slick's runners touched the ground, a heavily laden soldier, carrying what appeared to be a shortened M16 rifle, jumped out of the cargo area. He ran hunched over under his rucksack, clearing the circumference of the whirling blades. He was followed almost immediately by an equally burdened soldier with a rifle in one hand and the end of a short metal radio antenna in the other.

Then soldiers poured out of the grounded slicks.

Green was surprised by what he saw. Despite the loads the soldiers were carrying, everyone moved quickly, seemingly with purpose, but no one was shouting orders or giving directions. All the soldiers seemed to know just what to do.

To Green, they all seemed strangely faded, washed out, ghost-like soldiers from another world. Their tattered uniforms and helmet camouflage-covers were a uniform shade of dirty pale green and muddy brown. Even their faces were faded, pale, yellowish, dark stubble around the chin. Their eyes were alive, red-rimmed, looking everywhere, seeing everything. Their equipment and weapons shined black, glistening, strangely shark-like and menacing.

Green remembered a book he had read in high school, and he imagined was feeling the same thing that the young Langdon Towne felt when he first saw Rodger's Rangers at Crown Point, the faded men of the forests with black, glistening muskets and shining, silvered bayonets.

As the soldier with the short M16 passed the replacements, Green heard him shout over his shoulder, "Sergeant Taylor! Handle this!"

Another of the faded soldiers, this one tall and lean, walked by them. Without as much as a look or a pause, he shouted over the noise of the chopper, "You men, follow me!"

The replacements followed the tall soldier and moved toward the line of parked trucks.

As Green followed the tall soldier behind the line of deuces, he could hear the engines of the slicks begin to rev higher. He looked back and saw the line of birds simultaneously leap into the air, rise, and bank left in sequence flying back toward the mountains.

The faded soldiers were milling behind the trucks. Seeing this, the tall soldier shouted, "Jones! First truck! Williams! Number two! Davis! You got the third! Load 'em up!"

Then, he seemed to remember the gaggle of replacements clustered behind him. "Jones! Williams! Davis! On me! Now!"

The tall soldier turned to Green, "Who're you?"

"PFC Green, sir!" he answered.

The tall soldier grabbed Green by the suspenders of his web gear and propelled him toward one of the approaching soldiers. "This one's yours, Jonesy! And Green! Don't call me sir! My name is Sergeant Taylor!"

Green half stumbled into the faded soldiers called Jonesy, who caught hold of Green's web gear and steadied him before his rucksack tumbled him onto the ground. Behind him, Green heard Sergeant Taylor say to the next replacement, "Who're you?"

As he steadied himself, Green caught sight of a pair of blue eyes and an easy smile peering through the grime of a pale, weary face. "Come with me, Green. We're on the first truck."

As Green shuffled along behind the blue-eyed soldier, he heard Jonesy ask, "What the fuck are you carrying? Did you leave *anything* back at basecamp?"

He grabbed Green under his arm to help move him along. "I'm Richie Jones," the faded soldier said, "I got the first squad. Everybody calls me Jonesy."

When they got to the back of their truck, Jonesy helped Green wiggle out of his rucksack. Then both of them hoisted it onto the truck where another faded soldier grabbed it.

"What the fuck's the FNG humpin' in here. A mortar base plate," he grunted as he pulled Green's rucksack onto the truck.

Green handed his rifle up into the truck, put his foot into the stirrup on the tailgate and with Jonesy pushing and a couple of guys pulling finally arrived on top of layers of sandbags covering the bed of the truck. The wooden benches had been removed, so Green propped himself against the side of the truck. Someone had dragged his rucksack onto the pile of rucks in the middle of the truck bed.

Jonesy dropped down next to him. "This is the first squad, first platoon," he explained, "The tall guy back there is Sergeant Taylor. He's our platoon sergeant. Our six, that's what we call our platoon leader, is Lieutenant Lattimore. He's the short, solid-lookin' guy carrying the CAR-15. The way it works around here, you just call Taylor, "Sergeant"; Lattimore, "Lieutenant" or "LT"; and me, "Jonesy." No calling people 'sir' and no saluting. Save that shit for basecamp if you ever make it back there."

Green saw the soldier with the short rifle, whom he now knew was his platoon leader, Lt. Lattimore, double time up from the rear of the convoy. Then he turned and looked down the column of trucks. He raised his right arm and spun it in a circle. The deuce engines began to rev up. Then, as soon as Lattimore jumped into the cab of Green's truck, the convoy jerked forward. The soldiers in the back of the truck lurched into each other as their truck began to move.

"Delvecchio," Jonesy said to one of the guys sitting across from Green, "You're up!"

"Me! What's wrong with the Fuckin' New Guy," the one called Delvecchio challenged!

"I gotta talk to him!" Jonesy answered. "Now get up front, D!"

Delvecchio took his rifle and positioned himself behind the cab of the truck.

Then Jonesy said, "I want the rest of you guys split up on both sides of the truck, looking out!"

The rest of the squad re-positioned themselves, so they were watching the sides of the road.

"They're in a big fuckin' hurry to get us somewhere," said Jonesy to no one in particular. "That's never good news!"

As the truck bounced down the dirt road along the airstrip, Jonesy continued, "Like I was saying, this is first squad, first platoon. Lattimore's a good guy once you get to know him. He doesn't like chicken shit, and he knows what he's doing. So, whatever he tells you to do, just get it done. Taylor's a bit stiff, but he's no lifer. He's a good guy to have around in a fight. And he takes care of his people. If he doesn't like what he sees, he'll tell you. Just don't fuck up the same way twice. Then he'll really tear you a new asshole. Lattimore and Taylor are a good team. They know their shit, and they take care of their people. You could do a lot worse!"

The truck left the air strip and turned north onto a paved highway. Green saw that the jungle and all the foliage had been cut back and plowed a good fifty meters on both sides of the road.

"Keep an eye on that wood line!" Jonesy yelled out abruptly.

The faded soldiers watching out the sides of the trunk barely nodded.

"Probably didn't need to say that," Jonesy said to Green, "These guys know what they're doing, but sitting out here in the middle of a road on this big-ass truck gets me a bit antsy. The guy standing over the cab is Jimmy Delvecchio. Everybody calls him Jimmy, or Jimmy D, or just D. He's got Bravo team. They're the guys on the other side of the truck, Sweetie Gomez and Freddy Harris. Freddy's from Detroit and Sweetie's from LA, so D's got all my city boys. We're runnin' a bit short like the whole company, so I got the squad and Alpha team. You're with me to start. That guy next to you, that's Johnny Little. We call him 'Little Bit.'"

Green looked to his left and saw a guy, who looked more like Rosy Greer than a "little bit."

Little Bit kept his eyes glued to his sector of fire, but out of the side of his mouth, he said, "Welcome to paradise, Rook! Misery sure do love company." Then he laughed in a strangely humorless way.

The truck slowed suddenly. Jonesy got up and looked over the cab. They were approaching a built-up area.

"We're coming into Kontum," he told the others. "Keep a sharp lookout. Nobody gets near the truck. And don't let anybody throw anything at us."

Jonesy sat back down next to Green. "Okay! Until you get a feel for this shit, just keep your eyes on me. If the shit hits the fan, do what I do. I hit the dirt; you hit it. I open up, so do you. Just fire at whatever I'm firing at. I get up and run, you follow. Never stay up for more than about three seconds or someone's goin' to nail you. When you go down, roll. Try to get to cover first, then concealment. The fuckers know where you're at anyway. Never come up where you went down, or somebody'll be waiting. You getting this?" Green just nodded.

"Okay," Jonesy continued, "Keep your weapon clean and serviceable all the time. No more than eighteen rounds per magazine or you'll jam that damn tinker toy. Check your rounds every couple of days. Get rid of the dented ones and any of them with dirt or mold. Most important parts of the rifle are the chamber and the bolt. Swab out the chamber with a patch every morning right before stand-to. The dampness gets in it and gums it up. Check your bolt. Make sure the extractor assembly, that's the part in front, moves freely back and forth. And check your firing pin. Had a guy assemble his bolt and he forgot the firing pin. That was one fuckin' rude shock, I'll tell ya. If you don't have time to clean the bolt, slather some oil on it and wipe it down. But be sure the extractor moves back and forth."

Green imagined this is the way Langdon Towne learned his craft from "Hunk" Mariner before he moved out with the rangers to attack the Abenakis in French Quebec.

"Hey! You still with me, Green!" Jonesy interrupted Green's reverie. "This shit's important! Pay attention."

Jonesy looked up to see where the truck was, then he continued, "Make sure you have a magazine locked and a round in the chamber, keep the safety on and keep your thumb on the safety. If you run into a dink, drop your thumb and grease the bastard. If you run into a bunch of dinks, drop your thumb then push it forward, and grease 'em all. Hold the trigger back till you feel the bolt lock. Then release the magazine ... just let it drop ... lock another, slap the bolt release, you're ready to go again. Keep doing that until someone tells you to stop. How many magazines you got loaded?"

"I got the full load," he answered, "Ten. I got some ammo packed in my rucksack."

"Ten mags!" Jonesy responded. "That ain't near enough! When the shit hits, you ain't goin' have time to unpack your ruck! Hey, D! Give me one of your bandoleers!"

Joey D somehow managed to pull a bandoleer of ten magazines over his head and hand it back to Jonesy without taking his eyes of the road.

"I'm goin' to want them back, Jonesy," he said.

"Don't sweat the small shit, D," Jonesy answered.

Then he handed the bandoleer to Green. "Here put this on."

Jonesy looked over the side of the truck and realized they were in the town.

"Come on, Green," he said pulling Green to his feet, "I need you pulling security on this side."

Green untangled himself from the bandoleer, letting it just hang down from around his neck. He looked out from the truck. They were on a road passing what appeared to be rows of stores, restaurants and bars. Some buildings were made out of masonry; some seemed to be knocked out of tin.

There were colorful signs everywhere, a lot of yellows and reds, but Green could only read a few in a bizarre, tortured English, like "Happy Cowboy Bar" and "Shoeshine Barber," and "Go Go Girl Deluxe."

There weren't many people on the street. What few there were seemed to be ducking into the buildings or behind the three-wheeled Lambretta carts parked along the road as they passed.

"I don't like this," he heard Jonesy mutter beside him, "I got a bad feeling about this."

Jonesy turn his head, and yelled, "Look sharp!"

"What's wrong?" Green asked.

"When GI convoys run through these towns, they're usually mobbed by kids begging C rations, coke-girls selling sodas, beers and shit, and hookers trying to make a fast five bucks," Jonesy answered. "At least the people wave. These bastards are afraid to get close to us. I don't like this shit at all. What did they tell you back in the rear about the rules of engagement?"

Green thought for a second. "Uhh... you can return fire ... you can engage when you see enemy uniforms or equipment ... uhh ... if you kill a civilian or an ARVN, your ass is grass ..."

"Yeah," Jonesy responded, "That's the way they see the war back in basecamp. Whatever happens out here, don't take any chances. The dinks could hit us with an RPG from any one of those alleyways. We can't do shit about that, so don't worry about it. If it happens, it happens. What's more likely is they'll send some kid running out of one of these doorways with a grenade. You see anyone running at this truck, boy, girl, man, woman, I don't care if it looks like your baby brother, you put him down. Don't yell "halt" or any of that shit. Just put him down. You got that!"

"Yeah ... Yeah ..." Green answered.

He felt adrenaline kick in as he brought his rifle up. He looked out over his sights, and he could see everything, every little movement along the road. His eyes seemed to pierce through the darkness of the doorways and storefronts. He could hear the blood flowing through his veins and arteries.

This is how it was with the rangers when the French and Indians were stalking their retreat down from Quebec, he imagined. Any missed movement in the shadows was death.

The convoy finally cleared the town without incident ... no grenade-throwing kids ... no truck blown to bits by anti-tank rockets. Soon, they were back on the open highway with the jungle cut back on both sides.

Green realized his rifle was shaking. As his adrenaline drained, he felt exhausted the same way he felt after a three-mile reveille run back in Ft. Jackson. Jonesy pulled him back down into the bed of the truck.

"Okay. "We're through that," Jonesy said as they sat back down. "Better to be safe than sorry."

Then Jonesy continued, "Okay, a couple of things. Don't get your underwear in a knot if the guys aren't all that friendly at first. It's not because of that bullshit they tell you in the rear about the life expectancy of an FNG being fifteen minutes, so don't waste any time getting to know the poor fucker. We were all there once, and we're still here. Tell you the truth, you get your shit together, and you got a better than even chance of getting through this without a scratch. Especially here. This is a good outfit. The old man knows what he's doing. We take care of each other. And we don't put up with any bullshit. The deal is these guys don't know you yet. They don't know if they can trust you. They got to know that when the shit hits the fan they can depend on you, you won't come apart. That takes some time. When the guys know you're okay, they'll let you know."

"How?" Green asked.

"Easy!" Jonesy answered. "They'll call you by your name instead of 'rook' or 'FNG' or just 'get the fuck over here.' If they really like you, in other words you're competent, dependable, and a good guy to have around, they'll give you a nick name, like 'D' or 'Little Bit' or 'Sweetie.' Until that happens, you're just going to be the FNG for a while."

Green nodded. He wondered how long it took Natty Bumppo to become Hawkeye. Then, he heard the truck downshift and begin to slow. Jonesy looked over the side again.

"One last thing," Jonesy started, "And this is important, so listen to me on this. I don't know what your thing was back in the world. Out here don't let me catch you drunk or high, or I'll kick your ass into next week. We have beer and soda runs. Everybody pitches in a couple of bucks, and the supply guys send us a couple of cases of beer and soda from the rear. You'll get three or four cans of beer and soda every couple of days, if that's what you need. But that's it. When you're in the rear you can get as fucked up as you want on whatever you want. That's between you and the lifers. I don't give a shit. Out here you're my problem. So, you stay straight. If I can't get this through to you, I'll let Little Bit explain it. You with me on this?"

"Yeah! Sure, Sarge," Green stammered, "No sweat."

"It's Jonesy!'" Jonesy said.

"Uh ... yeah ... Jonesy ... no sweat ... I'm straight," Green faltered.

"Okay, good! Then we got no problem with that!" Jonesy said. "Looks like we're pulling off the road. I need you up and watching out the side of the truck."

Green got up. The truck pulled off the highway and was going down a dirt road that led straight toward a wall of trees.

Green wondered if Langdon Towne had kept a flask of rum in his pack for when things got rough.

Soon the truck followed a dirt track into the forest and the trees seemed to squeeze in around them blocking out the sun. For a few nervous seconds, Green couldn't see a thing. Soon his eyes adjusted. The jungle was within a few feet of the truck. Jimmy D yelled "Low bridge!" and they all ducked as tree branches swept down the length of the truck.

Green was surprised by the jungle.

It was dark but looked a lot like the woods near his grandmother's house in upstate New York, except it seemed more cavernous and un-fathomable.

He was expecting a jungle of ferns and vines like in *Tarzan* and *Ramar of the Jungle*. These trees seemed to be hardwoods, no pines or evergreens. Along the side of the road, the underbrush was thick, im-penetrable, mostly saplings, bushes. and brush, like back home in the states, just thicker, darker.

He couldn't see an inch beyond the edge of the forest. There could be battalions of dinks in there watching them, and he wouldn't see them.

Then the jungle suddenly retreated, and the sunlight flooded over them as the road ran along the side of a large clearing. The truck slowed, then stopped. Green saw that there were soldiers in the clear-ing and four mortar tubes set up.

Lt. Lattimore jumped down from the cab and was talking to an-other soldier with a shortened M16, a "CAR 15," Green remembered. The other soldier was pointing out into the clearing.

The meeting broke up and Lattimore walked down the convoy hitting the sides of the trucks with his fist and yelling, "Get 'em off! Dismount! We're here!"

Where "here" was Green had no idea.

The squad dismounted from the truck. Jonesy double-timed down the line of trucks to talk to Lattimore. The guys climbed down, then Green and Sweetie handed down their rucksacks to them.

When Green got down, he noticed that the other guys were helping each other on with their rucksacks. No one seemed interested in giving Green a hand, so he had to swing his rucksack on by himself. It hadn't gotten any lighter during their truck ride.

When Jonesy got back, the squad clustered around him. "We're going to be here for a while. They want us to assemble just on the other side of the mortars. Charlie company's got the perimeter, so we're just hanging out for the time being," he told them.

Jimmy D led the squad out across the clearing. Green did his best to bring up the rear.

Jonesy came up beside him and said, "Shit, rook, I can't believe the size of that ruck you're humpin'. We got to do something about that when we get a chance."

The squad filed across the clearing. Green couldn't believe how hot it was in the sun. Soon his sweat was stinging his eyes.

When they got past the mortars, D selected a grassy spot and just collapsed back onto his rucksack. The rest of the squad clustered around him in no particular order. In no time, the other guys were out of their rucksacks, dropped their helmets, loosened their gear, and were dozing in the sun. Green did notice that none of them let go of his weapon. The other two squads of the platoon followed and clustered around them.

Green didn't dare collapse onto his rucksack like the other guys. He didn't think the ground would stop him. He picked a spot near the squad, but not too close to anyone in particular.

Carefully, he shrugged the rucksack off his shoulders and let it slide down his arms onto the ground behind him. He laid his M16 against it and took off his steel pot. He took Jimmy D's bandoleer off from around his neck. He didn't know whether he was supposed to give it back, but D looked like he was already asleep, and Green didn't think he had enough seniority yet to wake him up. Green unbuckled his web gear and deposited it next to his ruck and threw his helmet and the bandoleer on top of it. Green figured he was undressed enough, so he left his protective mask strapped to his left leg.

Green picked up his rifle and sat down with his back against his rucksack. He held the rifle across his legs and checked his safety. Then, he pulled back the extraction handle just far enough for the ejector port door to pop open. He looked into the ejector port and saw the brass end of a chambered round grasped by the end of the extractor. He let the bolt slide back forward re-chambering the round, snapped the ejector port door closed, and re-checked the safety.

He laid the rifle across his legs and looked around at the deep forest that surrounded them. He felt his eyes getting heavy in the warm sun.

Jonesy walked up and snatched his rifle. Then he squatted down next to Green.

"Saw you check it," he said, "That's good. Always check. No surprises out here. But keep the business end pointed up when you're flaking out. Don't want this bad boy going off and hurting anyone."

Jonesy handed Green back his rifle vertically, bore pointing up into the sky. "Just tuck it under your arm, like your girlfriend after sex," he advised.

Green winced a bit at that, never having tucked his girlfriend, or any other girl for that matter, under his arm after sex. He took the rifle back from Jonesy and cradled it under his right arm, bore pointed up and over his shoulder.

Jonesy looked at Green's bulging rucksack. "Looks like we're going to be here for a while, at least until the rest of the company catches up with us," Jonesy said. "So, while the rest of the guys are getting their beauty sleep, let's see what we can do to lighten your luggage. What the fuck you got in there?"

"They told me back in basecamp I could pack anything I was willing to carry," Green defended himself.

"Yeah! I bet they did," Jonesy answered, "That's their idea of a joke. What you got in there?"

"Let's see," Green answered, I got a spare set of jungle fatigues, socks, skivvies, some towels..."

"Okay! Hold on," Jonesy said, "I think I see the problem. Let's unpack this thing."

Jonesy undid the straps holding Green's rucksack closed and started throwing Green's stuff in piles on the ground.

"Did you say you had an extra set of fatigues?" Jonesy asked. "Yeah, here we go."

Jonesy took Green's extra pair of trousers out of his pack, and called, "Hey Freddy! You still need a pair of trou?"

"Bet yo' ass!" Freddy answered. "My dick hangin' atta these!"

Jonesy tossed the trousers over to Freddy.

"Hey, Jonesy!" Green objected. "I'm signed for those."

"Don't sweat it, rook!" Jonesy said. "Combat loss! They send clean fatigues up to us, so you don't have to hump 'em."

Green saw Freddy loosen and remove his boots, drop his drawers, pull Green's pants on, and get back into his boots. Green noticed he wasn't wearing any drawers.

Freddy yelled over, "Fits real good! Thanks for the pants, rook. You may be of some use after all!"

Freddy laid back down and was asleep in seconds.

Green saw that Jonesy had emptied his rucksack and had his stuff in three piles.

"Okay," Jonesy told him, "The stuff on the left you got to keep. The stuff in the middle could be useful, if you want to hump it. The stuff on the right, I got no idea why you'd want to keep that shit out here."

Jonesy handed Green his waterproof bag. "Before you repack the ruck, put this bag in like a liner. It'll keep your shit dry when the monsoon hits."

Green fit the waterproof bag into his ruck, then started packing the pile on the left. It was his poncho, poncho liner, air mattress, field sweater, towel, extra socks, a shaving razor, his chow, toothpaste and toothbrush, heating tabs, insect repellent, salt tablets, lighter, flashlight, water purification tablets, the rifle cleaning kit, batteries, insect repellent, gun oil, whetstone, canteens, ammo, and the Vaseline.

"Pack the chow on top or in the side pockets," Jonesy instructed, "That way you can get to it quick when you get a chance to eat. Put the towel on top too. You can use it to wipe the sweat out of your face while we're humping the bush. A lot of guys lay the towel across their shoulders to cushion the rucksack straps. I'd put the heat tabs in with the chow. You can put the iodine pills, insect repellent and salt tabs in a side pocket too. Hang two of the canteens on your web belt so, if you have to dump your ruck, you'll still have water. Put 'em on your hips, not on your back, or they'll get in the way of the rucksack. Hang the flashlight on your web gear, or on the outside of the ruck. Keep your eye on it, or it'll walk."

"Should I keep the poncho near the top in case it rains?" Green asked.

"No," Jonesy answered, "Nobody *wears* a poncho out here. We use it to build hooches. If it rains, you get wet. Don't sweat it. Your skin's waterproof, and you'll dry out … eventually. If you're afraid of getting wet, buy yourself a rain jacket from one of the coke girls when we're near a town. Won't do you any fuckin' good to keep dry, but if it makes you feel better, go ahead and get one. While I'm thinking about it …"

Jonesy rummaged around in the middle pile and pulled out a pair or shoelaces. He tossed them over to Green. "Here! Tie these through the grommets of your poncho. That way you'll be able to tie it to trees and shit to make a hooch for yourself. Keep that extra ammo out too.

I'll look around for some extra magazines while we're here, and you can load them."

When Green had pretty much packed away everything from his "keeper" pile under Jonesy's supervision, he continued, "Okay, before you start rummaging through all that shit in the middle, I got to tell you something. Since you're the new guy, you get to hump some of the squad equipment. So, give me a minute here."

Green watched as Jonesy went through the squad, removing stuff from their rucksacks. He unstrapped a short-handled spade from Sweetie's ruck. Then, he went over to Freddy and removed a small, rocket launcher in a collapsed tube called a LAW, and a coil of rope. Then from Little Bit, he took what looked to Green to be a small, thick map case and a couple of small cylinders wrapped in green wire.

He brought the stuff over to Green and dropped it next to his rucksack. "The LAW fits real nice on the side of the ruck. Just strap it to the frame. The shovel should go on the back. Just don't strap it too low or the handle'll tangle up your legs. The rope can go on the side or on top. Just make sure it doesn't uncoil while we're moving. This thing in the carrying case is one of our claymore mines. You can strap that to your ruck, or just carry it over your shoulder by its strap. And last but not least, these little guys are trip flares. I'd put them in one of the side pockets. You may need to find them in the dark."

While Green was packing and strapping the equipment to his ruck, Jonesy went on, "Now sometimes we have to hump shit for the platoon or the company. You could get a box or two of machine gun ammo, or some batteries for the platoon radios, or a mortar round or two. So, think about that before you load yourself down anymore."

When Green finished, Jonesy said, "Okay! Let's try this bad boy on for size."

Jonesy helped Green on with his rucksack. When he had it on, Jonesy said, "Okay. Now jump up and down."

Green got the impression Jonesy was now fucking with him.

"No! I'm serious," Jonesy said, "Jump up and down. We got to make sure all this stuff is secure."

Green jumped up and down. Other than the rope coil hitting him in the back of the head, nothing hard hit him or stuck him in the back, and nothing fell off the rucksack.

"Good," Jonesy said, "A little noisy, but seems okay. How's it feel."

"A lot lighter than before," Green admitted.

"Good!" Jonesy said, "You may have to hump this bad boy twenty klicks up and down some mountains when we get going again. Now you can take whatever you want to carry from the middle pile."

Green shimmied out of the rucksack and went over to the middle pile. He felt he was looking at the graveyard of his former life. First, he grabbed his letters and his pictures. Somehow, he knew he couldn't let those go yet. Then he grabbed his writing stuff so he could write home. The soap seemed to be useful. He wasn't at all sure how that was done out here, but he stuck it into his ruck anyway. The shades were light, so they went into a pocket in his fatigue jacket.

He imagined that somehow Natty Bumppo was able to move effortlessly through the forests with nothing more but musket, powder, shot, knife and tomahawk, living off the land.

In a movie, Landon Towne only needed his map-drawing equipment, some jerky, and a bag of parched corn on his way to Quebec.

He picked his portable radio up from the pile. It seemed too expensive to just leave there.

"Hey, Jonesy! You think we can use this?" he asked.

"Already got one," Jonesy answered. "I think there's another one in the squad. Jimmy D's got one, I think. You want to hump it, it's up to you."

Green was about to put the radio back down into the pile, but then he thought he'd like to get the news from home on Armed Forces radio. The Mets were finally playing some decent ball. Maybe they'd do something next season. So, he slipped it into his rucksack. Then he grabbed the little camera and film. Judy and his folks would like to see pictures, he thought. The last thing he grabbed was the paperback novel. Somehow knowing whether Frodo escaped the dark riders was still important to him.

That's it, he thought, or I'll be trying to hang on to all this shit.

While Green was filtering through the debris of his former life, another convoy of trucks pulled in and some more faded soldiers piled out of them and filed across the clearing toward the first platoon.

Jonesy looked up at them, and said, "That's the third herd and the rest of the second platoon. We should find out what's going on soon."

While the new arrivals settled in, Green noticed Lattimore and Taylor in a conversation with other soldiers carrying CAR 15's, and a tall soldier with a large map case.

"The tall guy is the battalion operations officer," Jonesy said, "Major Modine or Modica, something like that. The guy to his left is our CO, Captain Jacoby. The rest are the other platoon leaders and platoon sergeants. We better get ready to move. Whatever's going to happen, it'll be soon."

Jonesy walked around the squad waking the guys up.

Green felt a flush of excitement.

His first combat mission.

This must be how Langdon Towne felt when the rangers got ready to pull out of Crown Point for their raid in Quebec.

When Jonesy got back to Green, he had a sandbag in his hand. When he dropped it next to Green, it made a metallic clack.

"Found some magazines for that spare ammo of yours," he told Green, "Let's get them loaded. I don't know how much time we got."

Jonesy dumped the empty magazines out on the ground, then picked one up. "When you get a new magazine," he told Green, "Pop off the bottom and check the spring for rust and tension." Jonesy showed Green how to do that. "Then look through the magazine for dents and obstructions. The M16's a good weapon when it works, but it's real temperamental. Magazine mis-feeds'll jam you up in a hot second. Put some oil on the spring then re-assemble the magazine."

Jonesy watched as Green complied.

"Okay, good job," Jonesy said when Green had the magazine re-assembled. "Let me show you something they don't teach back in the world about loading these things."

Jonesy took a small metal device out of his pocket and fit it on the back of the magazine. "This is an ammo clip," he told Green. "They come with the ammo. It fits on the back of the magazine like this. You can keep this one when we're done."

Jonesy took one of Green's spare boxes of ammo. He removed one of the ten-round clips and slid the metal rail into the ammo clip.

"When you have the rail attached to the clip," Jonesy said, "Just place your thumb at the rear of the top round, and push."

Jonesy pushed down with his thumb, and all ten rounds slid into the magazine.

"Now you try," he told Green.

Green picked up the next ten-round set, attached it to the clip and slid the rounds down into the magazine.

"Good," Jonesy said, "Now pop the two last rounds out of the magazine. You only want about eighteen rounds in a magazine. If you try and load the full twenty, the rifle'll jam on you. I don't know why, but it will. Put the extras in your helmet and load them into their own magazine when you got eighteen."

Green loaded the next magazine while Jonesy watched. When Jonesy felt Green knew what he was doing, he left him to it and walked over to where the other squad leaders were congregating and smoking, waiting for the operations briefing to break up so they could get their movement orders.

Green felt his excitement build.

He was loading his magazines like an old pro and any minute he would be moving out with his new comrades on his first real combat operation. He could almost visualize himself moving swiftly and silently through the forest, closing with the enemy.

He was loading the last of his spare ammunition when he heard what sounded to him like fireworks going off in the distance.

His first thought was that a live-fire training range had just opened up. Then he remembered where he was. There were no training ranges out here in the boonies.

When he looked up, he saw all movement in the clearing had ceased. Everybody had stopped what they were doing and were staring off toward the firing in the distance.

The first group to break out of the spell was the ops briefing. The meeting quickly broke up and the Alpha Company officers and NCO's double-timed over to where the company was waiting. As that happened, the soldiers around Green got to their feet and started checking over their equipment and adjusting their gear.

Then, over by the mortar section, Green heard the call, "Fire Mission! Fire Mission!"

The mortar pits suddenly broke out into a flurry of activity.

Green saw Lt. Lattimore talking intently to Jonesy and the other squad leaders. In minutes, Jonesy, map in hand, was trotting over to the squad, calling "On me, guys! On me!"

As soon as the squad gathered, Jonesy said, "That firefight to the north is Delta Company. They moved out earlier trying to make contact with the dinks. Looks like they found 'em."

Jonesy opened his map and pointed, "Delta's in contact here ..."

The rest of what Jonesy was saying was drowned out by a salvo of mortar fire. The squad had to pull in closer to hear what he was saying.

"Delta's in contact here. We're located here to the south of them ...."

Another salvo exploded.

"Alpha company's moving up to them along this trail ..." Jonesy's finger traced a line on the map. "When we get about here, we're swinging west to get around Delta's left flank ..."

More explosions from the mortars.

"... our job is to get around the dinks and sweep them out of here ..." Jonesy's finger swept across where Delta company's front should be ... more outgoing explosions... "Questions?"

Green felt his heart racing.

The firefight in the distance, the mortar fire, the mission briefing, moving out toward contact with the enemy, all this got him fired up.

He looked around at the other guys. He was surprised. They seemed to look grim, worried, even fearful. Green couldn't understand what was wrong with them.

This was Hawkeye hot on Magua's trail to the Huron village. This was Major Rogers and his rangers moving up on the Abenaki. They were going out to meet the enemy. They were going out to do what they were trained for.

"Okay," Jonesy continued, "We got Delta Company eighty-ones here. Battalion four-deuce and our eighty-ones are inbound and will be set up here to support our movement within the hour. Plus, there's a battery of One-Oh-Fives firing from just north of Kontum on call. We're pulling out of here in ten minutes. Third platoon leads off, then second, then us. We got a platoon of Charlie Company attached. They come last. We're trailing the platoon, second squad to our front, the Charlie Company to our rear. So, just get in behind second squad when they move out."

Jonesy spread his map out again in front of the squad.

The mortars continued to fire.

"Them motherfuckers gonna melt them barrels," Little Bit muttered.

"Fuckin' A," Jimmy D answered, "It's their guys out there in the shit."

"Okay! Listen up," Jonesy interrupted.

He pointed to a double black line on the map. "This is the road there at the west edge of the clearing. We're goin' to follow it north about a klick to where it intersects this trail running east-west." Jonesy pointed out the intersection. "This is our line of departure. Delta

Company should have pushed the dinks north of it by the time we get there."

"Man, if they ain't, that gonna be one fine cluster-fuck when we get there," Harris interrupted.

"We worry about that shit when we get there, Freddy," Jonesy asserted. "When we get to the intersection, we move west ... that's a left turn for you city boys ... until we make contact with some guides from Delta Company. They'll mark their left flank. From there, we keep moving west until our trail unit, that's the platoon from Charlie Company, clears Delta's flank. Then we turn north and advance in line until we make contact. Any questions?"

"Yeah," Green blurted, "Are we really going to use these trails all the way to contact?"

There was silence.

When Green looked up, he saw from the way the other guys were looking at him that he didn't really have enough seniority to be questioning Jonesy.

"Why do you ask," Jonesy responded?

"Uh ... they told us in the rear never to walk on trails ... booby traps and ambushes ..."

Harris actually snorted at that. The other guys just looked at Green silently.

"Okay! Okay," Jonesy responded, "Give the guy a break. That's actually a decent question. The reason we're walking up the trails, Green, is time. We got to get up to Delta Company as fast as we can. If they're pushing the dinks back, we want to hit them while they're still off balance and then finish the job. If not, we got to bail Delta out before they get their asses kicked. Any more questions."

No one spoke, but Green thought he heard Sweetie mumble something that sounded like, "fucking booby traps, you gotta be shittin' me."

"Okay," Jonesy said, "Get saddled up and get ready to move out. We're leaving the rucksacks here. Make sure you got enough water to last you the rest of the day and take at least two meals."

As the squad moved back to their equipment, Jonesy caught up with Green. "Don't worry about that shit," Jonesy told him, "You got a question, you ask it. But remember, stay close to me when we move out."

"Got it," Green responded.

Green got to his equipment. He checked his rifle — round chambered, safety on. He took his third canteen off his rucksack and attached it to his web belt giving him three quarts of water. He unpacked some cans of C-rations, but he wasn't sure what to do with them.

He looked up at the other guys and asked, "What's the best way of carrying these?"

"Sure they not booby trapped, rook?" Sweetie snickered.

"Just put 'em in your cargo pocket in your trou," Jimmy D answered, "That's where I keep my chow. And make sure you got a P38 with you. Those cans are hard to chew through, though sometimes that tastes better than the shit that's in 'em."

"Thanks, man," Green responded, and dug his P38 out of his rucksack. Green put his web gear on and picked up his ammo bandoleers.

"Hey, D," he called, "You want your ammo back."

"No! You keep it," Jimmy answered him, "I got plenty. Hey! Just drape those bandoleers across your chest like a bandito. Make sure the open sides are facing up."

"Yeah! Thanks, D," Green said. He draped the bandoleers across his chest. They lay there like a sagging X.

Sweetie looked him up and down. "You one sorry lookin' bandito, man," he said, and thumped Green on the chest, rattling the magazines.

Little Bit put his hand on Green's shoulder as he walked by.

"Show time," he muttered.

Jonesy started lining up the squad to move out. First his team, then Jimmy's.

"Stick close!" he reminded Green! "Just follow my lead. You'll be fine."

Green saw the company beginning to file toward the road.

This is it! This is it! he thought. We're going into combat! We're going out after these guys! We're going to kick some ass!

He checked his rifle again.

Soon Green was part of a column of soldiers moving up the dirt road through the jungle. He could clearly hear the firefight in the distance.

There didn't seem to be much attention paid to stealth. The column moved north at the quick time and sounded like a creaky, rattly mule train ... water sloshed in canteens ... magazines clanked together ... rifle slings jingled ... boots scraped and scuffed the ground.

Some guys were even smoking while they marched!

Green did not imagine Major Rogers or Natty Bumppo approaching their enemies in the forest like this!

They moved north for about forty minutes. Green could now distinctly hear the sound of the battle to their front.

Suddenly the column halted. The squad immediately split to both sides of the road, Jimmy D to the left, Jonesy to the right.

Jonesy walked up the road to talk to the lieutenant.

Green found himself just off the road in the brush next to Little Bit. When Green looked over, Little Bit pointed to his eyes and then pointed out toward the jungle to indicate "keep your eyes open for the enemy."

Green peered out into the shadows of the forest.

There was movement everywhere. Leaves turning in a light breeze, green, then silver, then green again. Smaller trees and saplings swayed. Patterns of light and shadow constantly danced between the trees. Flying insects flashed through columns of light. Green swore he could see ants moving across a vine ten meters to his front.

Green almost lost it when something dropped with a thud out among the trees.

When Jonesy laid his hand on his shoulder, Green's head snapped around as quick as a mouse trap.

"The head of the column is at the line of departure," Jonesy informed him and Little Bit, "They're making coordination with Delta. Then we'll be moving."

Jonesy sat down next to Green, his back against a tree. "Gimme your rifle," he said to Green, "I'll adjust your sling."

Green handed his rifle over to Jonesy. Jonesy began adjusting Green's sling so he could hang the rifle from his shoulder.

While Jonesy worked on the sling, he said, "Hear the firing up ahead? Notice now you can hear individual weapons firing, and they seem to be coming from different locations? That means we're about a hundred, hundred fifty meters away. Still too far away to worry about it. We're not under fire yet. But we're getting close."

While Jonesy spoke, Green heard a sharp CRACK, CRACK, CRACK to the north.

"That's an AK," Jonesy told him, "They sound heavier, sharper than M16's at this distance. But, when they sound like that, they're no real threat. You won't see guys ducking or hitting it when they hear that sound. But, if you hear what sounds like a whip crack beside your head, then they're close and comin' your way. That's when you hit it. It's that whip crack you gotta pay attention to."

"What if I don't hear it?" Green asked.

"Then you're about to meet St. Peter and the rest of us got to clean up the mess," Jonesy answered.

Green was not at all sure he was joking.

"Just keep your eye on me till you get used to this shit," Jonesy continued, "Looks like we're moving again."

Jonesy handed Green back his rifle, then yelled, "Okay, guys, back on the road! Let's go!"

The squad re-assembled on the road and moved out.

About a hundred meters ahead the column turned left onto a dirt trail, just a path through the trees. Green could hear the firing on his right now. The reports of the individual weapons were very clear, but no whip crack. So, Green just followed Jonesy into the woods.

The guys around him seemed to be more cautious now. There was no talking, no smoking, and less equipment noise.

Green stumbled on a root across the path. "Pick your feet up," Jonesy hissed back to him, "Weight balanced. Bring your foot down heel first than roll through the toes."

Green tried it. It seemed awkward at first, but he seemed to be moving silently, like Natty Bumppo sneaking up on a buck in the forest.

Soon the column stopped, and Jonesy waived the squad off the trail to the north. Green picked a sector to his front and watched. He was getting used to the natural movements of the forest. They began to form an expected pattern. He didn't feel as anxious as he did before.

Soon they were up and moving again.

Green began to notice signs of earlier activity in the area. Mostly, the brush along the trail was broken, crushed and pressed down. Then he saw some debris, empty rifle magazines on the ground, a US canteen still in its carrying case, a boonie hat lying under some brush.

Green felt his stomach tighten. They were close now, very close.

They stopped again, took cover. Green heard a POP, POP, POP immediately to his front.

"That's friendly," Little Bit hissed, "But keep your eyes open."

Then, they started to move again.

They went a few meters, stopped, and took cover.

"They're trying to coordinate shit with Delta Company," Jonesy whispered. "Find the flank."

Then he went down the line to tell Jimmy D's team.

Green looked out to his front, toward the firefight. Then out of the corner of his eye, he noticed something on the ground. When he looked, he saw it was an M16 magazine. Without thinking, he picked it up. Strange, he thought, the magazine's still loaded. Then he felt wetness on his fingers. When he looked, he saw a viscous, brownish-red liquid on his hand. He dropped the magazine.

Little Bit hissed over, "What you doin'?"

Green wiped his fingers on his trousers and looked down to where he thought he had dropped the magazine. He saw an American jungle boot lying there.

How could you lose a boot? he thought.

He reached out, grasped it and realized he was touching someone's foot.

Then he noticed the leg in army jungle fatigues.

Green moved forward to examine what he had found.

Little Bit whispered over, "What the fuck you doin', rook? You stay put!"

He moved towards Green's position.

Green discovered a GI lying in the woods.

He was still.

Green thought the guy must be sleeping. He didn't understand how anybody could sleep so close to contact.

Green put his arm on the sleeping soldier's shoulder and shook it.

"Hey! Wake up, man! Somebody's goin' to see you," he whispered.

Little Bit came up behind Green.

"Shit," he muttered, "Leave 'im alone! Leave 'im alone!"

Green didn't understand why Little Bit was saying that. He rolled the sleeping soldier over.

The soldier moved strangely for a sleeping man. Too limp, too loose.

Then Green saw the sleeping soldier's face.

His eyes weren't closed ... they were half open ... Green got the impression of blue eyes ... a mouth gaping open ... yellowed teeth ... his face was pasty ... white, tinged with green.

There were bugs crawling on his face ... in his eyes ... in his mouth.

He heard Little Bit say, "Oh fuck!"

Then Green smelled something.

It was pungent ... sweetish... like the back of a butcher shop on a hot day.

He looked back down at the gray-green face ... unfocused blue eyes.

He vomited ... he tried to suck some air into his lungs ... he tried to get control of his body ... he gagged ... then he vomited again.

Little Bit dragged Green back onto the trail, away from the dead GI.

Green vomited again. Only clear-yellow bile came up.

Little Bit called out, "Jonesy! Get over here! We got a KIA!"

Jonesy ran down the trail. "Who is it? Who is it?" he hissed.

He followed Little Bit into the brush off the trail.

Then Green heard him call, "Medic! Medic!"

What the fuck's a medic going to do for that guy, Green wondered.

Green tried to spit the taste of puke out of his mouth. The dead stink seemed to cling to him. Then, he saw the drying blood on his fingers and he puked again. Again, nothing but water and yellow bile.

Jonesy walked over to Green with two rifles in his hands. "This yours?" he asked Green.

Green nodded.

Jonesy tossed the rifle at him. "Don't ever walk away from your weapon!" he told Green.

Green fumbled with the rifle and nodded at Jonesy.

"Check your weapon!" Jonesy ordered Green.

"Check my weapon..." Green muttered.

"Don't argue with me, you fuckin' rookie," Jonesy hissed at him, "You dropped it back there in the dirt. Then you left it. Check it for damage. Make sure there's no fuckin' dirt in the flash suppressor. Check it down to the firing pin. And don't give me any shit!"

Green felt himself getting angry. He didn't deserve this shit. But he kept his mouth shut.

He cleared the weapon, checked the barrel for dirt, and started breaking the rifle down.

A soldier carrying a large square satchel double-timed down the trail.

"Who's hurt?" he asked Jonesy.

"You don't need the bag, Doc," Jonesy answered, "Follow me."

The medic dropped his bag and followed Jonesy into the woods.

Green worked on his rifle.

What the fuck did I do, he fumed, I found the guy.

The way the dead guy looked confused Green.

In the movies, when an American got killed, he looked like he was asleep; he was peaceful. The guy he found looked like he was still in agony … the bugs crawling all over him … and why was he left here alone … where were his buddies? In the movies your buddies stayed with you … consoled you … held your hand as you slipped away … said a little eulogy over you.

Green saw that Jonesy, the medic, and Little Bit were carrying, half-dragging, the dead GI out of the brush. They laid him out along the trail right in front of Green.

Doc was checking him over. He pointed at the dead GI's left breast. "There's the entry wound," he told Jonesy.

Then he rolled the guy over onto his left side. "And there's the exit wound," the doc said.

Green looked up. There was a hole the size of a melon where the guy's left shoulder blade should have been. Sticks of white bone, pink and red viscera, yellowish foam poured out of the hole in his back.

Green thought the wound was moving. When he looked closer, he realized it was crawling with ants.

Green almost lost it again.

Little Bit put his hand on Green's shoulder. He spoke to him almost like a father speaking to a frightened child. "He didn't feel shit," he said quietly, "He was dead before he hit the ground. Them bugs ain't botherin' him one little bit."

Doc dropped the dead guy on his back. He reached in under his shirt and pulled off his dog tags.

"Cohen, Gerald L," he read, "Oh Positive." "Jewish."

He broke off one of the dog tags and forced it between the dead guy's teeth. Then he went over to his bag, opened it, took out a tag with white string, sat down and started writing.

Jonesy re-emerged from the brush carrying an extra rifle and helmet. He cleared the weapon and dropped it near the medic.

"Here's his weapon, Doc," he told the medic.

He tossed the helmet near the body.

Jonesy walked over to Green. He handed Green the dead guy's mag and put his hand on Green's shoulder. "You back with us?" he asked.

"Yes, Sergeant! Rifle's operational," Green snapped.

"Yeah, I know," Jonesy answered, "And it's still Jonesy. Look, give Little Bit a hand with the KIA. We got to collect all his personal shit so the dinks don't get it. You can leave your helmet and rifle here for a minute. They ain't goin' anywhere."

Green crossed over to where the dead guy was. Little Bit was holding a plastic bag the medic had given him.

"We got to go through his pockets," Little Bit said, and nodded toward the dead guy, "You gonna be okay?"

"Yeah, I'm fine," Green muttered. They walked over to the dead guy.

"Roll 'im toward you," Little Bit told Green, "I'll go through his back pockets."

Green realized Little Bit was doing him a favor by not forcing him to see that exit wound with the ants again. Little Bit pulled a small square package wrapped in a C-Ration bag out of the dead guy's pocket.

"Wallet," he said to no one in particular and dropped it into Doc's plastic bag.

"Okay, that's it," Little Bit said, "Let him back down."

When the dead guy was on his back again, Little Bit pointed to his breast pockets and said, "You go high, I'll go low," and started digging through the dead guys trouser pockets.

Green unbuttoned the first breast pocket and found an unopened pack of C-ration cigarettes, a book of matches, two packets of sugar and a packet of instant coffee.

He showed it to Little Bit, and he said, "Give me the butts. You can toss the rest of that shit." Little Bit jammed the cigarettes in his own breast pocket.

Green opened the dead guy's other pocket and pulled out two letters, opened but still in their envelopes. He looked at the first, addressed to "SP4 Gerry Cohen, D Co 3/35 INF." He noticed the "I" was dotted with a little heart. It looked like the same stationary Judy used. The letter was from a Miss Rachel Singer, Skokie, Illinois.

There was some blood on the corner of the yellowish envelope.

He flipped to the second letter... "Love, Mom and Dad" ...

"Hey, Green," Little Bit interrupted, "We collect "em, not read 'em!"

Green handed the letters over to Little Bit and he dropped them into the bag. Absently, Green felt for Judy's letter in his own breast pocket. He was relieved it was still there. His hand closed around it, holding on to it.

The medic tied the tag into a buttonhole on the dead guys shirt.

"Doc! Where you want this shit," Little Bit asked.

"Drop it by my bag," Doc said without looking up.

"Sure thing, Doc," Little Bit answered, "Hey, we having a game tonight?"

"Anytime you got the money, I got the cards," the medic answered. "Just come on by my hooch when you're ready to part with your cash."

"We see about that," Little Bit chuckled.

Jonesy came back down the road.

"We're starting to move," he told the guys, "Doc! You got this?"

"Yeah," the medic said, "I got it. I'll catch up."

The squad re-assembled on the trail.

Sweetie came up to Green and said, "Don't sweat the small shit, rook. First time I saw shit like that, I pissed my pants. Hey Freddy! You remember that, bro?"

"Remember it?" Freddy chuckled. "Man! I can still smell it! Why does Mexican piss smell so bad."

They both chuckled as they stepped around the body of Spec-4 Gerry Cohen lying along the side of the trail.

When they halted again a few meters down the trail, Green's mind was still trying to put things together.

There was a dead GI lying out down the trail ... bugs crawling all over him ... they were just leaving him there ... joking with each other like nothing happened. What about the dead guy's parents ... his girl, Rachel from Skokie ... he's just lying out there dead ... alone ... they don't even know it.

Even in movies the heroes get it sometime, like Sergeant Striker in Iwo Jima... or Paul Bäumer reaching out of the trench for a butter-fly, their buddies take care of them ... people mourn them. Sad music plays.

This guy's unit just left him lying there ... like so much trash.

Major Rogers wouldn't leave anyone behind... didn't he even go back for Landon Towne eventually.

Then Green remembered a story he had read back in high school ... a story he really hated ... something about a lifeboat ... what was it ... Stephen Crane ... a brotherhood of men ... human survival in a hostile environment. There are no heroes! Anyone can be killed! There's no reason to it! Seven mad gods who rule the sea ... it just is ... it just happens. Shit happens.

Green rubbed Judy's letter again.

Jonesy dropped down beside him. "You did okay back there, Green," he said, "That's always tough. First time I saw one of ours like that, I froze, couldn't move. Taylor had to kick me in the ass to get me moving ... really ... it's always tough the first time."

"We just gonna leave him there?" Green asked.

"No choice," Jonesy responded, "We have a mission. The doc will tell his people where to find him."

"But why did his unit just leave him out there like that?" Green persisted.

"You haven't been in the shit yet," Jonesy said, "It's all fucked up ... nobody knows what's going on ... everybody's trying to stay alive. His guys may not have missed him yet ... they may not have had the chance to go look for him. When the shit hits, it's a real cluster-fuck."

"But the guys," Green said, "Sweetie and Freddy, they were standin' right there ... joking with each other."

"Green, I'm telling you," Jonesy responded, "When you've seen enough of this shit ... and you will see shit like that ... first thing in your mind is, 'thank God it ain't me'. I imagine there'll come a day when we can all sit down, get good and soused, and cry about this shit ... what we saw ... what we did. But it ain't today. Today we got a job to do ... we got to keep ourselves alive best we can ... and we got to keep each other alive. That's what we got."

Jonesy put his hand on Green's shoulder. "You did okay," he said, "Keep it together."

Green's head was spinning. This was not what he had expected. The movies, the stories, they're all bullshit. Wrong place ... wrong time ... you're lying alone dead in the woods with bugs crawling all over you.

Jonesy came down the trail. "Guys! On me," he called.

When the squad was around him, he said, "Lieutenant says we're standing down. Delta Company says the dinks have pulled back, so we stand down."

Green realized for the first time that the firing had stopped.

"We goin' back?" he heard Jimmy D ask.

"No," Jonesy said, "We're goin' to set up here on Delta's flank in case the dinks try to come back. Captain's got the third herd out looking for some high ground where we can dig it."

Green heard a rumble in the distance. Thunder.

"Monsoon's comin' in tonight," Jonesy said, "So we're goin' to get wet, not much sleep tonight. So, we go fifty-fifty till we move out. One guy sleeps, the other guy watches. How's your food and water?"

Nobody had any problems, so the squad settled in along the trail.

"Hey, Rook," Little Bit asked, "You want to catch some sleep first?"

"No! I'm okay," Green answered, "You go ahead. I'll keep watch.

As Little Bit settled in against a tree, Green caught himself rubbing the letter in his breast pocket again.

"Hey, Rook," Little Bit called over.

"Yeah," Green answered.

"You did okay, man!" Little Bit said. "Welcome to paradise!"

Jody

Sergeant First Class Mike Grieves was marching alongside his basic training company as they returned from the day's training. They were wrapping up their sixth week of basic, a couple of weeks from graduation.

Watching them march along the blacktop in cantonment, Grieves thought they were finally looking smart, looking like soldiers.

Grieves had taught them how to march like soldiers. They had no drummer beating out a cadence like some of the other basic training companies. His boys marched to their own beat, the beat of their feet hitting the pavement.

But Grieves also knew that you never pushed a good thing too far. After about five minutes of marching in silence, he had to give them the cadence to get their timing back or they'd lose their synchronization.

So, he sang out a cadence to them,

> "Left ... Left ... Left, Right, Left!
> "One, Two, Three, Four,
> "One, Two, Three, Four!"

Now Grieves could hear it, the rhythm tapped out as every left boot in the company hit the ground at the same time. Now they were ready.

He sang,

> "Momma, momma, look at me!"

They answered in unison,

> > "Momma. Momma, Look at me!"

> "I am in the Infantry!"

> > "I am in the Infantry!"

> "Momma, momma, ain't you proud?"

> > "Momma, momma, ain't you proud?"

"I am singin' mighty loud!"
 "I am singin' mighty loud!"
"Am I right or wrong?"
 "You're right!"
"Am I goin' strong?"
 "You're right!"
"Sound off!"
 "One, Two!"
"Sound off!"
 "Three, Four!"
"Bring it on down!"
 "One, Two, Three, Four"
 "One, TWO-oo, THREE, FOUR!"

Now they were hitting it on all pistons. Grieves could hear it; he could feel it coming back at him through the pavement they were pounding.

Other soldiers walking along the street were stopping to look, watching his company march down the street.

Time to stir them up, Grieves thought.

"Ain't no use in goin' home!"
 "Ain't no use in goin' home!"
"Jody's got yo girl an gone!"
 "Jody's got yo girl an gone!"
"Am I right or wrong?"
 "You're right!"
"Am I goin' strong?"
 "You're right!"
"Sound off!"
 "One, Two!"
"Sound off!"
 "Three, Four!"
"Bring it on down!"
 "One, Two, Three, Four"
 "One, TWO-oo, THREE, FOUR!"

Mick Dwyer was marching halfway down the left file of the first platoon. In the last letter he had gotten from home, his girlfriend, Lori, had let him know she was still upset with him for joining the army. He should have at least discussed it with her first!

Then, he heard his friend, Joey Simon, whisper behind him, "Hear that, Mick? Jody's got her by now!"

Grieves sang out again.

"Jody, Jody, six foot four!"

"Jody, Jody, six foot four!"

"Never kicked his ass before!"

"Never kicked his ass before!"

"Gonna take a three-day pass!"

"Gonna take a three-day pass!"

"Gonna kick ol' Jody's ass!"

"Gonna kick ol' Jody's ass!"

"Some college boy, six foot four, a shiny new car, and some foldin' green in his pocket," Joey whispered, "By the time you get home, he'll have her knocked up!"

"For Christ's sake, Joey, will you let it go!" Mick said a bit too loudly.

"No talkin' in ranks there!" Sergeant Grieves yelled. "I'll have your ass cleaning out grease traps with teaspoons all weekend!"

He sung out again!

"Your girl was home when you left!

"You're right!"

"Jody was home when you left!"

"You're right!"

"And now there ain't nothin' left!"

"You're right!"

"Sound off!"

"One, Two!"

"Sound off!"

"Three, Four!"

"Bring it on down!"

"One, Two, Three, Four"
"One, TWO-oo, THREE, FOUR!"
Yeah, Grieves congratulated himself, these boys are shaping up real fine. They'll make some damn fine troopers!

7

The Village

Tom Lattimore knew something wasn't right.

It was too quiet, too fuckin' quiet.

They had done sweeps through Montagnard villages before. This one was right out there in the dark, about a hundred meters down the trail in front of him.

When they got close, they usually heard the animals, the roosters, the pigs even. Then, the dogs smelled them, started barking.

But not now.

He heard nothing out there in the dark.

Something was wrong.

Lattimore had to admit to himself, he didn't like doing these sweeps. There was something wrong with a bunch of armed soldiers busting into someone's home and searching it. That, and being in the middle of a village, made him jumpy. It was too exposed and too constricted, all at the same time. There was no cover or concealment in the middle of a village. You found yourself surrounded by huts, where anybody could be hiding.

No, Lattimore didn't like these sweeps at all.

But the geniuses up in the Two Section, military intelligence, were convinced that the enemy was using these villages to infiltrate the area of operations and stockpile materials. He had to sit through a briefing where some REMF down from brigade explained that the 'Yards built their huts on stilts of sorts, so they were elevated off the ground.

From Lattimore's experience that was correct, and it made a lot of sense in so damp a climate, no flooding and things dried out faster when it rained.

According to the genius giving the briefing, the North Vietnamese army was hiding weapons and equipment in subterranean bunkers built underneath these huts so the Americans couldn't detect them from the air. So insidious were the NVA that these bunkers were virtually invisible even when standing right next to them.

The brain trust at brigade had issued the battalion long metal rods which they were supposed to drive into the ground to uncover these caches. Of course, the army didn't issue any hammers to drive the rods through the soil, rendering the whole concept virtually useless. And the rods themselves were a major pain in the ass to hump through the jungle, so most of them were quickly "lost" by the troops. Lattimore doubted that a single rod had survived to be used on this sweep.

This silence was strange, foreboding, he thought.

The company had arrived in the vicinity of the village around 0330 hours. Lattimore had deployed two of his platoons, the second and third, behind the village as a "blocking force."

The "search team," his first platoon, would enter the village from the east, make contact with the inhabitants, hopefully gain their co-operation, and conduct the physical search.

In Lattimore's experience, an American infantry company was never stealthy enough to pull off these maneuvers without being detected. The banging of equipment, the stumbling around in the bush, and the unauthorized talking probably sounded to the 'Yards like the circus had just arrived in town.

If there were any dinks in the village, they were long gone by the time Lattimore managed to cordon it off, which was fine with him.

Any day you didn't initiate a firefight with the NVA was a good day, as far as he was concerned.

Usually by now, the village dogs were going crazy, which stirred up all the livestock that the villagers kept penned near their huts.

Lattimore heard nothing out there in the darkness.

It was just about BMNT, Begin Morning Nautical Twilight, and the cocks should be crowing. But there was nothing but silence in the direction of the village.

BMNT was also when Lattimore had to get this show on the road. He looked out to the east. The sky was just beginning to lighten. He could begin to see the dark shapes of the trees around him. The trail into the village was just visible as a pale line leading off to the east through the forest.

The "rules of engagement" were to advance to the edge of the village, show themselves, and wait for the inhabitants to approach them.

He had two South Vietnamese military policemen attached to him as "interpreters." He could see them huddling among his headquarters section, the letters "QC" faintly visible on their helmets.

He considered them next to useless. They never understood what the 'Yards were saying in their own language, and the 'Yards typically refused to speak Vietnamese.

Lattimore continued to wonder why there was no sign of human habitation coming from this village.

Evacuation was his lead theory. The villagers had just upped and didi'd ... living in the middle of a combat zone couldn't be very pleasant ... or safe.

Brigade said that this was an *inhabited* village.

Brigade intel wrong?

Say it ain't so, Joe!

Another possibility was that the dinks had some sort of nasty surprise waiting for them down the road. If that were so, Lattimore couldn't understand how they even got the damn animals to cooperate with them!

Shit! All the answers were waiting just a hundred meters down this trail ... and it was time to move out ... just take it slow and careful.

Lattimore then realized he wasn't hearing any birds. They usually caused a racket this time of the morning!

Something was really fucked.

Lattimore spotted his first squad leader, Sergeant Jones, squatting near him in the gloom.

"Jonesy," he hissed, "Move 'em out!"

Pat Green was out on the point.

He was the newest guy in the squad, so he got stuck with all the shit details, of which walking point was the foremost followed closely by burning shit and being last for C-Rat selection. Pat was so sick of Ham and Lima beans he could scream.

He was leading the platoon down a trail, a path really, toward a Montagnard village somewhere out there in the dim light. The good news about walking along a trail ... movement didn't make much noise. The other news about being on a trail ... that's where the dinks set up booby traps and ambushes.

How he could be expected to spot a trip wire or a punji trap in this light, Green couldn't imagine. Would he hear a click when he stepped on something? Would he be able to feel a trip wire through his jungle boots before he triggered something?

There was just light enough that he could barely make out the path before him and the individual trees surrounding him.

If the dinks were out there, keeping low, not moving, how would he see them? What was he supposed to look for ... the silhouette of a helmet ... the shape of a weapon? Every time the trail seemed to jog right or left Green imagined he was looking right down the snout of an RPK machine gun.

In every movie he had ever seen the hero always had some sort of sixth sense about these things ... Dan'l Boone could smell the enemy out there waiting in ambush.

Jonesy had told him sometimes you could smell the dinks before you see them. They smell like fish from what they eat. Green imagined he could smell something fishy ... maybe ... but then it was gone.

Shit ... this whole damned country smelled like fish!

If they were out there waiting, he'd never see them.

Walking point down this trail, he'd just be in the wrong place at the wrong time when the shit hit.

Soon the forest seemed to open up ahead of him ... a clearing. Out in the clearing, he could see black, square-shaped silhouettes ... peaked roofs against the sky ... structures ... dwellings of some sort.

The village!

Green raised his hand with a clenched fist. The column halted behind him. He got down behind some brush.

Nothing seemed to be moving in the clearing. He heard someone approach his position and kneel down next to him. It was the old man, Lt. Lattimore.

"This is it," Lattimore said to no one in particular.

Then the LT stood up and walked straight out into the clearing.

Lattimore walked far enough out into the clearing so that anyone looking from the village could see him. He turned back toward his men still undercover under the tress, and said, "Send those QC's up here."

He heard some rustling behind him in the woods, some inarticulate talk, and suddenly the two South Vietnamese military policemen stumbled into the clearing as if somebody had shoved them from behind, which they probably had been. Hesitantly, they joined Lattimore standing out in the clearing. They stood close to him as if he could in some way protect them.

Nothing moved out there toward the village. There was no sound.

The protocol was to stand here, to wait for the villagers to approach them.

Nothing moved in the village.

Again, Lattimore was conscious of the silence.

Even the morning birds were silent.

The village was abandoned, he assumed.

He turned his head toward his men still skulking in the woods, and said, "Machine guns to me!"

Again, there was rustling behind him, some whispering as the word was passed down. Then his two machine gun crews emerged from the forest and joined him.

He pointed the first to take a position twenty-five meters to the right, just inside the wood line; the second, twenty-five meters to the left.

For a moment, he thought to call the platoon sergeant, Jake Taylor. Then he remembered that he had left Jake with the blocking force to assist his platoon leaders.

He called back, "Squad leaders to me!"

Again, some rustling and whispering in the woods behind him. Then, three soldiers emerged and joined him at the edge of the clearing. As they did, Lattimore took a knee.

The QC's took that opportunity to get back under cover. Lattimore could almost sense their relief not having to stand out there in the open with him.

When they were all together, Lattimore quickly briefed them. "Sam! You and second squad link up with the gun on the right. Set up along the wood line. Cover the village and our movement forward. José! You take third squad to the left, same deal."

Lattimore noticed that his two radio operators, RTO's, had joined him.

"Jimmy ... get on the horn to battalion ... report our position ... tell them the village appears to be abandoned ... tell them we're going in. Jackson ... get a hold of Sergeant Taylor with the blocking force ... tell him no contact made ... we're advancing into the village ... then get a hold of the mortar section ... talk to Lieutenant Desmond himself ... tell him the village seems abandoned ... I want fire plotted right on these coordinates ... set it up and be ready to go on my command," he instructed.

Lattimore turned to Jonesy. "Okay, Jonesy, first squad is going in ... clear the area and we follow ... you draw fire ... get down best you can ... we'll cover you ... then get the fuck out of there ... got it."

Jonesy nodded, taking a firm grasp of the shitty end of the stick he'd been given.

"Okay," Lattimore concluded, "Any questions?"

There was now enough light that he could see his squad leaders shaking their heads no.

"Okay, initially my CP will be here. I will displace forward as soon as first squad enters the village. Move out!" Lattimore ordered.

The squad leaders went back into the woods to brief their men. Within minutes the second and third squads were filing out of the forest, moving along the wood line and getting into position. Jonesy's squad was congregating at the head of the trail, waiting for the covering force to get into position before they began their advance.

Lattimore moved back to join them.

"Jonesy," he told his first squad leader, "If anybody's in that village, they know we're here, so take it slow and careful."

As soon as he said it, Lattimore realized how lame he must sound. If the dinks were in the village, Jonesy's squad was heading straight into a hornets' nest.

Jonesy just nodded, then called, "Green! Move out! Straight downtown!"

As he entered the clearing, Green immediately realized that there was something worse than walking point down a trail through a forest in the dark.

It was walking point across a clearing surrounded by buildings in the early light.

Green imagined that there were hundreds of pairs of eyes fixed on him, all waiting until he got just a little bit closer so they could not possibly miss him.

He felt his legs go weak; his abdomen seemed to turn into water.

He tightened his butt muscles so there'd be no "accident."

He wondered if this was anything like Major Rogers, Sergeant McNott, and Langdon Towne felt when they were closing in on the Abenaki village at dawn.

He wondered why those stupid novels he had read as a kid never talked about guys being so scared that they almost shit their drawers.

Green could see nothing moving. There were no sounds... complete silence ... not even birds.

When he came up to the first hut, he heard Jonesy hiss at him. He turned, and Jonesy gave him the signal to halt.

Green tried to find as much cover as he could.

He could see clearly into the village now. The huts seemed to be grouped around a central space with a couple of trees growing in it. To his left front, he could just see where the village had damned up a little stream that flowed past and flooded their rice paddies.

The village was absolutely still.

Green looked back and saw Jonesy briefing Jimmy Delvecchio, his B-Team leader. Jonesy pointed to the hut on their right and gave D the "cover" sign. D nodded and moved toward the hut. Sweetie Gonzales and Freddy Harris followed him. They seemed to disappear in the shadows under the hut.

In the distance behind him, Green could see movement from the wood line across the clearing. Then he realized that Lt. Lattimore was moving forward with his RTO's and the covering force. They had to displace because now the huts were screening the first squad's advance.

Come on and join the fun, Green thought.

Green was just wondering whether Jonesy was going to hold here until the old man and the machine guns caught up to them, when he saw Jonesy give him the signal to move out.

Green moved into the space between the huts. He was trying to stay right in the middle, but he knew that if there was a ambush, it wouldn't make a hell of a lot of difference where he was in this narrow space.

The light had increased. He was just able to perceive colors ... the greenish-grays of the trees ... the blackish-browns of the huts.

Then he spotted something, something that seemed to break the linear patterns of huts and trees. It was under one of the trees to his front. It looked like ... well it looked like a lump of something ... a bush ... no ... it was too solid ... too opaque ... hard, like a boulder.

Green gravitated toward it.

Then something about it moved.

Quickly, his hand shot up ... fist closed ... stop!

He got down on one knee; no place to hide out here.

He stared at the object. What had moved?

Then, there it was again ... it looked like a small creature on top of a rock ... or a flap of cloth ... yes... it looked like a piece of black and red fabric.

Green moved closer.

A smell hit him.

Meat! Rotten meat!

When he reached the object, the smell of decay and purification almost gagged him.

He examined his find. He suddenly realized he was looking at a human body. It was like no human body he had ever imagined. Black ... swollen to the point of stretching and straining the clothes that constrained it.

The face was the worst ... open eyes bulged out at him ... the mouth was frozen into a round, silent scream.

Green recoiled back from this horror ... he almost dropped his weapon.

He looked around himself ... he was surrounded by these black shapes ... they lay everywhere in the clearing.

The sun finally broke over the trees to the east. He heard something ... a buzzing ... flies ... thousands upon thousands of flies surrounding each of the dead black, with swirling, black aureoles.

Lattimore was double-timing across the clearing. He could hear the machine gun crew and covering force advancing behind him.

He saw the first squad's point man move into the village. Then he saw him freeze, signal the squad to halt.

Lattimore changed his axis of advance to get more concealment from the hut to his right. The covering force followed.

Something was going on up ahead.

The point man spotted something.

As Lattimore reached the hut, he immediately spotted the fire team in overwatch position. Just as he was pointing the position out to the gun crew and covering squad, he saw the point man in the clearing back away from something as if he were frightened of it.

Instead of getting under cover, the point man just stood there, right in the middle of the clearing, looking around, as if he were in shock.

He saw Jonesy move up to him.

The point man pointed to something in the clearing.

Both men just stood there, staring.

What the fuck, Lattimore thought.

"Keep your eyes open!" he instructed the overwatch team as he ran forward into the clearing.

As he ran, he saw a huge, black soldier with an M79 grenade launcher, "Little Bit" he remembered suddenly, rise up slowly and walk toward his two friends who were still just standing in the middle of the clearing between the huts.

When Lattimore reached them, he said, "What the fuck's going on? What're you doing?"

Jonesy just pointed and deadpanned, "Look!"

Lattimore looked in the direction that Jonesy was pointing.

He looked at the huts first, the black doorways. That was the primary danger area.

Nothing!

Then underneath the huts, in the shadows where the enemy might be concealed.

Nothing!

He noticed what seemed to be piles of cloth everywhere in the clearing. At first, he didn't know what he was looking at. Then he noticed the black, moving cloud around each pile of cloth ... then he heard the buzzing ... flies.

Then he realized what he was seeing.

He heard Jonesy say, "They're all dead ... the whole fuckin' village is dead!"

Lattimore pulled his men out of the village.

It wasn't a tactical decision; it was a human decision.

They all knew they had to get away from that horror. Everyone and everything in the village was dead, dead for at least a day, maybe more, putrefying in the heat.

No one would enter the huts. Seeing the bodies lying in the clearing was bad enough. No one wanted to discover what horrors lay waiting in those huts.

Green, Jonesy's point man, seemed to be in shock. Doc was looking at him. Even Jonesy, who had been through the shit a couple of times, was pale, withdrawn.

Lattimore was confused.

What had happened here?

The bodies were lying about individually as if someone had suddenly and instantly cut the strings of a score of puppets and they had all fallen to the ground simultaneously.

If they had sensed danger, wouldn't they have huddled together, Lattimore wondered. Wouldn't we have found the bodies in piles?

Even their animals were dead. Every one of them. Each lying alone as if they had all died at the same instant ... what could kill everything in an entire village instantly ... even the birds in the area surrounding the village seemed to be gone ... they were sitting in a dead zone ... an instantaneous dead zone.

Suddenly, a horrific thought formed in Lattimore's mind. He tried to reject it ... push it away ... but it kept coming back to him ... an instantaneous dead zone.

"Doc! Doc!" he yelled.

"What's a matter, sir?" Joe Ambrose, his head medic yelled over to him, "You hurt?"

"No! No! Come here! Quick!" Lattimore insisted.

As soon as Doc got over to his commander, Lattimore grabbed him by his equipment straps and hissed into his ear, "How much atropine we got on hand?"

"Atropine? Why do you ..." Doc jerked back and said.

"Keep it down, Doc, for Christ's sake," Lattimore said, pulling Doc close again, "I hope the fuck I'm wrong, but I think this village was hit with some kind of nerve gas."

"Nerve gas," Doc gasped, "No! That's not possible! Who the fuck ..."

"Doesn't matter," Lattimore insisted. "What matters is getting our guys out of here and treated. ASAP! How much atropine back at the firebase?"

"Shit ... I don't know ..." Doc calculated, "I think there's a box of ampules in battalion stores ... what ... twenty-four doses..."

"Okay," Lattimore said, "Get on battalion admin/log! Confirm that! Tell them to get on the horn to brigade! I need at least ... shit ... seventy-five to be safe ... yeah... seventy-five doses ... ASAP. Get on it, Doc!"

As Doc walked away, Lattimore yelled, "Squad leaders... RTO... on me... Now!"

Please, Lord ... please, Lord, he prayed ... let me be wrong about this ... please let me be wrong ... or please lord, don't let it have been a persistent agent ..."

He looked up and everyone was there with him. "Jackson," he said to his company RTO, "I want Sergeant Taylor on the horn! ASAP! Sergeant Taylor himself! Not his RTO. Not one of the lieutenants."

Then he turned to his squad leaders. Jonesy was still looking a bit green around the gills. "Saddle 'em up!" Lattimore started. "We're moving out..."

The RTO interrupted him. "Sergeant Taylor's on the horn LT," he said handing the handset to Lattimore.

Lattimore grabbed the handset.

"Jake! It's Tom! Listen up ... we may not have much time ... I think we've been exposed to nerve gas ... yeah ... you heard me correct ... nerve gas ... have one of your medics go around and collect up every ampule of atropine that your guys are carrying ... what ... yes ... atropine... right ... no ... don't tell them anything ... just make something up ... recall on a bad lot or some shit like that ... you can tell the platoon leaders ... no one else ... don't start a panic ... then you pull out ... head straight back to the firebase ... what ... no ... don't wait on us ... go straight in ... tell the platoon leaders that comes straight from me ... when you get back there ... decontaminate the men ... all the clothes, all the equipment ... use the water trailers ... battalion's got some of those canvas-bag shower heads ... wash everything down ASAP ... yeah... once you get back you can tell them the truth ... if any of your guys suddenly develop flu-like symptoms ... runny eyes ... runny nose ... tightness in the chest ... or disorientation, like he's drunk ... hit him with the atropine ... yeah ... right away ... atropine ... I hope the fuck I'm wrong ... get 'er done ... good ... see you back there ... out."

Lattimore looked up. His squad leaders and RTO were looking at him as if he had just sprouted a second head.

"Okay ... you guys heard that ... so, same message ... collect up the atropine ... give it to Doc Ambrose ... watch your guys for symptoms ... we're moving back to that stream we crossed on the way in about a klick from here ... it's upstream of this place, so it should be alright

... we're all taking a bath ... weapons, clothes, equipment ... everything ... into the water ... then we're heading in ... look, I'm probably wrong about this ... or whatever hit these people has already dispersed ... so we're safe ... better safe than sorry."

Pat Green was sitting up against his rucksack with his head hanging down between his knees. He was feeling a bit better. He didn't think he'd ever get the image of the black, bloated, putrefying corpse out of his mind ... the bulging eyes ... the round, screaming mouth.

Jonesy laid a hand on his shoulder.

Green's head jerked up.

"Green! You carrying any atropine?" Jonesy asked him.

"Atropine? Why you asking about atropine?" Green responded.

"The old man wants me to collect it up," Jonesy answered, "Something about a bad lot number or some happy horse shit like that."

"Couldn't this shit wait?" he grumbled.

He found his protective mask strapped down to his ruck and opened a pocket in the back. He pulled out a plastic ampule.

"Yeah ... here's some," he said and gave it to Jonesy.

"Great!" Jonesy said! "Oh yeah ... some good news ... the old man's going to stop and let as all take a little swim in that blue line we crossed this morning."

8

The Clean Lieutenant Pays A Visit

The clean lieutenant with the clipboard looked down at his boots.

Mud had spattered on the spit-shined toes of his Corcoran jump boots.

He turned his heel and saw that mud had also splashed up the boot and across the back of his starched, pressed and creased fatigue trousers.

God-damned pigsty, he thought, can't stay clean at all in this damned mud. I can't wait to get out of this stinking hole and get back to brigade.

The clean lieutenant knew better than to wipe the mud off the spit-shined toes of his boots. That would just ruin the shine by scratching the base of polish on the toes. The first chance he got, he'd rinse his boots off from the spigot on the water trailer.

The grunts in this place had plenty of drinking water.

When he got back to the rear, his hooch girl could take care of his uniform.

Meanwhile, he would just have to suffer through being on this tiny, filthy battalion firebase in the middle of God's armpit ensuring that army food-service procedures were being observed.

Not that the clean lieutenant gave a rat's ass about mess regulations. In fact, he didn't really give a rat's ass about anything in the army.

For the clean lieutenant, the army, this idiotic war, and being in the filthy, rotten fish-smelling country were just means to an end.

What the clean lieutenant did care about, if he cared about anything other than his own needs, was his political aspirations when he got back to the world.

Because there was a war on, and serving in a war always looked good on a political resume, the clean lieutenant had signed up for ROTC in college. He was commissioned in the Infantry at graduation. He could have chosen a non-combat branch, like the Adjutant Generals Corps or Transportation, but being in a combat branch during a war played better. He had been tempted to take Armor, but the thought of having to get involved in all that maintenance, repair, dirt and grease was a bit too nitty-gritty for him. He'd never get the grease out from under his fingernails, and how would that look when he was out shaking hands with potential voters.

Although the clean lieutenant was now in the combat arms, the trick was to keep out of actual combat. And, to keep out of having to spend time in places like this mud-spattered, fly-infested, filthy firebase up in the highlands of Vietnam.

Well, father was taking care of the combat part. For the man who decided who got elected to all the worthwhile political offices in Boston, the state of Massachusetts, and in Washington, keeping his only son out of harm's way should be a minor challenge.

The clean lieutenant was seven months into an obligatory twelve-month combat tour of Vietnam and, so far, the most violence that he had been exposed to was when a fight broke out in the O-Club on the Pleiku Air Force Base.

Since arriving in country, the clean lieutenant had had several staff assignments. At first, he had been assigned to Civil Affairs at division, the G5 Section. Life was acceptable in the division base camp. He had a room in a wooden barrack, and a tolerable bed to sleep in, once he found one that didn't sag in strange places. Of course, there was no plumbing to speak of, but what could one expect? This was a "hardship" tour. The bartender at the division officers club could mix a decent rusty nail, when he had the ingredients, and, when not, there was always plenty of ice to kill the taste of the beer that he was forced to drink.

The problem with this assignment for the clean lieutenant, was that civil affairs also meant actually visiting various Vietnamese villages around Pleiku. God, how those cesspits stank! The clean lieutenant could not understand why anyone would want to live like that, tin shacks, filth, snotty brats, and mongrel dogs everywhere. And the smell! It was like the fish market in Boston in August, but many times worse. He had trouble not throwing up every time he had to go into one of those stinking holes, and it took days to get the smell out of his uniform.

Then, for no reason he could imagine, or was told, the clean lieutenant was transferred to the division's third brigade. This meant moving from the division base camp to a somewhat permanent firebase ten kilometers west of Pleiku, near some Vietnamese cesspool, the name of which he could never remember. He was billeted in something the army called a SEA-hut, a wooden building with a floor elevated off the ground and under a tin roof. Instead of a bed, he was given a cot and air-mattress, which strangely was more comfortable than the lumpy mattress and sagging springs he had to endure at division. But, when it rained, which it never seemed to stop doing in this God-forsaken country, it hammered the roof like Gene Krupa on cocaine ... kept him awake for hours ... even after four or five cocktails! But he thought he could endure even that for the six months left on his tour.

At first, the brigade chief of staff didn't know what to do with the clean lieutenant. So, he did odd jobs around the Command Post, some typing, some filing, but mostly "go for" work for the Operations and Intel sections.

A sergeant actually had the audacity to ask him to take a turn fetching the coffee from the mess tent in the morning. That was the last time that sergeant, or any other enlisted man, made a mistake like that. He certainly made his position clear to the brigade commander.

Then, again for no apparent reason, the clean lieutenant was suddenly assigned to the S4 Section, Supply and Logistics. This meant moving again. This time from the CP to a location called the "Combat Trains." Now he lived in a tent, a "GP medium" as the army classified it. At least there were duck boards on the floor, and he paid some of the Vietnamese workers to build him walls for privacy. There were actually enlisted men living in the same tent as he! He thought that must be against regs, but he could probably endure even that for the remaining time left in his tour.

Again, at first the Four wasn't sure what to do with the clean lieutenant. So again, he spent his time at odd jobs, alphabetizing the clothing issue records, typing forms that were originally filled out by hand.

At least the people here had the good sense not to try to turn him into a coffee-boy.

Then, the brigade mess officer, some OCS lieutenant, who unfortunately had a Combat Infantry Badge and time-in-grade on him, came up with the idea of assigning him as the "brigade head-count officer." The OCS person explained to him that the brigade needed someone to ensure that army food service regs were being observed in the field. Specifically, he was to ensure that meals were being signed for by the troops in the field and that rations were accounted for.

"When a battalion mess sergeant signs for a hundred rations, someone has to make sure that a hundred rations are issued to the troops," the OCS person explained to the clean lieutenant. "The way the army keeps track of that is through signatures. Before a soldier goes through the chow line, he has to sign this "Signature Headcount Sheet." See ... DA FORM 3032 per DA Pam 30-32! Across each line, the individual prints his last name first, then first name or initial, then rank ... rank has to be by pay-grade. So, Sergeant Jones, say, writes in 'E5' not 'Sergeant.' The unit serving the meal, the date and time of the meal, and the meal designation goes onto the header of each form. If you have to use more than one form for a meal, you just start another form by reproducing the header from the first form, but on the top of the second form you write '2 of' and fill in the number of individual forms you use for each meal later."

"Now, if a battalion draws a hundred rations and collects a hundred signatures, no problem. What we're looking for are over-draws, like drawing a hundred rations and only serving eighty meals. Now, that's never good, but it happens. So, when that does happen, either the mess sergeant needs to fill out this other form that explains how he's managing leftovers, or the first sergeant fills out a form explaining why a solder assigned to the unit wasn't fed. They're pretty self-explanatory. Look them over when you get a chance and if you have any questions, you can ask me. But the essential point is that the number of rations issued must equal the number of rations served plus the number of rations used for leftovers, plus the number of soldiers not fed."

"Now you don't have to take the signatures yourself. You can have a unit NCO do it, but just keep an eye on him. While the mess hall is serving, keep an eye on portion control, make sure all the servers have head gear, general cleanliness, shit like that.

"Any questions? Good!"

"Last, make sure the troops going through the chow line are in proper uniform as much as makes sense under the tactical conditions. Division policy states that the troops being served chow will be in proper field uniform with steel pot and flak vest. Also, everyone should be carrying his assigned weapon. The SOP calls for troops to use their mess kits. But, a lot of the mess sections use paper plates, which is alright. There should be two garbage cans for waste material. Make sure the troops scrape their mess kits in one and dump the paper and plastic in the other."

"And, this is important, don't let them pitch the eating utensils from the mess kit in the garbage. Plastic stuff, okay, but no silverware. Check the immersion heaters and washing stations. Make sure the water is hot enough, just below boiling, one soapy for washing, one clear for rinsing. And make sure the troops use them, with the brushes. Make sure the immersion heaters are set up away from the chow lines. If one of those gas heaters blows, we don't want casualties. Are you getting all this?"

The clean lieutenant had stopped listening after DA Form blah, blah, blah.

He was noticing the mess officer's Combat Infantry Badge.

Like most junior staff officers, the mess officer had done six months with a line unit before getting a staff assignment.

The clean lieutenant already knew that he would get a Bronze Star for his service at the end of his tour. Since most civilians didn't know the difference between service commendation and one for valor in combat, he could expect them to think of him as a "war hero." But a CIB would really seal the deal.

He wondered if being in a brigade trains area was considered "field duty." Or, if an occasional mortar or rocket attack was considered "under enemy fire." He made a mental note to research that.

Or he could just slip a headquarters typist a few bucks to include him on the next set of CIB orders. He didn't think anyone would notice.

The undesirable part of the clean lieutenant's new assignment was that he actually had to go out into the field to inspect battalion mess operations. Luckily, due to the tactical situation in the highlands, mess operations were consolidated at battalion, and even the battalion kitchens weren't operating all the time. Most of the time, the soldiers had to eat C-rations and like it.

But even battalion firebases were a little too close to actual combat operations than the lieutenant wanted to be.

Being an infantry officer didn't obligate him to do infantry work. So, the clean lieutenant had become a master at "combat commuting," getting on the first supply helicopter out of brigade in the morning and getting on the last one back at night, even if he had to order some enlisted man to make room for him by dumping a couple of crates of ammo, boxes of rations, or some replacements.

On a couple of occasions, though, especially now that the monsoon season had started, the clean lieutenant had gotten stranded on a battalion firebase. Usually, they let him bunk in with the battalion CP. But, once he actually had to sleep in an infantry "hooch," just a couple of ponchos strung up with sticks with nothing between him and the wet ground but a leaky air mattress.

The battalion Ops officer told him to sleep with his boots on in case something happened at night! What that "something" was, the major never specified.

During the night, the 105 battery got a fire mission. When those guns went off, the lieutenant nearly shit his pants. He couldn't tell whether the stuff was going out or coming in.

When he finally got back to brigade, his boots and uniform were such a mess that his hooch girl wanted twice what he normally paid her to take care them.

But the clean lieutenant could endure all this for the few months remaining in his tour. Besides, spending a night or two on a forward firebase probably made his case for a CIB stronger.

During his last inspection, the clean lieutenant had had a real bad moment. The battalion he was inspecting decided to send hot rations out to a company out in the boonies. The battalion mess sergeant wanted to know whether the clean lieutenant wanted to ride out on the helicopter with the chow so he could collect his signatures.

The clean lieutenant had to think fast, finally telling the mess sergeant that according to army regs, once rations were broken down to that level, actual signatures were not required.

Whether that was true or not, the clean lieutenant had no idea, but the mess sergeant seemed to buy it. The clean lieutenant made an apparent effort to measure the number or rations placed in each marmite can and confirmed the strength of the unit being fed, then told the mess sergeant that everything met army standards.

It took the clean lieutenant a couple of hours to fudge the forms once he got back to brigade. But the brigade mess officer seemed pleased. Strangely enough, quite pleased, as the clean lieutenant remembered. That, and the fact that the brigade mess officer referred to the battalion mess sergeant by his first name made him feel like someone who had been left out of a joke.

But nothing in his seven months in Vietnam had quite prepared the clean lieutenant for what seemed to be unfolding before him at this battalion.

The mess hall was set up and ready to serve. They were only feeding the battalion's alpha company which had just gotten in from a three week sweep through the surrounding mountains. The meal, a breakfast ration, was delayed because the company had to hump into the firebase and had only come in a half hour ago.

The battalion mess sergeant had shown the clean lieutenant his paperwork confirming that he had drawn eighty-three rations for this meal. That seemed a little low for an entire line company, but the clean lieutenant knew that most line units in the field were under strength.

The refuse containers and the cleaning stations were set up and separated away from the chow line. The clean lieutenant had checked the cleaning stations and both immersion heaters were lit, and the water was almost to the boiling point. The mess line and serving utensils looked reasonably clean. The servers were all wearing steal pots in accordance with division policy.

It was the unit to be fed, the line company that had just pulled into the firebase, which shocked the clean lieutenant. They were beginning to form a line to be served chow, but had the clean lieutenant not known better, he would have thought he was looking at something halfway between a band of gypsies and a motorcycle gang.

All the men were filthy and unshaven, even their faces were streaked with mud. There wasn't a regulation haircut to be seen. The fact that he could see their hair indicated to the clean lieutenant that no one was wearing a steel pot in accordance with division policy. Their uniforms were filthy, and most were ripped and shredded. The clean lieutenant could swear one soldier was trying to stuff his testicles in what was left of his trousers.

But every one of them was carrying a weapon. In fact, not only did they have their weapons, to the clean lieutenant every weapon looked remarkably serviceable, clean and well-oiled despite the monsoon. Each one of them had a bandoleer or two of ammunition hanging from, wrapped around, or tied somehow to his body.

What really shocked the clean lieutenant was how pale the soldiers appeared. Their faces were a dull shade of grayish white. They looked like something that had crawled out of a Herman Melville nightmare — a ship's company of drowned men returned to muster out and collect their shares.

One of these ragamuffin soldiers, a tall, lean NCO, walked up to the clean lieutenant as if he knew him well and had just run into his old friend on the Boston common.

"The company's ready to be fed, LT," he reported.

"Huh ... what?" the clean lieutenant stammered. "Who are you? Don't you salute officers?"

"I'm Sergeant Taylor, the company field first sergeant," the tall soldier responded. "This is alpha company. We're supposed to get hot A's. And no ... I don't salute officers in the field. We're ready to be fed. What's the holdup?"

"The holdup?" the clean lieutenant answered unaccustomed to being talked to like this by an enlisted man. "Where's the rest of your company. I want the whole company here before I open the chow line."

"This is the whole company," Taylor stated. "I got five on sick call with the medics, but this is alpha company."

"That can't right be right, sergeant!" the clean lieutenant protested. "I've got eighty-three A-rations issued to Alpha company, 3rd Battalion, 35th Infantry to be accounted for. But I only see about fifty soldiers in this line! Chow can't start until I see your entire company!"

"Lieutenant, I don't know what the fuck you're talking about!" Taylor told him. "This is alpha company ... all of it ... and the old man sent us over here to get fed. These guys haven't had a hot meal in over three weeks, not even a fuckin' cup of real coffee. I need to get this fucking goat-rope moving. Besides, I got a bunch of guys standing in a line out in the open ... something that's not too good for their long-term health. So, instead of having them stand around smelling chow they can't eat and presenting nice targets for some dink sniper, let's get this show on the road!"

The clean lieutenant was shocked at the way he was being addressed by this filthy, enlisted man. So, he decided to put an end to this man's insubordinate attitude.

"Sergeant," he stated, with as much indignation and resolve he could muster, "I don't know who you think you are ... where are your officers"?"

"Officers eat after the men," the sergeant said, not at all impressed by the lieutenant's posturing. "I don't have the foggiest fuckin' idea where the platoon leaders are. The old man's over the CP with the battalion commander ... you wanna talk to him? Hey, Green!"

Another one of the drowned soldiers came over, weapon and magazines clanking, "Yeah, Sarge?"

"Green, hustle your ass over to battalion … it's the bunker with the antennas over there … get the old man … tell him there's a problem with the chow … I need to see him."

The one called Green muttered something under his breath that sounded to the clean lieutenant like "fuckin' army can't even organize a chow line," and then he doubled over toward the battalion CP, weapons and magazines clanking an accompaniment to his jog.

"While I have your attention, Sergeant… uh… Thomas, was it," the clean lieutenant continued, "Regs specify that soldiers on a chow line must wear steel pots and flak jackets. You need to get your men squared away."

"It's Taylor, Lieutenant, Platoon Sergeant Andrew Jackson Taylor! And we got no flak vest and I'm done with this conversation! Tell your story to the company commander when he gets here."

"You come to the position of attention when you address an officer, sergeant!" the clean lieutenant demanded. "I'll have you up on charges! You're being insubordinate."

Taylor didn't flinch. He looked the lieutenant right in his eyes and said, "You'd need a witness for that… *sir* … and you don't seem to have one … I got fifty hungry guys standing around wondering why they ain't getting fed who'll swear they never heard or saw a thing … besides … I hear the accommodations in Leavenworth are a hell of lot better than they are out here … *sir*."

The clean lieutenant was building up all his army-authorized indignation to respond, when the one called Green clanked over with another one of the ragamuffin soldiers. This one was carrying a carbine.

Before the clean lieutenant could react to this new event, the new soldier said, "What the fuck's going on here, Jake! Why aren't the men being fed. What's the problem that you had to pull me out of a meeting with the battalion commander?"

"I got no problem, LT," Taylor stated. "But this here REMF lieutenant's got a shit pot full of them. And he won't let the cooks serve."

The company commander turned on the clean lieutenant.

"Who the fuck are you, and why the fuck are you fucking with my people?" he demanded.

Before the clean lieutenant could respond, the battalion commander, Lieutenant Colonel Jack Byrne, who could smell a cup of army coffee at ten miles, wandered over from his CP and joined the growing cluster in front of the mess tent.

"Ah, Lieutenant Lattimore!" the battalion commander said, "Let me introduce you to our brigade mess ... uh ... head-count audit officer... did I get that right, Lieutenant? He's visiting us from brigade to make sure we don't waste any of the taxpayer's money by overfeeding the troops. Isn't that right, lieutenant."

"That's not quite why I'm here, sir ..." the clean lieutenant tried to explain.

Deciding that this conversation was completely out of his league, Sergeant Taylor said, "This shit's now way above my pay grade! Excuse me, sir! Come with me, Green!"

Taylor took one step back, assumed the position of attention in front of the clean lieutenant, and brought up a smart salute.

Being completely immune to any sarcasm being directed at him, the clean lieutenant also came to attention and returned the salute, thinking that he had won the chest-bumping contest with this insubordinate NCO.

The company and battalion commanders just looked on.

Taylor snapped off his salute smartly and said, "You have a great day, sir!"

He and Green walked back over to the company, clanking their weapons and magazines. The clean lieutenant could have sworn he heard one of them mutter, "What a dip shit!"

"Yes!" Colonel Byrne continued, "The lieutenant's quite a celebrity in the division. Seems his daddy's a congressman or senator up in one of them Yankee states. Isn't that right, Lieutenant?"

"No, sir. My father is the managing partner of a law firm in Boston ..."

"Yes, indeed," the battalion commander interrupted, "It is indeed a comfort to know that young men of the lieutenant's station have chosen to serve their country in this stinking, dirty, shit-hole of a war when they could just as easily have used their influence to stay out of it ... indeed it is."

"Thank you, sir," the clean lieutenant said with no sense of irony, "I'm just trying to do my duty ..."

"And a fine piece of work you're doing, coming all the way out here from brigade to assist us in feeding our own men," the colonel continued, "Is there anything I can do to make things work a little better for you?"

"Thank you, sir," the clean lieutenant answered, mistaking the battalion commander's offer as sincere. "I need to get these troops in proper uniform ... they need helmets, flak vests ..."

"Ah ... yes ... just like division wants," Byrne seemed to agree. "Well, you see lieutenant, these men have literally just walked out of the bush after humping the boonies for over three weeks ... and my battalion is suffering from an acute shortage of flak vests at the moment. Perhaps you could mention that to the Brigade Four when you see him. I'm sure he'd love to know that. But, back to your point, I think just this one time we can get the men fed and then take care of some of those other details after we've had a chance to settle them in and clean them up a bit ... just this one time, mind you ... that's okay with you, isn't it, Lieutenant Lattimore."

"Uh ... Yes, sir," Lattimore agreed, wondering where this was all going, "I'll see it all gets takin' care of."

"See how easy that was, Lieutenant," said the BC to the clean lieutenant. "Is there anything else?"

"Yes, sir," the clean lieutenant continued, thinking he was finally making some progress! "It seems that there were eighty-three rations drawn for this meal and this company's strength is well below that. I will not be able to account ..."

"Excuse me for interrupting, Lieutenant," Byrne said. "But, if I understand you correctly, you need at least eighty-three signatures on that form you got there on that clip board. Is that correct?"

"Yes, sir! But they must be valid ..."

"That won't be a problem, Lieutenant," said the battalion commander, plucking the clipboard from the clean lieutenant's hand and passing it over to Lattimore, "I'm sure we can find a couple of extra people on this firebase to feed. Can you also take care of that little detail for us, Tom?"

"Affirmative, sir!" Lattimore responded.

"There! I think that takes care of all the critical issues we have before us at the moment," the battalion commander said, "Now can we get these men fed, Lieutenant?"

"That's fine with me, sir," the clean lieutenant conceded, "I'll just observe the operation."

"That's fine ... fine indeed," Byrne tutted.

Then he sprung his ambush.

"Oh. By the way, lieutenant. How long have you been in country? I seem to remember someone telling me over six months. Is that right?

The clean lieutenant was surprised, in a not too pleasant way, that the commander of a light infantry battalion operating in the field knew that much about him.

"Seven months this week, sir," he answered.

"That's what I thought ... that's what I thought ... but I'm a bit confused," the colonel said, actually managing to look somewhat perplexed.

"About what, sir?" asked the clean lieutenant, not liking at all where this conversation seemed to be heading.

"I see on your collar that you're an infantry officer," said the BC. "But, seven months in country, on brigade staff, and you're not wearing a CIB. How can that be?"

The conversation was now taking a very unpleasant turn, and the clean lieutenant felt himself get a bit flushed, but he wasn't sure why.

The nascent politician answered, "I haven't yet been offered the opportunity of serving with a line unit."

"Really! What a waste!" the battalion commander said in apparent shock. "An officer of your caliber and talent! And so many line units in need of good officers! Hmm ... Tom! Don't you need officers?"

"A platoon leader and an XO, sir," agreed the alpha company commander.

The clean lieutenant was now sweating freely. His stomach seemed to be tying itself in a slip knot, and he knew why.

"That's what I thought, Tom," said Byrne nodding.

Then he turned to the clean lieutenant and said, "I could fix this right up for you with brigade, Lieutenant. You wouldn't even need to go back. You could join alpha right here ... are you all right, lieutenant?"

The clean lieutenant looked as pale as one of the drowned soldiers, whom he had tried to refuse to feed, just somewhat cleaner.

"I'm ... uh ... I'm fine ... sir. I've... I've just been standing out here most of the morning. I think the sun's getting to me a bit."

"Oh, we can't have that, Lieutenant. We can't have that at all," the colonel seemed to fret. "How could I explain to the brigade commander that I let one of his most promising staff officers get sun stroke!"

The battalion commander patted the clean lieutenant on his back as if they had reached some sort of an agreement, secret to just the two of them.

"Why don't you grab some coffee over at the mess tent and head on over to my CP," Byrne offered. "Sit down in the shade. Relax until your head clears. We'll keep an eye on things out here for you. Won't we, Tom? You just go over to my CP. Get off your feet for a bit ... get out of the sun."

With seemingly benevolent and concerned smiles on their faces, both the company commander and the battalion commander watched the clean lieutenant shuffle over to the battalion CP, picking his way carefully around the puddles and mud.

When the clean lieutenant was well out of hearing, Lattimore broke the silence without breaking his fake smile. "Were you serious, sir? I mean about putting that REMF in my company."

"I wouldn't have that useless piece of shit in my battalion if my life depended on it, Tom ... not if my life depended on it," Byrne answered. "And I certainly wouldn't fuck up a good leadership team like yours by assigning him to it. For Christ's sake, not only would I need someone to change his diapers every time something happened, but I'd also spend the rest of my career writing letters to some fuckin' political bag-man in Boston about how I'm taking care of his baby boy."

"That's a relief," Lattimore said. "For a minute there I thought you were being serious, sir."

"No. We can do without the likes of him," the BC concluded. "Annoying little bastard! The Four probably sent him out here because he can't stand the sight of him and didn't want him fucking up anything important. But, Tom, that little, snot-nosed son-of-a-bitch is connected, and I imagine he could stir up quite a shitstorm if he wanted to. I have enough on my plate without having to worry about ration accountability. So, you make sure I have enough names on that form. I'm sure our nice, clean lieutenant will be on the first bird out of here as soon as he has his signatures. And, I have a feeling we won't be seeing his starched and spit-shined ass again anytime soon."

9

Why We Fight

"So, Greenie," Sweetie Gonzalez said through a mouthful of powdered eggs, "Tell me again about these dominoes!"

Sweetie was engaging in two of his favorite pastimes, eating and busting Pat Green's balls.

"It's not 'dominoes,' Sweetie," Green tried to explain while wolfing down his second bacon sandwich, washed down with gulps of steaming, brown army coffee, "It's the 'Domino Theory'. It's how the government explains why this war's so important."

"Because of them dominoes, right?" Sweetie questioned.

Then he laughed with an explosion of powdered egg. "Who gives a fuck about dominoes, man?"

"Can it, Sweetie! I'd like to hear this," Jonesy, their squad leader, said.

Jonesy wasn't eating, but he was on his second cigarette and third canteen cup of coffee, with enough sugar in it to make the plastic spoon stand up.

Green chewed quickly and hard, then swallowed like a boa constrictor downing a small deer. He put the rest of his sandwich down on the paper plate balanced on his lap. Then, he took a big swallow of coffee to wash the lump down out of his throat so he could talk.

"It's like this," he explained. "It's like a row of dominoes. When you knock down the first one, all the rest fall in a row." Green mimicked falling dominoes with his hands.

"First, the communists took over China. Then they tried to take over Korea, but we stopped them, and they only got the north. Now, they're trying to take over South Vietnam. If we let them have Vietnam, then they go for Laos, then Cambodia, then Thailand, then Malaysia. One country falls after the one before it, like a row of dominoes. Soon, the communists got all Southeast Asia. Australia's threatened, Japan's threatened, even Hawaii."

"No shit," said Freddy Harris, one of the squad's riflemen, "Hawaii, eh? These commies got it all planned out like that?"

"Well, that's what the government claims," Green answered, picking up his sandwich. "My history professor in school said it's all bullshit. The government made it up so they could have this war. It feeds the 'military-industrial complex', he said."

"The what?" Jimmy Delvecchio, the Bravo Team leader, stopped eating long enough to ask. "What the fuck is a military, industrio ... whatever the fuck you said?"

"The military-industrial complex," Green answered, despairing of getting his sandwich down quick enough to get back to the mess tent for a third, "It's a conspiracy between the government, the army, and the arms industry to keep this war going. Businesses make political contributions to the politicians, who then support the war and approve all the defense spending. So, the politicians get re-elected; the government gets more taxes and power over people; the army gets bigger, gets more equipment and weapons; and industry makes a bundle manufacturing all the shit needed for this war. That's what my professor said, anyway."

Green took a quick bite out of his sandwich.

"So, this war is part of some dark, secret government conspiracy?" Doc Ambrose, alpha company's head medic, asked.

Doc had pretty much finished off his plate of bacon, eggs and toast, and was stuffing some brown, shaggy tobacco down into the bowl of his pipe.

"Hell, back home in Ohio where I come from, we see this as part of the fight against global communism. Korea was round one; this is round two," Doc added.

"Yeah," Little Bit agreed. "Them fuckin' commies're no good ... Hey, Greenie! You gonna finish that?"

"Let Green eat his sandwich, Little Bit," Jonesy said, "There's plenty more over at the mess tent. So, Doc! You think this is all about communism? Not sure I get that. These guys we're up against aren't Russians or Chinks, so what makes them commies?"

"It's an ideology, not a nationality," Doc said, lighting his pipe, "A belief, like a religion. Except these guys believe that the government should control everything, industry, education, people's lives. There are no individual freedoms like we have back in the world. No freedom of speech, no freedom of religion ..."

"They got the freedom to get laid?" Sweetie quipped.

Sergeant Taylor, their platoon sergeant, came over to the group.

He handed Jonesy a clipboard and a pen, saying, "Jonesy, I need twelve signatures from your squad for the chow."

Jonesy was momentarily confused, "But I only got ..." Then he got it... "Okay, Jake, twelve it is!"

"When you're done, bring it back to me. I'll be over by the CP." With that, Taylor walked away.

Jonesy filled out the head-count sheet as himself, "Jones, Richard T., E5". Then on the next line he wrote, "Smith, Johnny P., E4". Jonesy quickly scanned the sign-in sheet and realized that he was the fifth or sixth "Spec 4 John Smith" in the company.

Then, he passed the form over to Sweetie.

"Everybody signs it twice," he said, "First your name ... your real name ... then make something up."

Then he asked Doc, "So, Doc! Did you get into the army just to fight commies."

Doc thought for a second, puffing on the pipe, then answered, "No ... not really ... I think the thing for me was serving my country during wartime, but preventing them from forcing communism on the South Vietnamese people ... they should have the right to choose ..."

"What if they choose to be commies?" Harris quipped.

"Well ..." Doc mused, "I don't see that, but ..."

"Who gives a shit about that!" Sweetie interrupted, "Commies ... you see the way these people live ... they don't even have enough food to feed themselves ... they beggin' from us all the time ... 'GI! GI! C-Ration, GI!' ... what the fuck do they have that the commies want ... what difference does any of this shit make to them ... or to us ... it's all bullshit!"

"Why did you go in the army, Freddy?" Jonesy interrupted "You join, or you get drafted?"

"Me? I joined up ..." Harris started.

"RA All the Way!" Sweetie ribbed him!

"Why you join?" Jonesy asked.

"Shit," Harris said, "Opportunity, man! I made it through high school, but there were no decent jobs around Detroit. The unions had the auto industry all sewed up, and I'm the wrong color for that bunch. Want to drive a truck in Detroit, you better be a Teamster, and me and my kind ain't on Jimmy Hoffa's Christmas list. Lotta guys in my high school just hangin' round the neighborhood. The ones ain't usin' smack, are sellin' it. That shit's not for me. So, I went down to the recruiter and the army took me. Not a bad deal. Every now and then I gotta put up with some cracker bullshit, and bein' in Nam sucks the big one but, all and all, army's not a bad deal. I'm thinkin' I might be a twenty-year man."

Sweetie passed the sign-in sheet to Green.

After Green signed it, he noticed that there was a "Bell, Tinker" in the outfit, two "Mouse, Mickeys" and one "Duck, Donald." In fact, one of the "Mouse, Mickeys" appeared to be an o5, a Lieutenant Colonel. Somehow that seemed appropriate.

Then, he heard Jonesy talking to him.

"What you say, Jonesy?" he asked.

"I asked how'd you get here?" Jonesy repeated.

"Me?" he answered. "I got drafted!"

"Drafted!" Sweetie challenged. "I thought you was a college boy?"

Green bristled a bit at that. Being called a "college boy" was not a compliment in the infantry.

He remembered when his drill sergeant in basic had got up in his face one morning at reveille and yelled, "Green, y'all know what the difference is between a dumb-ass and a college boy?"

Of course, Green knew, but he had also been in the army long enough, six weeks at the time, to know how the game was played.

"No, Drill Sergeant!" he responded sharply.

"Well, Green," the sergeant answered, "After you tell a dumb-ass somethin' twice't, he gets it. After you tell a college boy somethin' twice't, he still askin' you dumb-ass, fuckin' questions!"

"I took a semester off," Green explained. "Soon as I did, the draft board got me."

"Yeah, but why'd you go?" Jonesy asked. "Lotta college guys these days run off to Canada, I hear."

"Canada!" Green said. "I couldn't do that! My dad was in World War Two. I had cousins in Korea. I couldn't run away! I couldn't disgrace my family! Besides, I agree with Doc. It's like President Kennedy said, 'Ask not what your country can do for you. Ask what you can do for your country.'"

"Kennedy!" Sweetie exclaimed. "I don't see no fuckin' Kennedys in this place. Just suckers like you and me!"

"So, Green," Jonesy persisted, "Now you been here a few weeks, what you think of this domino, military-complex, bull-shit war we got goin' on?"

Green thought about it for a few moments while he passed the sign-in sheet over to Freddy Harris.

Then, he spoke, "It's fucked up ... it doesn't make any sense."

"How's that?" Jonesy asked.

Green responded, "I mean, in Europe, there were front lines ... a direction to go in ... when you got there, you won ... the war ended ... even in Korea ... we were always trying to keep the gooks north of this line ... north of that parallel ... here ... we're just running around in fuckin' circles ... it's like hide 'n' seek with the dinks all the time ... we move in, they pull back into the hills and hide ... we leave, they move back in ... shit ... what do they expect us to do ... kill them all ... that ain't gonna happen."

"So, why you do it," Jonesy asked.

"Don't know," Green said, "Cause I'm here ... I do what I'm told to, I guess ... that and the fact that you guys are all doing it ... I guess I just don't want to let you guys down ..."

"Ah! That's sweet," Gonzales interrupted, making a kissing sound. "Come here, bro! I give you a big kiss!"

"What about you, Sweetie?" Jonesy asked. "You seem to have a lot to say. Let's hear what you think."

"What do I think, man!" Sweetie shot back. "I think it's all bullshit! Back in the world, I got this real sweet job. I work the bar in my uncle's restaurant in Echo Park near the stadium. I makin' pretty good money, get my drinks for nothin', and after them Dodger games when those blonde *chicas* from the valley come in half in the bag from drinking beer at the ball game, I have some really good times, you know! Then I get this letter from the fuckin' draft board, and my whole life goes to shit! What the fuck does anybody care about that? Just another Chicano off the streets of east LA, right?"

"Hey Sweetie," Jimmy Delvecchio called over, rubbin' his thumb and forefinger together, "You know what this is, man ... it's the world's smallest violin ... you're breakin' my heart, bro."

"Fuck you, D," Sweetie responded.

Then he continued, "The college boy here got one thing right. This fuckin' war's bullshit, the way they got us fightin' it. Best bet, keep your head down! Stay alive! Do your twelve months and get your ass back to the world!"

"Oh, that's real fuckin' comfortin'," Freddy Harris responded. "So, when the shit hits the fan and I'm dependin' on you to cover my ass, where the fuck you gonna be? Hiding down in some hole, tryin' to keep your ass from getting' shot off."

"No, man," Sweetie protested, "Ain't like that, bro ... you my friend ... you all my friends ... I be there for you ... you know that ... but think about it, bro ... who they send over here to fight this fuckin' war ... people like you and me, that's who ... even the college boy here ... you don't see no rich boys end up in this place ... no politician's kid ... hell ... they pull strings ... take care of their own ... get their kids in the National Guard or some shit like that..."

Jonesy was just about to say something, when Sergeant Taylor came back over, this time with a clean and shiny FNG in tow, a fuckin' new guy.

"This is your lucky day, Jonesy," he announced, "I got this here replacement ... what you say your name is, rook..."

"Dwyer, Sergeant. PFC Mick Dwyer," the soldier answered.

"Good," Taylor continued, "Private First Class Dwyer now belongs to you, Jonesy. The old man sent him over here because he's another one of them New York City boys, and you already got a couple of those to make Private First Class Dwyer here feel right at home while he's with us. You got that sign-in sheet ready for me?"

"Whose got the sheet?" Jonesy asked.

Little Bit passed it over to Jonesy. He looked it over to make sure they had put down enough signatures.

"Okay," Jonesy said, "Which one of you idiots wrote down "Minh, Ho Chi" ... ah ... shit... "Ho, I. M. A?"

Taylor snatched the clip board from Jonesy.

"Don't matter. Long as we got enough signatures. Nobody actually gonna read through this shit anyway," he said.

Then he turned to Dwyer, "Okay rook … this your new home. Have fun!"

Then, Taylor walked back toward the CP.

"You get anythin' to eat?" Jonesy asked the new guy.

"Not yet, sergeant," Dwyer responded.

"Okay, drop your shit and get over to the mess tent before they stop serving," Jonesy instructed him, "And it's Jonesy, not sergeant."

Dwyer dumped his weapon, helmet, ruck and web gear, and turned to go to the mess tent.

Jonesy stopped him, "Hey… uh…" He couldn't remember the new guy's name.

"Mick Dwyer, sarge… uh … Jonesy," he answered.

"Your weapon," Jonesy said, "Never walk away from your weapon, Dwyer!"

"Oh shit," Dwyer said and picked up the M16. "Sorry, sarge … uh … Jonesy."

Then, he walked toward the mess tent.

"Jesus Christ," Jonesy mused, "Was I ever that green."

Then, not to waste a good pun, Jonesy said, "Green, take this guy under your wing, will you … show 'im the ropes … he's from your hometown … you speak his lingo."

"Okay, boss," Green agreed.

"Okay … where were we …" Jonesy asked himself, "Oh yeah… Little Bit … you join or get drafted?"

Little Bit looked up from a paper plate overflowing with eggs, bacon, biscuits and SOS. For a second, Jonesy wondered how much food Mrs. Little had to put on the table every morning to get her little Johnny off to work.

"Me, boss," Little Bit choked out from around a mouthful of toast, "They drafted me."

"What'd you do before the war," Jonesy asked.

"Worked the farm with my daddy," Little Bit said.

I bet you pulled the plow, Jonesy imagined, then asked, "Your daddy own a farm?"

"Own the farm," Little Bit said, "Hell no! Ain't no nigg ..."

Little Bit stopped suddenly. Freddy Harris shot him a look.

Then, Little Bit continued, "Ain't no black man in Coatahoula Parish, Louisiana own any land. My daddy farm for the judge. He own the land."

"How's that work?" Green asked. "You pay rent?"

"Hell no!" Little Bit answered. "The judge take part of the crop, my daddy keep part, and part go to the ..." Little Bit seemed to struggle for a word "... part go to the levy."

"The levy?" Jimmy Delvecchio asked. "What the fuck's that ... like a dam on a river?"

"No," Little Bit said, "My daddy pay the levy, and the white boys in the parish leave us alone."

"The white boys," Delvecchio persisted, "You mean the Klan."

"Yeah," Little Bit answered, "The Klan, the sheriff, and the rest of them ofay crackers. My daddy pay the levy, and they leave my daddy and my fam'ly alone."

Hearing this, Green was amazed. This was share-cropping, like some ancient tale from the days of reconstruction. And the Klan! Little Bit was as big as any three people Green had ever met, and he was a trained, combat-experienced infantryman. Yet, he was okay with paying protection money to a bunch of crackers in bed sheets. What kind of cultural brainwashing caused him to accept that?

"So, why would you want to go fight this war?" Green blurted out.

"This my country too!" Little Bit explained to Green as if he were a three-year-old. "I got my pride. When I get back home, I goin' put on my green uniform, an' walk right into Harrisonburg, an' everybody say, 'There go Johnny Little, old Augustus Little's boy. He went an' fought that Asia war, an' he come back.' Then the judge his self gonna come down out of his office, and he gonna shake my hand, right there in front of the courthouse, in front of all them white people, an' he gonna say to me, 'Good job, boy! You served your country!'"

"Then everything goes back to the way it was?" Delvecchio asked.

"Sure, Jimmy," Little Bit said, "Why wouldn't it?"

Freddy Harris seemed about to say something, then stopped and went back to eating his food.

It was then that Mick Dwyer got back from the mess hall with a plate of bacon, shit-on-a-shingle with a bright yellow, powdered egg garnish floating on it, and two pieces of buttered toast balanced on top.

Before he could get a bite into his mouth, Jonesy asked him, "So, Mick ... you join or get drafted?"

"Me?" Dwyer answered, looking longingly at his untasted powdered eggs, congealing into a solid, yellow lump on his paper plate. "I joined."

"Oh, Christ," Sweetie groaned, "Another fuckin' hero!"

Mick looked a bit embarrassed.

Jonesy asked him, "Why'd you join up."

Now Mick's cheeks got a little red, "I joined because my best friend did."

There were a few seconds of stunned silence.

Then Jimmy D said, "That's it? You joined the fuckin' army during a fuckin' war because some friend of yours did?"

"That's pretty much the way it was?" Dwyer confessed, wondering if he'd ever get a chance to eat.

"So, where's this guy now, this buddy of yours?" Freddy Harris asked.

"Oh ... Joey ..." Dwyer said, "He's up north with the hundred and first ... been there for about three months now."

"Ah ... the pukin' buzzards," Harris continued, "He a grunt, like you?"

No ... not really," Dwyer confessed, "He came in country as an eleven bravo, but he scored some job in division ... admin, I think..."

"Oh, that's fuckin' rich!" Harris chuckled. "You join the fuckin' army because you're buddies with some guy. and he winds up spending his time sharpenin' pencils in basecamp while you out here poundin' the boonies. You just gotta love shit like that."

About an hour later, word still hadn't come down what the army wanted the squad to do next. So, after a good, hot meal, their first in over three weeks, and a cigarette or two, the squad was crapped out, napping in the sun.

That is, except Pat Green and the rookie, Mick Dwyer. Green had given Dwyer the lowdown, and they were unpacking his rucksack into the traditional three piles of a light infantry load: "shit you had to keep," "shit you're not keeping," and "shit you can keep if you got the strength to hump it."

Green asked, "Where you from?"

"New York," Dwyer answered staring at a third pair of socks and wondering what pile to put them in.

"I know that," Green answered, "Where in New York?"

"Queens ... Astoria," Dwyer answered, finally tossing the socks into the "shit you can keep if you got the strength to hump it" pile.

"No shit," Green responded, moving the socks into the "shit you had to keep" pile. "My grandparents live in Astoria."

"Oh yeah ... where?" Dwyer said, staring at some pictures of him and his girlfriend, Lori.

"Who's that?" Green asked looking at Dwyer's picture. "Your girl?"

"Yeah," Dwyer said, "Lori."

"Then, you should keep them," Green advised, "But wrap 'em up in plastic so they don't get ruined. My grandparents live on Broadway, in an apartment building across from the hospital."

"I know where that is," Dwyer answered, placing the pictures on the keeper pile, "I live on Crescent Street, a couple of blocks down for Our Lady of Lourdes."

"No shit!" Green said. "Our Lady of Lourdes! I was baptized there! My folks were still living with my grandparents when I came along."

"Yeah!" Dwyer said! "Me too! And I went to school there. Eight years."

"So, critical question?" Green asked.

"What?" Dwyer responded, a bit worried by the "critical" part.

"Mets or Yankees?" Green asked.

"Mets all the way," Dwyer said! "I come from two generations of Giants fans. No way I could be a Yankee fan!"

"Keep the batteries," Green advised, "They always come in handy. Mets! Okay! A right-thinking lad! Don't ask Delvecchio. He's still hoping the Dodgers move back to Brooklyn. Hates the Yankees, can't stand the Mets."

"So," Dwyer asked, "You play any ball?"

"Yeah! High school," Green answered.

"Me too," Dwyer continue, "I played outfield for St. Agnes."

"No shit!" Green said. "I played for Xavier."

Dwyer stared at Green for a couple of seconds, then said, "That's why you look familiar. You pitched the last inning of the Bishop Cup's game in '65, right? That was you, wasn't it?"

"Yeah ..." Green started.

"I was the last batter you faced ... in the seventh," Dwyer said.

"No shit!" Green exclaimed. "I remember you ... tough little hitter ... couldn't get anything by you."

"Yeah, well, not tough enough," Dwyer said.

"No, man," Green insisted, "You hit the shit out of that pitch ... nine times out of ten, Alphabet doesn't make that play."

Dwyer could still see the white ball arching through the blue sky ... falling toward the grass ... the right fielder running ... stretching ... diving ... the ball and the glove meeting less than a foot off the grass.

Then he said, "Yeah ... but he did that day ... Alphabet?"

"Yeah," Green continued, "His real name was Stan, a Polish kid from St. Stanislaus parish. His last name seemed to have every letter in the alphabet in it. When he said it, it sounded like he was clearing his throat. So, we just called him Alphabet."

"Hell of a game," Dwyer said. "We kicked the shit outta you guys in '66, got the cup back."

"Yeah ... I heard," Green said, "That's baseball. It's just the way the game is. Alphabet plays two more steps to his left, or you hit the ball in a different spot, he never catches up to it. Right time, right place, good things happen. Wrong time, wrong place ..."

Green left the statement unfinished.

Then he said, "Okay, Mick, let's get this shit packed up. I'm pretty sure the army isn't going to let us just hang around here snoozing in the sun all day."

10

The Legend of Crazy Rodriguez

The squad was just standing down from evening stand-to. It was fully dark now.

Jimmy Delvecchio, the Bravo Team Leader, had first watch. He was sitting on top of his fire team's bunker, but close enough so he could hear the rest of the guys who were gathered together behind the bunker.

Jonesy was fiddling with his transistor radio trying to tune into Armed Forces Radio. It was Saturday night, and the Grand Ole Opry was coming on soon.

The city boys, Pat Green, Freddy Harris, Jimmy, and Mick Dwyer, and the Mexicans, Ebodio "Sweetie" Gonzales, and Domingo "Ding" Alvarez, didn't give a shit about the Opry, though Pat did get a kick out of Minnie Pearl.

For the country boys, like Jonesy, Little Bit, Doc Ambrose, and even Sergeant Taylor, their field first sergeant, it was almost a religious thing, some sort of an obligatory experience, like Mass on a Sunday for a Catholic.

More importantly, it had become one of the squad's rituals, like stand to and putting out the trip flares in the evening. When the Opry came on, it marked another Saturday, another week gone, seven days closer to going home.

It was against the company SOP, and every shred of common sense, to be gathering around a radio right behind the line bunker at night. But, the old man, Lieutenant Lattimore, had a good sense of when to give a little on things. As long as the guys kept it down — and since the bunker was nowhere near the chicken shit factory over at the Battalion CP — the old man didn't take much notice of these nightly gatherings.

Besides, they were on a well-established battalion firebase with slicks and shithooks going in and out all day, and with a battery of 105's, a section of four-deuce mortars, and two sections of 81's popping off day and night.

If the dinks didn't know where they were and hadn't mapped and surveyed the entire perimeter, they were deaf, dumb and blind. And, if that were true, the stinking war would have been over years ago.

So, no harm as far as Lattimore was concerned.

Jonesy wasn't having much luck getting his radio to work. He popped open the battery compartment and pulled out the batteries.

"Hey, Green! Hand me your flashlight, will ya?" he asked.

Green reached back and pulled the flashlight off his gear and handed it to Jonesy.

"Fuck," said Jonesy, "Battery compartments all corroded. Don't know if this battery's good or not."

"What kind of batteries does it take?" asked Freddy, hoping Jonesy wouldn't get the thing working, so he didn't have to listen to an hour of that damned cracker music. To him it sounded like a bunch of hicks strangling pigs and screaming while they did it. Freddy would take Motown any day over this shit.

"BA30's," Jonesy said, "You guys got any?"

General mutterings of "no," "fuck no," "don't know," "all out."

A figure joined them out of the dark.

"Hey, guys, where's the Opry?" It was Doc Ambrose, the head medic.

"Can't get the radio working, Doc," answered Dwyer.

"Yeah, no fuckin' music, *gracias a Dios*," said Sweetie.

"Oh, that's too bad," said Doc, "I was looking forward to hearing a little George Jones. Somebody said Tammy Wynette was going to be on tonight."

Doc was from Ohio, and to the city boys the entire state qualified as "country," since it was west of Jersey and wasn't Chicago, Detroit or LA.

"Well, Doc," said Jonesy, "Unless you got some BA30's in your bag, we're shit outta luck tonight."

"BA30's! They're impossible to get out here," answered Doc, "Only ones I got are in my flashlight, and I need those."

"Yep! Probably a good idea ... a medic with a workin' flashlight," said Little Bit.

He was a country boy from someplace in Louisiana, and he did enjoy listening to bluegrass. But, because he was black, he didn't feel comfortable pushing too hard to promote what in his mind was essentially cracker music, the same stuff pouring out of the whites-only bars in his town.

He did enjoy sitting with the squad. Black, brown or white, they had all seen some shit together. He knew they had each other's six.

Like a family, Little Bit thought, like brothers. None of that Jim-Crow shit out here in the boonies.

"Wouldn't make much sense you poking around inside somebody without a light," Doc Ambrose concluded.

"Hey, Doc!" Freddy said, "There a game goin' on over at the medics."

"No point, Freddy," Doc answered, "A week before payday. Nobody's got any money. Besides, you looking for another excuse to get cleaned out by Little Doc?"

Little Doc was the platoon medic ... a good medic and a world-class poker player.

"His luck's gotta change someday, Doc. And he's carrying around a lot of my money," Freddy answered.

"Freddy," Ambrose warned, "I don't think Little Doc's luck is going to change as long as he's using his own deck. And, as far as I know, that's the only deck we got."

"Yeah, well, we'll see 'bout that," Freddy answered, "we will see 'bout that."

"Hey, Sweetie," Green interrupted to get the conversation going in a direction other than Little Doc's deck of cards, "Tell that story about the guy you knew. What's his name? The guy with the machete? I don't think Dwyer's heard that one yet."

"Oh! You want to hear 'bout that Crazy Rodriguez?" Sweetie said. "That dude, man, he was one crazy motherfucker."

"Yeah, that's the one," Green said, encouraging Sweetie to tell the story. "The guy with the machete, right."

"Yeah, he got one bad-ass machete, sharp like a razor, and that motherfucker liked to use it, bro," Sweetie confirmed.

"Yeah, tell us that one, Sweetie," Jonesy urged.

"Sweetie" Gonzales and his buddy, Ding Hernandez, were both Mexicans from LA. In fact, Sweetie wasn't even a US citizen. He got drafted on his green card.

Sweetie wanted to make a life for himself in the States. So, instead of taking a powder back to Ensenada, down in the Baja where he had family, he reported and eventually wound up behind a sandbag bunker in the highlands of Vietnam with a bunch of city boys and country boys trying to catch a broadcast of the Opry with dead batteries.

Sweetie didn't get his nickname from his disposition, but from his culinary preferences. When he was a rookie, the squad got a ration supplement pack, an "SP" pack, which was full of various hard-to-get, and, in Nam, strangely exotic goodies like candy, writing pads, pens, cigarettes, and paperback books.

Now, since SP packs were distributed strictly by rank and seniority — time on the field — and, since Sweetie was a PFC with less than a month on the line, by the time it was his turn, all the good stuff was gone. In fact, the only stuff left, except for pads of writing paper and some ballpoint pens, was a carton of Kent cigarettes, and a box of something called Tropical Chocolate.

Since Sweetie didn't smoke, he had no use for the cigarettes, but he kept them anyway to trade with the dinks. But he couldn't believe his good fortune in getting an entire box of chocolate all to himself. The other guys in the squad wouldn't touch the stuff — it tasted soapy wax, wouldn't melt, and was rumored to cause the shits and make you sterile. But one man's garbage is another's treasure.

Now, Sweetie's propensity for the indigestible would have gone unnoticed had he not made a point of telling the rest of the guys that they were nuts for not having scarfed up the tropical chocolate delicacy when they had a chance.

"Ey! What's a matter with you guys? This stuff's good ... so sweet ... it's chocolate, bro ... sweet!"

So, based on that rather surprising and shocking event, Ebodio Gonzales acquired his *nom de guerre* in the squad, "Sweetie," because as one of the guys put it, "Anyone who could eat that shit had to have a terminal sweet tooth."

Ding was actually assigned to a different squad, but he and Sweetie were pretty much joined at the hip ... if you saw Sweetie, you saw Ding ... if you saw Ding, you saw Sweetie.

Ding never said much. And, when he first joined the platoon, he pretty much kept to himself. The common theory was he didn't speak English. But, when someone said something to him, he seemed to understand.

This went on for about two weeks, and finally Sweetie went over to Ding's hooch. They jabbered in Mexican for a few minutes, hugged, and ever since then ... joined at the hip.

To the guys in the squad, this made more sense than actual unit assignments, since Sweetie and Ding were both Mexicans, and both spoke Spanish, and both were from LA, and they seemed to understand each other.

"So," Sweetie was saying, "You want to hear about this Crazy Rodriguez dude, ey? That was one crazy motherfucker, I tell you. I never meet this guy, thank God. He gone when I get in country. He in second platoon, not this one."

"Was he a Mexican, like you, Sweetie?" interrupted Mike Dwyer.

"Fuck no!" said Sweetie, "That crazy motherfucker a Puerto Rican. Don't even speak my language right! He from some place up north ... New York, I think. 'Ey, Dwyer! You from New York. Maybe you know him, bro?"

"I don't think so, man," Dwyer answered, "I went to high school with a Mike Rodriguez. But I don't think he ever went to 'Nam."

"I don' know what this fucker's first name was," Sweetie continued. "Everybody just call him Rodriquez. He with the unit long time, eight, nine months, regular guy, just do his time like rest of us. Then the company workin' down in the Ia Drang. Bad place. Full a dinks, all over. They build this firebase near this dink village. You know how that go. Pretty soon dinks from the village coming in the wire to sell shit, cokes, cigarettes. So, there these really ... uh ... really ... 'Ey, Ding, ¿Cómo se dice 'linda' en inglés?"

"Cute!"

"Yeah, thanks, bro ... this girl, she real cute... Rodriquez like her a lot ... so they start hanging round together all the time ... guys they know what happens ... maybe Rodriguez get some. Nothin' wrong with that ... so, soon Rodriguez sneaking down into the village ... but nobody say nothin' ... everybody OK with this ... but then Rodriquez start talkin' crazy ... he say he gonna take this girl back to world, marry her ... everybody say 'Hey, Rodriquez! You crazy. You no marry dink!' But, Rodriquez, he say he in love! He say this girl gonna have his baby. Everybody think no sweat, we pull out soon. Rodriquez forget about this girl. But, one night, VC come to this village. They want to fuck up this village for bein' nice to GI's. In the morning, when sun come up, all unit on stand-to, they see Rodriquez' little dink girlfriend hanging in wire, throat cut, dead. Rodriguez, he go crazy. He want to go into village, kill dinks, kill VC. He say they kill his girlfriend. They kill his baby. Well, we pull out, leave this place, but Rodriguez, he not same ... he crazy now ... he get these machete ... he spend all his time sharpen it. All night, he sit in hooch with ... "Ey Ding, *¿Cómo se dice 'afilador'?*"

"Whetstone."

"*Si*, wet stone. He run these wet stone up and down, up and down the machete ... wsht, wsht, wsht ... all fuckin' night, everybody hear ... wsht, wsht, wsht ... he make these machete like a razor ... wsht, wsht, wsht ... he oil it up good ... wsht, wsht, wsht... his machete it shines, even in dark ... wsht, wsht, wsht ... pretty soon, all this wsht, wsht, wsht all the time make other guys pretty crazy too ... they tell the lieutenant... not the LT, the guy before him ... you gotta do something about this guy ... he crazy with the wsht, wsht, wsht all the time. But, the lieutenant he no listen ... he do nothin'... then Rodriquez start going out at night on LP but *alone* ... nobody else ... with these fuckin' machete of his ... good news, no wsht, wsht, wsht all night ... bad news, where the fuck he goin'... what the fuck he doin' out there in the dark ... nobody know ... guys tell the lieutenant, you gotta do something about this guy ... he crazy ... boo coo dinky dau ... lieutenant, he do nothing ... when it time for Rodriquez to go home, he tell the captain he no wanna go ... he wanna stay in Nam ... everybody say get rid of this guy... he fuckin' crazy ... but the captain, he no listen ... he let Rodriquez stay in Nam with his machete and his wsht wsht wsht ... one day, lieutenant has whole platoon on sweep in the Ia Drang ... bad place ... lots of dinks everywhere ... the platoon crossing this open area ... bad place ... then this dink machine gun open up ... they pretty much fucked ... no cover ... machine gun fuck up couple a guys ... rest hit the dirt ... no place to hide ... machine gun go down the line ... shoot this guy, then shoot this guy ... go right down the line ... fuck up everybody … the lieutenant on the radio, tryin' to get artillery, smoke, anything before this fucking machine gun kill everybody … then it stop … no more shooting … the lieutenant he don't know what to do … he think maybe dinks want to trick him … break cover … but he got no cover … the lieutenant he think dinks run away before artillery get there … so lieutenant get the platoon back into trees … then he count up who there … no Rodriquez … he gone … lieutenant think Rodriquez he get hit … find him later … got to take care of that fuckin' machine gun now … the lieutenant he moves up where he think that machine gun is … he hear nothin' … he thinks dinks they all gone … then he find the machine gun … sittin' right on its tripod … still smoking … the crew, three dinks, all dead … but get this … they got no heads … then the lieutenant he hear something … he look … there is Rodriquez with that machete of his … and he … he … 'ey Ding, *¿Cómo se dice 'roer'?*"

Sweetie pantomimed what looked to be a giant, buck-toothed, Mexican squirrel eating an ear of corn.

"Chew."

"Yeah … he chew on that dink's head."

"Whoa! Stop, man!" interrupted Dwyer, "You tellin' me this guy was chewing on some dink's head?"

"Yeah, he chewing on it … blood all over him … then the lieutenant he know these Rodriquez crazy … and the captain he know these fucker's *muy loco* … can't stay in the army no more … can't stay here no more … so the army want to send him home … send him back to New York or wherever he come from … don't worry 'bout his ass no more … but get this … the day Rodriquez supposed to get on bird … go home … he no show up … army don't know what to do … never nobody go AWOL from going home … they look round for him … can't find him … he gone … so, they stop looking … what the fuck … he gone … but every now and then … some unit up in these hills … at night … they hear this wsht, wsht, wsht out there in the dark … this Rodriguez he still out there, man … up in these hills … he lookin' for more heads."

"Aw, bullshit, Sweetie!" said Dwyer, "There's no crazy Puerto Rican out there with a machete!"

"Ah, you don' have to believe it, bro. But, next time you out there in the dark on LP, you listen ... wsht, wsht wsht..."

The other guys had had enough and started drifting back to their hooches. They were getting sleepy, and they all had to pull a four-hour guard shift before morning stand-to at oh-dark-thirty.

Dwyer grabbed Green by his sleeve. He kept his voice low so none of the other guys could hear him. "Pat, that's all bullshit, right. There's no crazy GI running around out there with a machete, right."

"I don't know, Mike," Green answered, "I heard that story when I first got in country. But, as I recall, the guy had been in the third platoon and his name was Reilly."

11

A Very Bad Day

I

Pat Green sat on the edge of his fighting position, his legs dangling down into the hole. Green could see the sky in the east almost imperceptibly shifting from black to deep purple.

About another hour until dawn.

An hour and a half until the end of stand to.

Green could see his fire team's other fighting position to his right and the silhouettes of Mike Dwyer and the Puerto Rican kid from Chicago, Perez, a replacement they picked up right before going on this mission, sitting on the edge of their hole.

Green knew that they should be down in their dug-out fighting positions, but grunts never liked getting down into those holes unless they had to. Too claustrophobic. The smell of wet soil. Too much like standing in a grave ... chest deep, two rifle-lengths long, and one rifle-length wide.

Alpha company had been in this position for only two days. So, their defenses were still basic, fighting positions for every two men around the perimeter. At this point, these were essentially two-man holes with logs and some sandbags piled in front for cover, no overhead. Interlocking fields of fire were plotted and staked for every position. The M60 machine guns were mounted on tripods, and had final protective fires locked in, cutting across each platoon's front. Fields of fire were cleared out about thirty meters to the edge of the jungle. The 81mm mortars within the perimeter had set up their sandbagged firing pits and had dug deep, sandbagged bunkers for the ammo.

Every morning and every evening, the entire company stood stand-to on their defensive positions, a hundred percent alert and ready to fight. The rest of the time, a minimum of thirty percent security was maintained around the perimeter.

Every grunt knew the three requirements for an effective defense: security, security, security. The rest were just details.

Green looked to his left and saw the silhouette of Johnny Little, or "Little Bit" as everybody called him, one of his guys manning a position for Jimmy Delvecchio's alpha team. The perimeter was stretched a little thin this morning.

There were two men from the platoon out on a listening post, an LP, about fifty meters in front of their position. They'd come back in as soon as it was light enough to see.

Yesterday, the old man, Lieutenant Lattimore, had sent Jonesy, Green's squad leader, out on a long-range listening post with Jimmy Delvecchio's fire team. They were about three klicks out somewhere to the north and west toward a hill everybody called the volcano, because on the map it looked like its summit was hollowed out.

Lattimore had sent a new lieutenant out with Jonesy. Green didn't know the new lieutenant's name. He just seemed to appear suddenly when they left the battalion firebase on this mission. Green imagined that, since Lattimore had taken over the company, the new lieutenant would become their platoon leader. So, it made sense the old man was getting him some experience on a patrol with Jonesy's squad.

The sky was turning pale gray, and the morning chorus of birds was in full swing. Green could distinctly see the guys on both sides of him now.

This was a tense time for grunts in the field.

The racket the birds were making could cover the sound of approaching movement. And you could get a pretty accurate sight picture on a guy from about fifty meters.

Green slid down into the fighting position. He noticed that the other guys along the perimeter did the same.

When Jonesy took Jimmy D's team out for the patrol yesterday, Green felt a bit put out that his team didn't go. D was a good NCO, and he had a good team, Sweetie Gomez, Freddy Harris and some FNG, Fuckin' New Guy.

Green didn't know the rookie's name, but he did notice that the guy looked a bit strange. His face was pale, almost grayish. He had something wrong with his eyes. He blinked a lot, even in the shade. Guys were starting to refer to him as "Blinky."

D's team was solid, and Jimmy had more experience as a team leader than Green. So, Green had to admit, it made sense for Jonesy to take Jimmy D's crew out with him, especially since the old man had saddled him with the new lieutenant.

But Green still felt... how could he put it ... left out ... something like choosing up sides for a game of stickball and not getting chosen for either team.

Until the new lieutenant showed up, Sergeant Jake Taylor had run the platoon.

When Green had joined the unit, Lattimore was his platoon leader and Taylor was his platoon sergeant; Taylor was also acting as the company's "field first sergeant," the top NCO in the field.

Taylor was the "real deal," a Sergeant First Class, an E7, a career man, but he wasn't a "lifer." He certainly didn't take shit from anybody, but he wasn't into the chicken shit either. Everything he told you to do served the two-fold concern of every grunt in the field had — get the job done, and keep you and your buddies alive.

When Lieutenant Lattimore got kicked upstairs to be the company commander, Taylor took over the platoon.

Jonesy kept the first squad. That made sense. Jonesy had been in-country almost seven months, all that time in the field, and he knew his shit.

Green still remembered Jonesy's very brief, very to-the-point introduction to life on the line. "Keep your weapon clean and serviceable. Never walk away from it. If we hit the shit, keep your eyes on me. Go where I go. Do what I do. If you need to worry about anything else, I'll tell you."

That was it.

His welcome to the first squad, first platoon, Alpha Company, 3/35th Infantry.

The surprise came when the old man offered a fire team to Green as a Spec 4 with only a few months in-country.

Jonesy had been running alpha team as well as the squad. But the squad had "fattened up" with a couple of replacements since then.

The deal Lattimore made Green was that he'd be an "acting jack," an E4 Sergeant. He could wear sergeant's stripes - not that anyone in their right mind would wear rank in the field -but get paid as an E4. When he had enough time in grade, Lattimore would promote him to E5.

Green remembered when he was a kid, he used to wear his father's World War II Eisenhower jacket. His old man was a Tech-5 in ordinance with Patton's 3rd Army in Europe. So, Green felt pretty good when he wrote home and told his dad he had made sergeant after only a couple of months in-country.

He was a "hard five," an infantry sergeant.

Green and the old man, Lt Lattimore, had a bit of history. It was pretty much standard that rookies walked point — a rite of passage — and Green did his fair share of it when he first got to the unit. But, after a few weeks, when some replacements came up, Lattimore kept putting Green out on point.

At first Green thought the old man had it in for him. Why, he couldn't imagine. But, after a while, Green figured that, for some reason, Lattimore trusted him up there.

Walking point through the forest, being out in front of a line company on the move, made Green feel a bit like Hawkeye, the legendary hunter and scout Green had read about in a novel when he was a kid.

After a while, Green began to realize that he was one of the few guys Lattimore trusted on point.

Not that everything went all that smoothly.

Green remembered one cocked-up mission, when some moron in brigade thought it would be a grand idea to send scout dogs out on sweeps with line units. Green had to share point with a German Shepherd, whom Green didn't mind that much, and his handler, who tripped, cracked, and popped every stick, root, and vine in the highlands.

Not that an infantry line unit was all that stealthy in the bush. In fact, it sounded like a gypsy caravan of banging canteens, ammo magazines and cursing, and smelled like a cloud of insect repellent, Old Spice and cigarettes.

One of the charms of walking point, in Green's estimation was, if the dinks focused on the oncoming racket, the point man was past them before they even noticed. That was Green's theory, anyway.

He hoped he'd never have to put it to the test.

But this clumsy dog handler climbing up Green's butt was a real pain in the ass.

The company was moving up on a ridge. The basic rule was "going up, ambush front; going down, ambush rear." So, Green usually got twenty to thirty meters out in front of the company going up a hill.

As Green, the dog, and the dog handler climbed the ridge, the dog seemed to become increasingly agitated, a situation that was not making Green feel very good about his next few steps up the ridge. The dog growled and struggled against his restraint, but the ridge was too steep for Green to see over the summit.

Green grabbed some cover and looked down toward the bottom of the ridge where the old man was waiting with the rest of the company.

Lattimore pointed Green up the ridge.

Before Green could move further, the dog handler pulled Green's sleeve. "I want to let the dog off the restraint," the handler hissed in Green's ear.

Green re-evaluated his opinion of the dog handler, the dog handler's mother, and anyone who ever knew him.

Green glanced down the hill at the old man and pointed to the dog. Lattimore just shrugged and again pointed up the hill.

Green gave the dog handler the thumbs up. The dog handler released his dog. It charged up the hill and over the summit.

Then silence.

Green looked at the dog handler. He just shrugged.

He looked down the hill at Lattimore, who again pointed up the hill.

Green was just about to his feet, when the dog, running full tilt down the hill and yelping, ran right into him.

Green and the dog rolled and tumbled all the way down the ridge stopping at the bottom in a tangled mass of equipment and fur at the feet of Lieutenant Lattimore.

The dog continued his journey, running down the entire length of the infantry column and into the jungle, followed closely by his handler.

Green picked himself up. He found his rifle, cleared a clod of dirt and grass out of the bore, checked to make sure all his grenades were accounted for and still contained their pins, and picked up his helmet.

He turned towards the old man.

Lattimore just pointed up the hill.

This morning, the eastern sky was turning bright orange, the sun was just below the horizon. Since it was almost full light, they needed to pass the LP back into the perimeter.

The guys knew the drill, but Green caught Little Bit's eye, then Dwyer's, pointed out toward the edge of the tree line and hissed "LP." Both guys acknowledged the warning. After the LP got in, stand-to was pretty much over. They could pull in the claymore mines and the trip flares, and grab a little chow, this morning's C-Rations.

They wouldn't be seeing any hot chow or coffee for a while. But at least they were on a firebase and not out humping the boonies. There was plenty of water and plenty of C-Rations.

Green saw that they had brought in some sandbags the day before. The good news — looked like they would be staying put for a while. The bad news — now they had to start filling the damned sandbags and building bunkers.

But there were certainly worse things they could be doing.

Green was looking forward to a day of working his ass off, digging, shoveling and pounding sandbags into a bunker. Except for the sweat bees that stung every time they landed on exposed flesh, not at all a bad day for a grunt in the field, not a bad day at all.

II

Sub-Lieutenant Tran Trung Thanh of the People's Army of Vietnam was finally doing his patriotic duty to free his comrades in the American-occupied south of his country. He was leading a platoon-sized reconnaissance patrol against the capitalist bandits on a sweep some five kilometers south of his regiment's basecamp in an extinct, weathered volcano near the border with Cambodia.

The volcano, his captain had told him, was of strategic importance to the People's Army of Vietnam because, from its heights, they could control traffic on Highway 14, the major North-South logistics route in the highlands. As long as they held the volcano, the Americans and their traitorous Vietnamese puppets could not move supplies from Saigon to the occupied cities in the north.

To counter, the Americans had moved troops down from their bases near the occupied city of Ban Me Thuot. They had fortified the old French airstrip near the village of Duc Lap. There they had placed their artillery and heavy mortars. Now, they were pushing what regiment believed to be company-sized units out toward the regiment's basecamp in the volcano.

Sub-Lieutenant Thanh's mission was to take out a twenty-man patrol and sweep through a one-kilometer square area to detect any enemy activity. His job was to observe and report. He was not to initiate contact with the Americans. If he were to make contact, he was not to become decisively engaged. He was to break contact as soon as was tactically feasible, withdraw his patrol back to the base camp, and report.

The captain had assigned a sergeant major named Trinh as Thanh's assistant patrol leader.

Sergeant Major Trinh was a legend within the regiment and within the People's Liberation Army. It was said that he had fought the Japanese, the French, and now the Americans. Sergeant Major Trinh, they said, ruthlessly killed whoever opposed the will of the Vietnamese People, be they Japanese, be they French, be they American, be they Chinese, be they Russian, or be they Vietnamese. Sergeant Major Trinh had no family except the People's Army of Vietnam and had no purpose in life except as a soldier of the people.

Sergeant Major Trinh's presence on Sub-Lieutenant Thanh's first combat patrol made him very anxious.

On the one hand, Thanh suspected that the sergeant major would kill him if he did not meet the ideals of the People's Army of Vietnam. On the other hand, Thanh was determined to demonstrate to Trinh that, despite being a newcomer to the people's struggle in the south, he could command a mission that even a sergeant major of Trinh's stature would approve, if not admire.

The first night of the mission was a surprise, if not a disappointment, to Sub-Lieutenant Thanh.

He envisioned their moving silently and stealthily through the night, approaching the very edge of an American position, listening to their inane conversations, then creeping back to the regiment with critically needed information - the size and the location of the enemy units. Perhaps, they would slit the throat of an unsuspecting American sentry to spread terror and awe of the People's Army of Vietnam among the Americans.

An hour before dusk, Sergeant Major Trinh led the patrol out a few kilometers out from basecamp. By the time it was fully dark, he had the men positioned just below the summit of a small ridge. There, Trinh put the unit on fifty percent alert, one man sleeping, one man watching.

Thanh could hardly believe that the sergeant major was not diligently seeking out the Americans. And he was letting men sleep while on a combat patrol in proximity to the enemy. Trinh told the men simply to be silent and listen for movement. If they detected any movement, they should alert him and the sub-lieutenant immediately.

After the men settled in, Sergeant Major Trinh explained to Sub-Lieutenant Thanh that what got men killed in the jungle was noise and movement. Movement, especially at night, was deadly. You could hear an enemy long before you saw him.

The sergeant major told Thanh not to believe what they had told him in training, that the soldiers of the People's Army of Vietnam could move like wraiths in the night, find their objective undetected, and surprise and destroy their enemies. Trinh said that was a myth. Nothing can move silently in the dark through this terrain.

At night, you settle in and listen. If the Americans were foolish enough to come to them, they would die. Besides, the sergeant major told Thanh, the Americans rarely moved about at night. Even they were not that foolish.

Sub-Lieutenant Thanh listened attentively to what the sergeant major told him. Although part of his mind understood the wisdom of

Trinh's instruction, another part of him suspected that hiding in the dark with their enemies near was cowardly.

In fact, much of what Sub-Lieutenant Thanh had experienced since leaving the replacement depot in the north had surprised and disappointed him.

At the patriotic rallies at university, he was told that victory in the south was near. All that was left, after the great peoples' victories in the glorious Tet offensive, was the mopping up of the shattered remnants of the Americans and traitorous Vietnamese bandits in the south.

Sub-Lieutenant Thanh began to suspect the inaccuracy of these portrayals during his journey south to join his unit through Laos and Cambodia.

There was no triumphant march of strong, determined young heroes down a broad and smooth highway under the fluttering red banners of the Socialist Republic of Vietnam, singing "Nothing is more precious than independence and freedom!"

Instead, he rode in a convoy of battered trucks, that travelled only at night without any headlights, stop and start, bouncing down a bomb-pocked trail just wide enough to accommodate the width of the vehicles.

There was evidence that, despite their recent defeats, the Americans were still vigorously attacking the supply routes into the south.

One night during his journey, his convoy unexpectedly halted. The trucks got off the road as best they could. Soon, Thanh could feel the earth shake. Ahead, he saw the sky flash with bursts of brilliant white light.

The driver of his truck just said, "The Americans are bombing."

"Quickly," said Thanh, "We must get the men off the trucks and into cover!"

"No need," said his driver, "The Americans are over a kilometer away. Their bombs can do us no harm here."

A kilometer away, thought Thanh! But this truck is bouncing like a ball with every impact! What are the American planes dropping?

"If we were any closer," continued the driver, "Getting under cover would do us no good. The American bombs are too big."

Later that morning, Sub-Lieutenant Thanh saw evidence that the Americans did not accept that they had been defeated.

The area where the bombs had struck was devastated. The forest and the terrain were shredded. The trees were blasted into tangled piles of branches, jagged splinters and foliage. There were great smoking craters on and along the road.

The engineers of the People's Army of Vietnam were clearing the road and clearing a path through the destruction for Thanh's convoy to continue its journey to liberate their comrades in the south. As they slowly picked their way through the destruction, Thanh saw what was left of a truck protruding from one of the craters. Then, to his horror, he realized that a convoy had been caught under the American bombs.

"Where are the medical units?" he blurted, "There must have been survivors!"

"Survivors?" snorted his driver, "There are no survivors when the Americans bomb. Not even bodies. Just smoking craters and blasted trees like you see. In a few days, the engineers will have cleared this place and filled in the holes. There will be no indication that our comrades died here. It will be just another stretch of road to drive over. Until the Americans come back."

Finally, Sub-Lieutenant Thanh arrived in a disbursement center near the border in the hills of Cambodia. The convoy that had delivered him unloaded and immediately turned back north for its next trip.

There, Thanh was informed that he was assigned to the 324A *Dac Cong*, Special Operations, Regiment.

Thanh was filled with pride. The soldiers of the *Dac Cong* regiments were the heroes who spearheaded the defeat of the Americans and their cowardly Vietnamese puppets in the great patriotic victories in Saigon and Hue.

Then, Thanh was informed that he was fortunate. His regiment's base camp was less than seventy kilometers to the south, right across the border.

What was a *Dac Cong* regiment doing on the border, wondered Thanh? Should it not be participating in mopping up the remnants of the enemy around Saigon and the other major cities in the south?

When a group of replacements was assembled for their march to the regimental base camp, Sub-Lieutenant Thanh and seven enlisted men, Thanh was shocked to discover that they would also have to carry supplies and ammunition to the regiment on their backs. Each of the enlisted men, in addition to their personal weapons, ammunition and equipment, was fitted with a special back harness to which was attached four rounds for the 82mm mortars. Also, some of the men carried a sacks of canned rations while others carried crates of small-arms ammunition, mostly the 7.62 shorts for the rifles and machine guns.

As an officer, Thanh was spared much, but he was given a dispatch case for the regimental commander and a sack of mail for the regiment. Although he was the tutelary commander of the replacement detachment on the march, Thanh was assigned a combat-experienced non-commissioned officer, a corporal, to assist him.

Corporal Ngo, he was told, was returning to the regiment after recovering from wounds heroically received while defeating the American terrorists near Ban Me Thuot. At last, thought Thanh, a man who has been in combat against the Americans, a hero of the struggle to liberate our country.

Sub-Lieutenant Thanh's expectations were disappointed almost as soon as he met Corporal Ngo.

Corporal Ngo was a little man, even by Vietnamese standards. His uniform, in which Ngo seemed to be lost, was dirty and torn. The most remarkable thing about Ngo was the ruin of his face. The left side of his face was burned and scarred as if melted by some great heat. His skull was furrowed above his left ear. His left eye was an uncovered, puckered ruin.

Yet, through with all the damage to Ngo's face, he seemed to display a constant sarcastic smirk, at least that's how Sub-Lieutenant Thanh interpreted it, although the "smirk" may have been the result of his burns.

Ngo briefly reported to Thanh and immediately led their little detachment of human pack-mules down a trail into the jungle. Thanh noticed that Ngo was carrying no extra equipment.

At the end of the first day's march, Sub-Lieutenant Thanh estimated that they had covered less than twenty kilometers, which was most unsatisfactory.

When he pointed this out to Ngo, the corporal just shrugged and said it is better to get to a destination slowly than not get to it at all. Thanh was not sure what Ngo meant by this, but he was sure that he was unsatisfied with the response.

That night, Corporal Ngo arranged the men in a small circle with him and Sub-Lieutenant Thanh in the center. He told the men that only one of them needed to be awake at any one time. The rest could sleep. Each man would be on guard for half an hour, then he would awaken the man to his left to relieve him, and so on around the circle. He said when man on guard heard the birds signing, he was to awaken Ngo, who would be sleeping in the center of the circle.

One of the men said to Ngo that he did not have a watch. So, Ngo borrowed Thanh's watch with its luminous dials and gave it to the first man on guard and told him to pass the watch along as the guard relief moved around the circle.

Ngo told the replacements that if they heard anything at night, especially voices or people moving, or if they smelled anything, especially food cooking or cigarette smoke, they were to awaken Ngo immediately.

They were not to fire their weapons unless ordered to or unless fired upon. In fact, Ngo made every replacement clear his weapon in front of him and re-attach the magazine with the bolt closed.

Finally, Ngo told the men if any of them snored, whoever was on guard was to awaken that man immediately. If they could not sleep silently, they could not sleep.

When Corporal Ngo re-joined Sub-Lieutenant Thanh in the center of the circle, he said, "There's no point in you staying awake, comrade sub-lieutenant. I do not sleep soundly anymore. I will keep an eye on our little charges tonight ... keep an eye ... I guess that's a joke now. Besides, I do not think any of them will be sleeping much tonight."

"Comrade corporal," said Sub-Lieutenant Thanh, "Tell me about our regiment."

"Our regiment?" answered Ngo. "A bunch of good guys. Good soldiers. They know their shit. The commander, Captain Phan, if he is still alive, is a first-rate officer. Tough, but fair. You will learn much from him, sir."

"Captain Phan?" questioned Sub-Lieutenant Thanh. "Why is a captain commanding a regiment!"

"Because he's still alive, and he's the best man for the job," stated Corporal Ngo simply.

"Tell me about the great victory over the Americans," demanded Thanh.

"Victory!" exclaimed Ngo. "There was no victory! We got our asses kicked. What have they been telling you back home?"

"Surely that is a lie, comrade corporal! Are you a defeatist? I could execute you now for treason!" hissed Thanh. "We have the Americans and their puppets on the ropes. We only need to move in and finish them off."

"Execute me?" chuckled Corporal Ngo. "If you execute me, how are you and this pack of children going to find your way out of these woods. There was no victory, Sub-Lieutenant. Yes! Initially we caught the Americans by surprise! But, to what end? What is the old saying?

'Never kick a sleeping tiger.' That's what we did; we kicked a sleeping tiger. And this one savaged us. When the regiment first attacked Ban Me Thuot, we were almost at full-strength. By the time we managed to extricate ourselves and pull back into the hills, we had barely enough men to field four companies. That's where I got hit. Now, I have no idea how many of us are left, or who commands, a captain, a sergeant, a corporal like me for all I know. A victory? We ran into a meat grinder. If you want to execute me, sir, go right ahead. Either you kill me tonight, or the Americans kill me tomorrow. Either way, I'm already a dead man."

Sub-Lieutenant Thanh didn't know how to process this information; neither Corporal Ngo's lies about the war — they had to be lies certainly, the Party would not lie to the people, — nor Ngo's attitude about his patriotic duty to the Vietnamese people.

Ngo certainly did not resemble the cleanly uniformed, well-fed, handsome heroes that Thanh had seen in the newsreels, movies, and patriotic posters.

But that was all in Hanoi.

Here he was in the combat zone with a dwarfish, scarred, one-eyed corporal telling him that everything that he had been told was a lie. Victory was defeat. Heroes are cowards. For the first time since joining the People's Army of Vietnam, Thanh was confused.

They travelled through the forest at Corporal Ngo's leisurely pace, making about fifteen to twenty kilometers each day depending on the terrain. Sub-Lieutenant Thanh noticed that not only did Ngo not push the men very hard; he marched them for no more than an hour at a time, then let them rest, drink water and smoke for about ten minutes.

Thanh was sure that they could make better time if Ngo didn't mollycoddle the men.

One morning, before they pushed off, Corporal Ngo got the men together. "We are close to the border now, comrades. We must be careful of American patrols. Up here, the Americans only use their special operations troops. These soldiers are very good. They can move without making a sound. You will not see them unless they want you to, and at that point, you don't want to. So, stay alert on the march. Two of you will act as our scouts. You will move about twenty meters out in front of us. Your job is to detect the enemy before they can ambush the main column. You will carry only your weapons and ammunition. The rest of us will carry your equipment. The officer and I will march between the scouts and the main column to coordinate and to keep you on the right course. Remember! Our mission is to get ourselves and this equipment to the regiment. If the scouts get ambushed, we will break contact and then continue our mission. Are there any questions?"

The men had none.

Sub-Lieutenant Thanh had many. He could not ask them in front of the others. An officer of the People's Army of Vietnam was supposed to be competent in all situations. The men needed to have confidence in his leadership.

That night, after Corporal Ngo had set the guard, Sub-Lieutenant Thanh said, "Comrade corporal, tell me about the Americans."

"The Americans? What do you want to know about the Americans?" answered Ngo.

Thanh noted that the farther they got into the jungle, the less often Ngo addressed him with the proper military courtesy.

"In training, we were told that the Americans are cowards," stated Thanh, "They will not stand up to us in a fight. They cower in their bunkers and fortifications like the cowardly French did in our great war of liberation."

"Ah ... so those are the fairy tales they are telling children in Hanoi these days!" answered Ngo. "It's not an issue that the Americans will not stand up to us, lieutenant, it's an issue that they do not have to stand up to us."

"Explain, comrade corporal!" ordered Thanh.

"The Americans' strength is their firepower," explained Ngo, "Not just the weapons they carry with them, but the weapons they can control. If they can fix our position, they can call down artillery, helicopter gunships, even air-strikes, sometimes in minutes. So, if we are foolish enough to concentrate our forces to attack them, and try to press our attack, their soldiers do not need to defeat us themselves. They get under cover and let their firepower destroy us."

"Then how can we defeat them, comrade corporal?" asked Thanh.

"One way is to close with them. Get up right in their faces," Ngo answered. "The Americans are squeamish about shooting artillery, and even their mortars, too close to their own soldiers. If we can get under the artillery and close with their infantry, then we can defeat them in a fight. But I tell you, Sub-Lieutenant, because I do not know what you have been told, the Americans are dangerous in a close fight. Their weapons are first-rate, their defenses well-planned, and they will rarely break. If you get in close with them, you are going to take punishment. Win or lose, they will hurt you badly. And, if you get close in, there is no retreat. If you break contact and attempt to withdraw, they will call in their artillery on you. Withdrawing is sometimes worse than the battle itself."

"Then how can we fight them?" asked Thanh.

"Hit and run is best," answered Ngo, "Hit them, cause some casualties, and get out of there. We do not have to defeat the Americans, comrade sub-lieutenant. We simply must prevent them from destroying us. As long as we are here in the south fighting, we are winning. The Americans are far from their homes, and these are not their people. They will tire of this fight eventually."

Again, Sub-Lieutenant Thanh did not know how to process this information. This picture that Corporal Ngo was painting of hit and run combat with the Americans did not resemble the images in the sub-lieutenant's imagination. There, he was riding on a captured American tank waiving the red, golden-starred flag of the Socialist Republic of Vietnam. Along the road the liberated peoples of the south were acclaiming him, acclaiming the great victory of the Vietnamese people. Behind his tank were columns of defeated, captured, shamed Americans, their heads hung low, their arms bound behind their backs, marching off into captivity.

This was nothing like Ngo's picture of hiding in the forest, sniping at unsuspecting American patrols, then retreating back into the underbrush. For the first time since joining the Peoples' Army of Vietnam, Thanh was feeling doubt.

"Do the Americans have any weaknesses that we can exploit to defeat them?" asked Sub-Lieutenant Thanh.

Corporal Ngo thought for a few moments, then answered, "Their loyalty to each other! Yes! That is a weakness that we have often used to defeat them."

"Loyalty?" questioned Thanh. "How can loyalty be a weakness?"

"Their loyalty to each other is very strong," stated Ngo, "So strong that I have seen Americans get themselves killed trying to recover the body of a comrade who was already dead. That, I know, sounds very strange, but it is true. I have seen it. In Ban Me Thuot, we had a wounded American down in front of our position. Every time he stopped screaming, we shot him again, not to kill, but to wound. Soon, the other Americans facing us couldn't stand it any longer. One of them, he was a medic because he was carrying a big bag of medical supplies, broke cover and tried to get to his wounded comrade. So, we shot him. Luckily, he was only wounded and started yelling for his comrades to rescue him. I think we could have kept this going all day, but we were ordered to pull out. We killed both Americans before we left."

"When you get to the regiment," Corporal Ngo continued, "You will meet our sergeant major, if he is still alive, Sergeant Major Trinh. He is a most experienced and competent soldier. You should listen to Sergeant Major Trinh very carefully if you wish to stay alive, comrade sub-lieutenant, that is, if Sergeant Major Trinh considers your staying alive of value to the regiment, no disrespect, comrade. Sergeant Major Trinh has a favorite tactic for defeating the Americans. When he detects one of their small patrols, Sergeant Major Trinh will engage the patrol. But he will not destroy it. He will kill some but leave the rest to call for help. He will leave three or four men to stay in contact with the patrol, literally firing over the Americans' heads. He tells his men to stay very close to the Americans, so that they cannot use their mortars or artillery against them. Sergeant Major Trinh then deploys his main force in an ambush between the patrol and their parent unit. Always, the Americans send a relief force to rescue their comrades. Always, Sergeant Major Trinh ambushes them. But he does not stay long in contact. He springs the ambush, kills and wounds as many of the Americans as he can, and withdraws. Sergeant Major Trinh usually kills the survivors of the American patrol as he withdraws. Sergeant Major Trinh is also careful to recover the bodies of any of his fallen comrades and his wounded. After Sergeant Major Trinh is gone, the Americans are left to recover their dead and wounded. They can find no trace of Sergeant Major Trinh and his patrol. They can find no trace of any casualties caused by their fire. This is very bad for their morale. If you can accomplish this feat a few times against an American unit, they do not even dare to send out patrols. Sergeant Major Trinh is a most competent soldier. If you are wise, you will listen to him when we re-join the regiment."

Sub-Lieutenant Thanh was peering out into the darkness toward where he knew the Americans had established their bases.

At last, he was fulfilling his duty to the Vietnamese people and the party. He was in combat against the enemies of the Socialist Republic of Vietnam. There was nothing between him and the enemies of the Vietnamese people but a few kilometers of forest.

Thanh felt all the doubt and confusion that had been building in him melt away.

Tomorrow, when the sun rose, beside stalwart comrades like Sergeant Major Trinh, Thanh would lead his men into combat.

He hoped it would be the most glorious day of his eighteen-year-old life.

III

Sergeant Richie Jones, "Jonesy" as everyone in the unit called him, had completed seven months of his twelve-month tour in Vietnam.

Sergeant Taylor had promised him that he would find Jonesy some sham assignment in the rear for his last month in country. Subtract that, and the two to three weeks he'd burn up on R&R, Jonesy figured, worst case, he had about fourteen weeks left in the field.

His sense of things was that the worst was behind him.

He had come into country right before the Vietnamese new year holiday, called Tet. There wasn't much going on then. The dinks seemed to have disappeared. Guys were beginning to think that the bombing was beginning to have an effect. The war was beginning to wind down.

Then the shit hit the fan.

The battalion was operating in the Ia Drang valley, when, without any warning, they were moved north to the division base camp just south of Pleiku. As the choppers brought them in, Jonesy couldn't believe his eyes. The city of Pleiku was burning. Black smoke hung low over the tin huts and masonry buildings marking the downtown area.

When they landed inside the division base camp, they were immediately trucked out to the perimeter bunker line.

When Jonesy first came into country, he had had to pull guard here. Then, it was almost like doing sentry duty in the States. He stood inspection in a guard mount while some officer quizzed him on the General Orders. He was issued an old M14 rifle and one magazine of ammo. The Sergeant of the Guard had told him under no circumstances was he to load the magazine into the rifle unless ordered to do so.

He stood guard in a plywood, sandbagged bunker that was built above the ground. While he was on duty, some guy he had never seen before came into the bunker and smoked a joint. He even offered Jonesy a toke. Then he left.

Now a couple of the stand-up bunkers in their sector had been blown to shit. Plywood and sandbags were obviously no match for an RPG. Jonesy wondered if some poor son of a bitch was standing guard in the bunker with an unloaded M14 when it got hit.

The soldiers ignored the ruined bunkers and began digging in on the perimeter of the base camp. He and a couple of guys were detailed to string concertina wire in front of the bunker line to replace the stuff that was taken out by the enemy's bangalores and satchel charges.

Jonesy wondered what had happened to the chicken-shit guard mount he remembered from a few weeks back.

That night the base camp was hit with mortars and rockets, but the dinks didn't try to get through the wire. On the third day, they could hear a hell of a firefight in the direction of Pleiku City, but they never got a call to move out. The unit spent its time strengthening its position, bunkering the fighting positions, stringing wire, and trenching.

They stayed on the base camp for about a week. Just when things were starting to get good — hot chow a couple times a day and even access to the division shower point — they got rounded up and trucked over to the helicopter pad.

This time they got loaded onto shithooks and moved up north. They landed at a beat-to-shit air strip up in the mountains and had to hump ten klicks to a mountain overlooking some river and a bridge along Highway Fourteen.

Just getting up the mountain nearly killed Jonesy.

For the next three weeks they chopped down trees until the shithooks had enough room to drop in a battery of 105's. Then more chopping, more digging, until there was room for the heavy mortars and two sections of 81's. Then more digging and more chopping until there was room for the battalion CP.

The good news was that with battalion came the mess hall, so they were again eating prime.

The bad news, all that noise, hardware and activity had gotten the enemy's attention.

The dinks waited until the monsoon came in. The clouds literally sat on top of the mountain. The guys could hardly see from one bunker to the next.

Then the dinks hit them with everything they had.

The battle lasted all night.

At one point the dinks overran the west side of the perimeter. The company had to pull back to the artillery pits and counterattack to reestablish the perimeter.

When the sun came up, they could see how much damage was done. They had lost one of the artillery pieces and a couple of mortars. The battalion CP was flattened and the battalion operations officer, the S3, was running the show from the Charlie Company CP.

The first and second platoons of Alpha Company had taken the brunt of the assault.

The first platoon was down to Lieutenant Lattimore, Sergeant Taylor and six other guys. Jonesy was one of them. Somehow, without so much as a scratch, he had come through one of the worst firefights the battalion had seen since the Korean war, when they were regularly beating off hordes of Chinese regulars.

After that there were some flare ups around the cities of Kontum and Dak To, but the fight seemed to have gone out of the enemy. They became increasingly hard to find and didn't seem to have enough interest, or enough ammo, to throw more than a couple of 82mm mortar rounds at the company every few weeks. The casualties that the dinks took after Tet and the constant bombing of their supply routes seemed to be having an effect.

Things seemed to be winding down.

Although Jonesy didn't have any delusions about the war ending, he just hoped it stayed relatively quiet for the next couple of months until he got out of the field.

Jonesy was now the senior squad leader in the first platoon. So, it came as no surprise to him that Taylor assigned him and Jimmy Delvecchio's fire team to take a new lieutenant out on his first patrol.

Jonesy's patrol wasn't going out that far. It was just a short recon sweep west of the company's position toward what looked like on their maps an extinct volcano. Battalion thought there was enemy activity in the vicinity of that hill. They were just to sweep the area a couple of klicks out in front of the company's position to see if any dinks were trying to get close.

As a squad leader, Jonesy normally wouldn't take out a four man patrol himself. Jimmy D was more than competent, a good NCO. But the new lieutenant was the Joker in the deck.

The new lieutenant was obviously slated to take over the first platoon now that Lieutenant Lattimore had the company. So, this short and relatively low risk mission was a good opportunity for him to get his feet wet, get to know some of the men, and give them a chance to get to know him.

No one wanted a rookie, officer or not, calling the shots on his first patrol. So, one of Jonesy's jobs was maintaining control of the mission without showing up, or pissing off, his new platoon leader.

Jonesy had enough rank and reputation, being one of the few survivors of the mile-high battle left in the company, to pull this off. Jimmy D didn't.

Besides, Jonesy had the "pedigree,"; he was regular army, and D was a draftee.

Jonesy had joined up in a spasm of teenaged, patriotic exuberance with a couple of his classmates right after graduation from high school. They all saw this as somehow fulfilling a call to service to the nation made by the recently murdered President Kennedy.

Now, Jonesy wasn't quite sure that joining the army had been a good decision for him. Even after all the shit he had gone through in Nam, he wasn't ready to call it a mistake. Part of him still believed in what his country was trying to accomplish in Vietnam.

But he was pretty sure he wasn't going to re-up when his hitch was over. The way this war was being fought made no sense. Ironically, it just seemed to make things worse for the Vietnamese people.

He'd get through the rest of his tour in Nam, probably take a stateside assignment for the rest of his enlistment, then go home to Tennessee and figure out what to do with the rest of his life.

He just hoped things would stay quiet for the next few weeks.

Jonesy's other mission that day was to get the measure of the new lieutenant.

He expected Jake, Sergeant Taylor, would be questioning him closely about how things went as soon as they got back to the firebase. Lt. Lattimore would probably be a fly on the wall for that conversation, before he made his mind up what to do with the new lieutenant.

Their first day out was uneventful.

The new lieutenant asked some questions about what Jonesy was doing and why. But, other than that, the new lieutenant acted like any other rifleman on patrol.

The squad's replacement — Jonesy didn't remember his name but had started calling him Blinky because of his squinty eyes — was carrying the radio, the PRC-25. He was a little confused at first whether he should stick close to the new Lieutenant or Jonesy, but after the first hour he had gravitated to Jonesy.

One of the questions the new lieutenant asked Jonesy was how to identify the enemy. Someone in the rear had told the new lieutenant that if he fired on friendly Vietnamese or Montagnards, he would be court-martialed and sent to Leavenworth for twenty years.

Jonesy explained that in this AO, there were no friendlies. The South Vietnamese army, ARVN, didn't operate up here. They didn't have the balls for it. And the dinks had exterminated any Montagnards not smart enough to get their asses out of the area. So, no friend-lies.

Jonesy explained that the dinks typically wore khaki or olive drab uniforms – but their OD looked different than ours, darker. They sometimes wore pith helmets, like in the jungle movies back home, but they may have Russian steel pots or boonie hats. Most of them carried AK's but there were still a few SKS carbines out there.

Jonesy told the new lieutenant that if they shoot at you, you shoot back. If you see pith helmets, shoot ... AK's, shoot ... red collar tabs, shoot ... khaki uniforms, shoot ... when in doubt ... shoot. Twenty in Leavenworth was better than dead forever. Besides, the chow was better in jail, and you didn't have to sleep out in the rain.

Anyway, their mission was recon. They were to avoid contact. If they detected any enemy activity, they were to get the hell out of there, preferably without the dinks knowing they were ever there.

Jonesy noticed that the new lieutenant seemed a bit concerned about this issue. Someone in the rear must have really put the fear of God in him about the rules of engagement.

Jonesy had to admit that pulling the trigger on another human being was difficult, at least the first time. Hell, he still had problems accepting the fact that other human beings were trying to kill him, even when it happened.

You get over that.

You had to.

Don't think of them as people.

Think of them as targets.

Think of them as dinks.

Do your job.

Stay alive.

Around dusk, Jonesy found a good position for the night, high ground along a ridge facing north with plenty of cover. He established commo and reported the patrol's location to the company using the radio's "short stick" antenna.

Jonesy made sure the radio was set to silent mode. The hissing of the squelch could be heard for meters at night and was a dead give away of their position.

While Jimmy D, Sweetie, and Blinky put out some claymores around their night laager, Jonesy checked the patrol's location on his map and located the pre-set targets plotted by the mortars in case he had to call for fire support or illumination at night.

Jonesy set the watch rotation, only one guy up at a time monitoring the radio.

The guys ate some cold c-rats and settled in for the night.

The new lieutenant seemed to be observing and learning the routine, a good sign. Jonesy asked him if he wanted to take a watch and he agreed, which meant more sleep for everyone else. Jonesy assigned the new lieutenant the first watch, because most of the guys would probably still be awake.

Jonesy explained to the new lieutenant how radio communications worked while they were on the patrol. The patrol did not initiate any calls at night unless they were in contact, detected movement, or had to re-locate. Throughout the night, the company CP would initiate periodic calls for a situation report, a "Sit Rep." The command station would call their call sign, Romeo Tango One One X-Ray, and say, "If your sit rep is negative, break squelch twice."

At that point, whoever was on watch, would depress the push-to-talk button on the radio handset twice. Company would acknowledge by saying, "One One X-Ray, understand negative sit rep, out."

The new lieutenant asked what if they had something to report.

Jonesy just said, "If you think you hear anything, wake me up, LT."

With that, Jonesy was done for the day and settled back on his ruck. The monsoon had pretty much petered out, so he didn't expect any rain during the night. Good for hearing what was around you and good for staying warm and dry all night.

In the darkness, he could sense the closeness of his fire team huddled around him in the dark. Good guys, he thought. Know their shit. The new guy, Blinky, seems to be shaping up. The new lieutenant seems to be getting it too.

As Jonesy drifted off, he thought it was strange that this place, these highlands of Vietnam, reminded him of the hills and mountains surrounding Jonesborough, Tennessee, his home. He often felt at home in these heavily wooded hills. He had hunted in hills and forests just like these as a kid with his dad and brothers.

Just a couple of months more and he'd be back there. He knew exactly what he was going to do when he got back.

All the guys had a "coming-home fantasy" about what they were going to do during their first few hours home. But his had nothing to do with the sexual gymnastics some of the other guys talked about. Hell, most of that stuff was physically impossible any way.

No, this had nothing to do with that.

He was going to borrow his daddy's truck and drive over to the hamburger stand on the highway just outside of town. There, he was going to order himself a strawberry thick shake, one so thick with ice cream he couldn't pull it up through a straw until it had melted some. He was going to drink that thing until it gave him a headache.

He could almost taste it!

A nice, pink, creamy, frozen shake, that's what he wanted.

Jonesy drifted off to sleep, another day gone and another day closer to going home.

IV

First Lieutenant Thomas Jefferson Lattimore never felt more alive than when he watched his company execute a morning stand-to in the field without his having to do a thing.

His company!

That's what they were. His company!

He had melded a good, effective combat team out of a collection of career soldiers, first term enlistees, and draftees. He had country boys, city boys, college grads, illiterates, whites, blacks, Mexicans, Indians.

None of that mattered.

Not in this place.

They were all Alpha Company.

They were a team.

They knew their shit.

They did the job.

They took care of each another.

And they were his boys.

Lattimore was finishing his tenth month in country, all of it in the field, all of it with Alpha Company.

He had arrived in-country not long after graduating Infantry OCS, green and scared shitless, just like the new lieutenant he had recently sent out on patrol. His first day in the field, his commander, Captain Jacoby, told him to listen to his NCO's; learn how things were done; get the routine down; say little; listen a lot.

He was lucky to have a solid squad leader, Jake Taylor, a career NCO. Taylor was also new to combat and Vietnam, but he had been pounding ground in places like Germany, Panama, and the back reaches of Ft. Benning for the last ten years of his life. He could run an infantry platoon in his sleep.

Lattimore got his cherry busted just after Tet on the mile-high firebase up near Dak To. That was a tough fight. But at least the dinks had to come to them.

Fighting on the defense was always an advantage. But it was a tough fight. A lot of good people got fucked up.

Then, there were a series of firefights around Kontum and Ban Me Thuot.

By that time, Lattimore had finished six months in the field and was expecting to get re-assigned off the line. But the battalion commander threw him a curve ball.

His company commander, Captain Jacoby, was getting ready to DEROS back to the states. So, instead of taking Lattimore off the line, the battalion commander offered him the company.

"Feel free to say no," he told Lattimore, "In fact, feel free to say fuck no. You've done your share, and I'm sure I can find you a nice safe spot up at brigade or division. But Alpha's a good company, and with both you and Jacoby leaving, that would put a big hole in that leadership team. So, I'd like you to step up and take the company."

Lattimore was both flattered and terrified by the offer.

Flattered that the battalion commander, a ring-knocker from the Academy, had that much confidence in his competence and leadership.

Terrified of being responsible for a hundred guys and a company-sized combat mission.

For one thing, there was his inherent infantryman's belief in never tempting fate. For the last six months as a platoon leader, he had avoiding getting himself killed and getting a lot of his guys needlessly fucked up. Now he could be done, finished with combat. He could get out of the field with his hide intact.

Why would he want to stay when he didn't have to?

He was just begging the "Wrong Time Wrong Place" principle to rear up and screw him.

But who was going to take care of his boys when he left?

If he turned it down, the army could stick some captain from a mess kit repair depot out with his company, who'd totally screw the pooch, and get a lot of his boys fucked up doing it.

"I'll do it, sir. I'll do my best," he said.

"I know you will, lieutenant," the battalion commander told him, shaking his hand, "Thanks for doing it!"

In a crazy way, Lattimore thought that running a company was easier than running a platoon.

He felt he had broken some secret code of combat leadership that they didn't teach at OCS.

"Trust and verify."

Trust your subordinates and let them do their jobs. Watch it happen. Intervene only if you must.

Before Lattimore joined the army, he had never given any serious thought to what he wanted to do with his life.

He had enrolled in the University of North Carolina as an engineering student. But, in his second year, he decided that all the time he had to spend on calculus and physics was getting in the way of partying and trying to get laid. So, he switched his major to something less time consuming, Political Science.

His father, who was an executive with IBM and who was footing the bills for Lattimore's experiments in hedonistic academics, didn't seem to care one way or the other as long as he got decent grades and graduated on time.

When Lattimore did graduate with a Bachelors in Poly Sci, and was re-classified 1A by the draft board, he realized that, with the war on, he wasn't going to be able to get a serious job until he took care of the military obligation hanging over his head.

An army recruiter told him that, if he joined instead of waiting to be drafted, he could pick his job in the army. Besides, with his college degree, he was almost sure to become an officer.

So, Lattimore joined the army requesting an assignment to the Signal Corps, so he could learn about computers, and to the Army Language School, so he could learn French.

He had heard French girls were hot and easy.

One of the first of many shocks that Lattimore received when he got to the army reception station at Ft. Benning, Georgia, was that having a college degree didn't mean the army was going to make him an officer.

First, he had to take a lot of Mickey Mouse tests to see if he qualified to be an officer. After passing these, Lattimore found out that he would still have to go through basic and advanced training as an enlisted man, a Private E1 recruit, and only then could he attend Officer Candidate School, or OCS as the army called it.

Then the army threw him another curve ball.

If he accepted OCS, he could request a branch, but the army would assign him to a branch based on its needs. And, with a war on, the army was always in need of infantry officers.

So, if he opted to go to OCS, he was taking his chances of becoming an infantryman, which meant a tour in Nam.

But Thomas Jefferson Lattimore just could not envision himself, a college grad, spending his three-year army career as an enlisted man. So, he signed up for OCS, stated Signal as his preferred branch, France as his preferred duty assignment, and headed off to basic.

Lattimore finished basic at Ft. Benning and then was shipped off on a Greyhound bus to Ft. Monmouth, New Jersey, for Advanced Signal Corps training.

For a guy who had spent his entire life no further north than northern Virginia, New Jersey was the coldest annex of hell that Lattimore had ever experienced. The old World-War-II barracks, where Lattimore and his fellow trainees slept, was so porous that, when the wind blew, there was a five mile-an-hour breeze blowing right down the center of their squad bay.

The good news, though, was that a weekend pass could get him to New York City, where Lattimore's slight southern drawl attracted the ladies like bees to honey. It almost made up for his GI haircut and his inadequate funding on army pay.

The training at Ft. Monmouth was what the army called a "gentleman's course."

After the first week, the drill instructors and cadre didn't yell at or harass the trainees much at all, as long as the barracks were clean, boots polished, uniforms presentable, they had haircuts, were properly shaved, showed up for class on time, and repeated the pattern every day.

And, after week three, weekends were free for expeditions to New York City.

Lattimore actually found the science of telecommunications fascinating: analog multiplexing, frequency modulation, bandwidth, things like that. He tolerated having to memorize certain facts, "The signal-to-noise ration of the AN/PRC-25 radio at 41.0 mc is no less than 40 dB blah... blah... blah..."

As far as Lattimore was concerned, such trivia was only useful for passing quizzes; and passing quizzes was useful in not flunking out of the course; and not flunking was useful in not being reassigned to the infantry.

So, he memorized what he was told to memorize.

Lattimore was in his ninth week of training, just three weeks shy of graduating, when the army lowered the boom on him. His OCS orders came down. He was granted one week's leave after graduation, before reporting back to Ft. Benning, Georgia, for Infantry Officers Candidate School.

Lattimore asked his unit commander if there was anything that could be done about the assignment. The lieutenant said nothing short of turning down OCS and getting an enlisted assignment in the Signal Corps. Then his commander reminded him that Signal Corps guys went to Nam, too.

Lattimore asked about his request to be stationed in France.

His lieutenant just laughed.

Infantry OCS was one of the toughest experiences Lattimore had ever had up to that point in his short life. It made basic training seem like a day at the beach.

The training cadre screamed at him, ran him, starved him, deprived him of sleep, and screamed at him some more.

Curiously, through it all, Lattimore made a discovery about himself. He had a backbone.

Although he had no interest in becoming an infantry officer — in fact, the concept scared the shit out of him — there was no way he was going to let these petty-assed bastards in the blue helmet liners run him out of OCS.

Lattimore completed the course and was commissioned a Second Lieutenant, Infantry, in the US Army Reserve.

In fact, Lattimore must have impressed someone, because they assigned him to Benning as a small arms/tactics instructor.

2LT Thomas Jefferson Lattimore was in fat city on Benning. He essentially worked a nine-to-five job on post, had all the perks of a junior officer, and the ladies at the Officer's Club were fine indeed. And, every day that passed, was one day out of his three-year commitment to Uncle Sam.

Then, one dark afternoon in November, he was summoned to his commander's office. There, he was told by his captain that he had been granted thirty-days leave before reporting to the Oakland Army Terminal for deployment to Vietnam.

The rest is, as they say, history.

Lattimore did six months as a rifle platoon leader and was now a company commander. His days as a college student and in the stateside army seemed like they had happened in a different life, a different world.

But, while Lattimore was commanding Alpha Company, he discovered another curious thing about himself.

He liked the work!

In college, he had never given much thought to a career. And, he always had considered the army something he had to get done with so he could start a career.

But since taking over Alpha Company, he discovered that he liked the work.

Not the filth he had to live in, and not the constant fear of combat he had to endure, although that did seem to give everything he did a bit of an edge. It was working with the men, molding them into an effective team, watching them perform.

What was it that grunts said, "Doing the impossible, for the ungrateful."

Lattimore was considering making a career in the army, in the infantry.

He had a great leg up on it. Combat and command experience, and he was only twenty-four. He had a college degree, and he could apply for a Regular Army commission when he got back to the States. He was sure his battalion commander would endorse his application.

The old man was a West Point grad. That had to count for something.

There was one fear that constantly lurked in the back of Lattimore's mind.

It wasn't getting himself killed.

If that were going to happen, it would. Wrong time, wrong place.

And he didn't doubt his competence as an infantryman and as a commander.

What could really scare Lattimore, if he were to let it, was doing something stupid in the heat of the moment; making a decision, or failing to make a decision, that got a lot of his people fucked up, then surviving to realize he had gotten them killed.

At least, that's how his mind would play it back to him, over and over, for the rest of his life ... if he survived.

There were worse things than getting yourself killed in this fucking place, he realized. It was getting a bunch of guys who trusted you killed.

But Lattimore just refused to let his mind dwell on such thoughts. That would ruin him as a commander.

That morning Lattimore watched as his first platoon brought in their LP. Then, they sent some men forward to recover the claymores and trip flares. Never leave that stuff out in the daylight where the enemy could mark their locations.

He still had a patrol out. The patrol had heard nothing last night and had made their last sit rep about thirty minutes ago.

Maybe brigade was wrong about the volcano.

Maybe there were no dinks anywhere near this place.

Sergeant Jones should be packing up to head back around now. They should call in their movement back to the firebase any minute now.

Lattimore wondered how the new lieutenant had liked his first night out in the boonies.

He wondered what Sergeant Jones thought about his new platoon leader.

It was just about full light.

Today, they would strengthen their position. A lot of digging, filling sandbags. He'd like to get overhead cover on all the fighting positions today. Get the CP and the mortar FDC into the ground. Maybe send out a squad to sweep around the perimeter.

That's what the infantry did a lot of … walking and digging. But, if that's all they had to do today, it wouldn't be a bad day, not a bad day at all.

V

Sub-Lieutenant Thanh roused his men and moved them out of their night position as soon as there was enough light to see.

Of course, Thanh did not have to rouse Sergeant Major Trinh. He was already awake. Thanh was not sure that the sergeant major had any of the needs or any of the weaknesses of a human being, the need to sleep, the need to eat, the need to drink, the need for human companionship. If he did, Thanh could detect no evidence of it. The man was not human. He was a total soldier of the peoples' liberation army.

Sub-Lieutenant Thanh would have been quite shocked to know that Sergeant Major Trinh's father had taught French literature at a *ly-cée* in Hanoi before the Japanese came. In fact, Trinh could quote from memory much of the poetry of Apollinaire that he and his father had shared those many years ago.

> *Me voici devant tous un homme plein de sens*
>
> *Connaissant la vie et de la mort ce qu'un vivant peut connaître*
>
> Here I am before all a sensible man
>
> Knowing of life and death what a living being can know

When the Japanese came, they rounded up anyone they thought would be a threat to them. Intellectuals were the first to go.

Trinh's father was arrested one evening and never seen again.

A few days later, Trinh's mother went to the Japanese headquarters to demand information about her husband, and she never returned.

At fourteen years of age, Trinh had lost both his parents to the foreign invaders of his country. Trinh went to live with his mother's cousin in a village ten kilometers north of Hanoi.

At first, he was afraid that the Japanese would come for him. When they did not, his fear gradually distilled into hate for the people who had murdered his parents.

> *Ayant perdu ses meilleurs amis dans l'effroyable lutte*
>
> Having lost his best friends in the dreadful combat"

Then, Trinh heard about a leader, Ho Chi Minh, who was fighting the Japanese and their Vichy French stooges. Trinh wrapped some food and his father's book of Apollinaire's poetry in a large *serviette* and started walking north into the hills.

It wasn't long before the soldiers of the Viet Minh found him.

Trinh quickly discovered two things about the Viet Minh. First, their goal was the complete independence of the Vietnamese people. They did not discriminate between the Japanese occupiers and the French occupiers. Both had to go. Second, they wanted to establish a Marxist state in Vietnam.

Ideology was as important to them as military competence. As a recruit, Trinh spent as much time in political and ideological classes as he did in weapons and tactics training.

One of Trinh's instructors, who called himself a "political officer," discovered Trinh's book of Apollinaire's poems. Calling it the "residual trash of a bourgeois, capitalist, colonial oppressor," the officer forced Trinh to burn the book in front of his fellow trainees while denouncing the French and those Vietnamese lackeys who clung to the culture of their oppressors.

Trinh did not care at all for this "communism" that the Viet Minh movement considered so necessary, so precious. But he would tolerate it as long as it gave him the opportunity to take revenge on the people who had murdered his parents.

After the war had ended, the Japanese withdrew from Vietnam, but the French remained.

Ho Chi Minh declared that the struggle of the Vietnamese people was not over until the French had been driven out and a socialist republic established.

The defeat of the Japanese had not restored his parents to him, so Trinh had no place to return to and no family other than the soldiers of the Viet Minh. So, he remained with Uncle Ho and the Viet Minh throughout the French war, the partition, the establishment of Ho Chi Minh's socialist state in the north, the Democratic Republic of Vietnam.

Now he fought in the war against the Americans to free their comrades in the south.

> *Nous ne sommes pas vos ennemis*
> *Nous voulons vous donner de vastes et étranges domaines*
> *Où le mystère en fleurs s'offre à qui veut le cueillir*
> We are not your enemies
> We wish to offer you vast and strange domains
> Where the mystery in flowers offers itself to anyone who wants to gather it

If Trinh allowed himself to think of such things, he would admit that he would gladly trade all the days left to him just to be able to spend one evening with his father reading from the book of Apollinaire's poetry that Trinh had burned so many years ago in the mountains near the Chinese border.

Such things are not possible.

His father's body was rotting in some undiscovered pit outside Hanoi where the Japanese had dumped it. His mother had probably died in one of those horrid "comfort houses" where the Japanese forced Vietnamese women to service the sexual needs of their soldiers. The ashes of Apollinaire were scattered across the dark hills that sheltered Vietnam from the Chinese.

Such thoughts were dangerous.

They serve only to distract Trinh from his duty, weaken his resolve, confuse him.

Sergeant Major Trinh's only reality was that on this morning, he was on a wooded ridgeline with twenty soldiers of the People's Army of Vietnam, a snot-nose sub-lieutenant with a party card and a university degree, the enemy near. and a mission to accomplish.

That was the limit of Sergeant Major Trinh's allowable reality.

> *Voici que vient l'été la saison violente*
> *Et ma jeunesse est morte ainsi que le printemps*
> Suddenly summer comes the violent season
> And my youth is as dead as the spring

Sub-Lieutenant Thanh decided that the patrol would sweep a small ridge some five hundred meters forward of their position on his map. Then, if they found nothing, they would return to the regiment. When he announced this plan to Trinh, the NCO made no comment. He just asked Thanh what time he planned to move out.

Thanh accepted this reply as the sergeant major's tacit approval of his plan.

On this day, Sub-Lieutenant Thanh was determined to find the enemies of the Vietnamese people, determined to destroy as many of them as he could, determined to demonstrate to Sergeant Major Trinh that he, Sub-Lieutenant Thanh, was a true soldier of the people.

That would make this day glorious.

VI

It was just about light enough to move out of their night position.

Jonesy saw that Jimmy D, Freddy and Sweetie were starting to pack up their rucksacks for the move without needing to be told. The new guy, Blinky, was emulating his team leader. This kid's going to work out fine, thought Jonesy. The new lieutenant was by the radio.

As soon as they were packed and about to recover their claymores, Jonesy planned to pull straight back to the company firebase. They were only about three klicks out over fairly easy terrain. They should get back in by late morning without having to push it.

Then he heard something!

Movement!

Out along the ridge, below their position.

Definitely human.

Moving left to right across their front.

The members of the patrol froze.

Maybe two, three people moving left to right, twenty meters below their position.

Should miss their position.

Should walk right by.

Point element?

Larger unit behind them?

Entire patrol?

Jonesy signaled Jimmy D, watch front. Freddy and Sweetie, watch flanks. Blinky, rear.

A large element may have flankers out.

Jonesy checked his map for the mortar pre-plotted targets.

Let them go past.

Call in mortars.

Break contact.

Get the fuck out of here.

Get back to the firebase.

Out of the corner of his eye, Jonesy detected movement, close to him ... too close.

He turned.

The new lieutenant was rising out of his crouch.

What the fuck!

What the hell was he doing?

Trying to get a better look down the hill?

Identify the movement?

No!

Jonesy moved to pull the new Lieutenant back down.

He had just reached him, when the new Lieutenant shouted a challenge down the hill, "Halt! Who is there?"

Then all hell broke loose!

VII

Sub-Lieutenant Thanh was surprised when his point element made contact with the enemy.

He could have sworn he heard a voice shouting in English. How foolish! We may have walked right by the enemy position without ever having detected them.

Sergeant Major Trinh came up to Thanh's position.

"They are about thirty meters to the front and above us. Sounds like no more than a squad. A small patrol," he stated.

"Move ten men up the hill," commanded Thanh, "Get in above them and sweep down on them."

"There is no need, comrade sub-lieutenant," responded Trinh, "We have discovered the Americans' forward positions. We should break contact and return to the regiment."

"What! Leave the enemy alive when we can destroy them! Never! Follow my orders, comrade sergeant major," commanded Thanh.

Sergeant Major Trinh thought that, if they could execute this maneuver quickly, they may be able to overrun the American position before the Americans could bring their artillery to bear on them.

He quickly instructed his sergeant to move up the hill with his section, bypass the enemy position, and get into position above them for an assault.

The men were just beginning their move up the hill when there was a series of explosions that seemed to devour the sergeant and two of his men. The others immediately went to ground.

"What was that! Have the Americans fixed their artillery on us that quickly?" demanded Sub-Lieutenant Thanh, his eyes wide with fear and surprise.

"No," responded Sergeant Major Trinh, "Those were command-detonated mines. We must proceed carefully. Again, comrade sub-lieutenant, I point out that there is no need to stay in contact. We should return and report as instructed."

"Never! Never! Look what these Americans have done to our men! I will not leave their deaths unavenged. I will not allow the Americans to escape!"

Thanh consulted his map. "This is a small patrol. If we hold them here, the Americans are sure to send in more men to rescue them. You, comrade sergeant major, will stay here and keep the enemy pinned down. I will take the machine gun and the rest of the men and move behind their position. When the Americans send up reinforcements, I will be waiting for them. Pin the enemy here, but do not kill them. I want them begging for help on their radios. When we have savaged their rescue force, then you will move in and finish the Americans on this hill. Then we will withdraw. Is that clear, comrade sergeant major!"

"Comrade sub-lieutenant," answered Trinh, "Let me again remind you. Our mission is reconnaissance. Find the enemy and report. That is all. We should break contact and return to the regiment."

"Sergeant Major Trinh," hissed Thanh, "I will ignore your insubordination this one last time. I command here! The mission of every soldier of the Peoples' Army of Vietnam is to find the enemy and destroy him. You have your orders! Now carry them out!"

"Yes, comrade sub-lieutenant," responded Sergeant Major Trinh.

As Thanh moved down the hill to organize his ambush, Trinh arranged his men around the American position. Firing up hill meant that, as long as the Americans kept down, his men would not have clear targets. He reminded his men to fire only short bursts or semi-automatic to conserve ammunition. Do not move forward up the hill because the Americans may have more mines deployed. Be careful of the enemy throwing grenades down the hill.

His men were experienced soldiers. They quickly found multiple firing positions with cover and concealment. Their movement between firing positions would make the enemy believe that there were more of them than there were, and his men would not offer any targets for heavy weapons, if the Americans possessed them.

His men were good soldiers. But, to Sergeant Major Trinh staying in contact served no purpose. Killing these Americans served no purpose. His instincts told him they must break contact, withdraw.

But the Sub-Lieutenant had ordered him to stay, pin the Americans to this spot, so the Sub-Lieutenant could provoke a larger battle. Trinh knew this was a mistake. Men would die this day for no purpose.

This fight, this day, was quickly slipping out of control.

VIII

Lt. Lattimore was heating some water in his canteen cup for a jolt of C-Ration coffee when he heard it.

Small arms fire north and west of their position.

Exactly where Jonesy's patrol should be.

All activity on the firebase stopped when the men heard the firefight, as they realized some of their own were in trouble.

Immediately the PRC-25 radio in the company TOC came to life.

"Romeo Tango One Six! Romeo Tango One Six. This is Xray! We have contact! We have contact!"

Lattimore forgot about his cup of boiling water and rushed over to his CP.

"Romeo Tango One Six! We are in contact! Over!"

"Who the fuck is that on the horn?" demanded Lattimore.

"I don't know," answered his RTO, "Sounds like the new guy."

Lattimore grabbed the handset. "X-Ray. Six. Report your situation."

"We got small arms incoming ... down the hill..."

Lattimore turned to his RTO. "I want the platoon leaders and the mortar section leader here... NOW!"

He went back to the radio. "Calm down ... give me the size of enemy force and location."

There was a hesitation. "Wait one."

Then the voice came back up on the radio. "We have at least a squad-sized element to our front and left. We have small arms incoming. The dinks are within ten, fifteen meters of us straight down the hill."

"What is your situation?"

"We have three down ... two KIA, I think ... one wounded... grenade fragments to the face ... "

"Are the dinks moving up on you ..."

"Negative ... they seem to be holding a position to our front and left ..."

Lattimore pulled out his map and laid it on some sandbags. He pointed to the last reported position of the patrol.

"Can you shoot?" he asked the mortar section chief.

"Got the range, but those dinks are too close to our guys," the sergeant responded, "Less than fifty meters with tree cover ... shit ... that's too fuckin' close ..."

Lattimore went back to the radio. "Put Sergeant Jones on!"

"Jonesy's down ... I think he's dead ... the new lieutenant's dead too ..."

"Is Delvecchio there?"

"Wait one ..."

Lattimore looked up at his platoon leaders. "First and second, saddle up, weapons, ammo, water, one meal. Third platoon, take the perimeter when first and second move out. Move it ... I don't know how much time we got..."

The radio came back. "One Six. X-Ray. Over."

Sergeant Delvecchio.

"Can you break contact? Can you move toward us?"

"Negative ... they got us pinned ... we got high ground ... I think we can hold 'em ... but not long ..."

"Give me your situation!"

"We have a squad-sized element to our front ... they tried to flank our left but we stopped them with the claymores ... they are firing on our position ... small arms, AK's, nothing heavier ... no visible targets ... they don't seem to be trying to get up the hill at us ... Jonesy and the new lieutenant are down ... Sweetie's hit in the face ... he can't see... "

"Any activity to the south?"

"Negative ... no incoming from that direction ... couldn't hear any movement..."

"Good copy! Wait one."

Lattimore gave the horn to his RTO. "Get up on the battalion command push ... give them a contact report ... tell them I want gunships ASAP ... then get the radio back on the company push ... I don't want to be out of contact with my guys."

Lattimore saw the first and second platoons saddled-up and gathering around the company CP. He knew he had to get moving if he had any chance of pulling his guys out. How fast could he cover three klicks? Why were the dinks just sitting on his guys ... that didn't make sense ... they should be trying to get up the hill at them, get around a flank, or just pull out? Why would they just sit there?

The RTO came over. "Battalion says the closest gunship support is sitting in Ban Me Thuot. They'll try to get something in the air, but they don't think they can get anything up here for two, maybe three hours."

"Am I ordered to hold my position until they get a read out on the birds?" Lattimore asked.

"Battalion didn't say anything 'bout that, LT. Want me to ask?"

Lattimore could hear the small arms fire raging to the north, his men in contact.

What were the dinks up to?

Why were they holding off?

He had almost forty men, two platoons, gathered around his CP, ready to go, ready to get their buddies out of the shit, just waiting for the word.

Were the dinks just baiting him?

He could be leading two platoons into a trap.

He didn't know how many dinks were out there ... the smart thing was to wait ... play it safe ... hold his position and wait for the gunships.

But he would be leaving the patrol to be overrun.

Lattimore knew as soon as the firing in the distance stopped, his men would be gone.

Every man in his company would know it ... know he just sat here safe in the perimeter.

"No," Lattimore answered him, "We'll call them if we need them. We got to get moving."

IX

Green was about halfway through a can of C-Rat peaches when he heard the firefight erupt to the north.

He and Dwyer looked at each other.

"That's Jonesy. It's got to be," Dwyer said.

"Got to be," Green affirmed.

"Get ready to move out ... weapons, ammo, water," he told his team.

It didn't take long for the team to saddle up. It never did.

Green strapped two bandoleers of M16 magazines and a claymore bag with some more. He checked his belt. Four frags. He made sure the pins were bent back and tied down.

Green saw the platoon leaders gathering at Lattimore's hooch. He heard the old man yelling something into the radio.

Taylor came over and confirmed the order for the platoon to saddle up and to get ready to move.

Green handed his two canteens to Perez.

"Collect them up from the other guys and get them filled at the water trailer before everybody else gets over there and it becomes a cluster fuck," he told the replacement.

Green slipped a couple of cans of C-Rat peanut butter, crackers and fruit into his cargo pocket on his left leg then stuffed a towel in so they wouldn't rattle too much while he moved. He made sure the guys had some smoke grenades. Green stuck one down in his right cargo pocket.

"Little Bit," he said to the team grenadier, "Got enough M79 rounds."

"Locked and loaded, boss," Little Bit answered.

"Good! Bring some extra shotgun rounds in case it gets thick out there."

Green could still hear Jonesy's firefight out to the north. That's good news, he thought, they're still holding on.

Why weren't the mortars firing, he wondered?

Perez came back with the canteens and handed them out.

Taylor came by and told the fire team to gather at the CP.

"Here we go, guys," Green said.

He led his team over to Lattimore's hooch, rifle in his left hand, two twenty-round magazines taped bottom to bottom in his right. He'd lock and load the magazines as they left the perimeter.

Green and his team took a knee near the company CP with Taylor and the rest of the first platoon. Green saw the second platoon starting to gather opposite them. The third was starting to spread out around the perimeter.

The sound of the small arms continued in the distance.

The mortars remained silent.

Finally, the old man came over to talk to them.

"You guys can hear the firing in the distance. Those are our guys, the patrol I sent out yesterday. We are in communication with them. They say they're in contact with at least a squad of dinks. Our guys have some high ground, and they say they can hold the dinks off for a while. How long, I can't tell."

"The dinks are in too close to our guys to use our mortars, and we don't know when we can get gunships up here. Our guys say the dinks are too close to disengage. As I said, I don't know how long they can hold out. I don't know how many more dinks may be out there between us and our guys. I assume every dink within twenty klicks is hearing the same thing we are, so our guys may have more dinks on their hands than they can handle real soon."

"So, we can't wait. We're going out to get them. We got to cover three klicks to get to our guys. I want to do that as fast as we can, in less than two hours. First platoon leads out. Second follows. I'll be up front with the first. Sergeant Taylor's got the first. Lieutenant Jackson, second. Lieutenant Franks, third and the perimeter until we get back. Medics stay with your platoons. Doc Ambrose, you're with me."

"Keep the radios on the company ops push. Go ahead and transmit in the clear. I don't think we'll be surprising anybody. Look guys! Battalion's got two companies at Duc Lap. I'm sure they'll reinforce us as soon as they can get the birds. We can't wait on that. Those are our guys out there catching shit. They need help. We're going out to get them. Any questions."

"Sir!" It was Ding Hernandez, Sweetie's buddy from the second platoon, "What about casualties. Anybody hit out there?"

"Not clear," the old man answered, "I think they got some wounded, but it's not clear who or how bad. Any other questions?"

Nothing.

"Okay! Saddle up! Let's get moving! Sergeant Taylor! I want to see you and Green at the head of the column."

Green followed Taylor out to the bunker line. His fire team followed. They simply walked toward the sound of the firefight.

At the bunker line, they stopped and waited for the old man. The rest of the two platoons filled in behind them. Lattimore, the second platoon leader, Jackson, his platoon sergeant, and their RTOs caught up with them.

"We're moving out on an azimuth of three-two-zero degrees," the old man briefed, "I want Green's team on point. Just move toward the firing, Green ... get us there! I'll be behind Green. Sergeant Taylor, I want you down the column with your last squad. If the head of the column gets hit, you'll be out of it and still able to maneuver the rest of your platoon.

"Lieutenant Jackson, if I get hit or get pinned, can't command, you take over. Sergeant Taylor, you're number three after Jackson."

"Green, I want you to take the point. Just stay oriented on the fire. Move fast. I don't know how much time we got. Get me within a hundred meters of the firefight. I don't know how many dinks're out there. I don't know what they're up to. If you see or hear anything that makes you nervous, stop! Look back at me. I'll be right behind your team.

There may be an ambush out there. I wouldn't put it past these little bastards to be using our guys as bait. So, stay alert. Any questions?"

A chorus of "No, Sir!"

"Okay, rejoin your platoons!

Green! Move out!"

X

Sub-Lieutenant Thanh found what he considered an excellent piece of terrain to ambush the Americans.

A ridgeline near an open field created a narrow belt of concealment through which Thanh was sure the Americans would have to pass to reach their comrades. Even the Americans were not stupid enough to cross open terrain so close to contact, but they were lazy enough to avoid climbing the ridge. So, they would file along the narrow band of concealment between the high ground and the open space, file right into the kill zone of Thanh's ambush.

Behind him, Thanh could hear the controlled fire of his men keeping the American patrol engaged. The whip crack of the AK 47's and the ripping tears of the answering M16's.

That was the bait for his trap.

Thanh had positioned his Russian RPK machine gun at the head of the corridor through which he expected the Americans to rush. The gun was equipped with a seventy-five round drum magazine and his crew had two more in reserve.

The rest of his team, his riflemen, were positioned on the high ground to the right, above the kill zone. Their job was to prevent the Americans from escaping. They were to keep them in the kill zone so that the RPK could do its work.

If the Americans tried to escape the kill zone across the open area to Thanh's left, the machine gun had an clear field of fire to make quick work of them.

Thanh had sent one rifleman forward to scout for the American relief force. If the Americans were moving toward the trap, the rifleman
was instructed to retreat before them without being detected. But, if
the Americans began to move off Thanh's intended course, the rifleman was to fire at them, get their attention, then lure them into the
kill zone.

Sub-Lieutenant Thanh was very specific when he briefed his men.
The RPK was to initiate the ambush. The riflemen along the ridge
were to hold their fire until the machine gun opened up on the enemy.
Their job was then to keep the Americans in the kill zone.

Thanh positioned himself with the machine gun team. He would
wait until he had as many Americans in the kill zone as possible before
he gave the order to fire.

Thanh expected the Americans in the kill zone to try to take cover
when the RPK opened up on them. They would lie there on the
ground trying to call for their fire support to save them.

That would be their fatal error.

Thanh had seen to it that there was no cover in the kill zone that
could protect the Americans from machine gun fire. Staying in the kill
zone was certain death.

The signal to break contact was the machine gun fire ceasing and a
repeated series of three short blasts on the whistle that hung around
Thanh's neck. Then, the RPK team and the riflemen would fall back
toward Sergeant Major Trinh's position. They would sweep up the
hill behind the trapped American patrol, finish off whoever survived
there, link up with Trinh's element, and return quickly to regiment
before the surviving Americans could call in their artillery.

It would be a magnificent triumph!

Earlier, when Sergeant Major Trinh seemed to oppose Sub-Lieutenant Thanh's plan to ambush the Americans, the sub-lieutenant was
confused.

Was this tactic not practiced by Trinh himself?

Was it not the duty of every soldier in the People's Army of Vietnam to damage the enemy as much as they could?

Did the Sergeant Major have no confidence in him?

Certainly, Trinh could not be a coward, a traitor.

Then, Sub-Lieutenant Thanh realized that Sergeant Major Trinh was testing him. Testing his resolve. Testing his devotion. Testing his determination. That was why Trinh had forced Sub-Lieutenant Thanh to order his cooperation.

Sub-Lieutenant Thanh was confident that he had passed Sergeant Major Trinh's test of his leadership. Now, he would demonstrate to the Sergeant Major that he was an effective combat leader, an effective tactician. A comrade in whom Sergeant Major Trinh could have confidence.

On this glorious day, Sub-Lieutenant Thanh would win a great victory for the Vietnamese people.

XI

Pat Green had never moved through the bush like this.

Usually it was a slow, cautious walk, one step at a time. Lift the lead foot high not to trip. Lay the foot down heel first, then roll the weight forward along the blade of the foot toward the toes. Don't break any brush or twigs. Stay low. Look, look, look. Take the next step.

Now he was almost jogging!

Ignoring the noise of the cracking twigs, dislodged rocks, breaking branches. Ignoring the sounds of his ammo magazines clanging, branches hitting the plastic hand grips of his rifle, and a circus parade jogging behind him.

Every time he had a thought of slowing down, of being more cautious, he heard the rattling gunfire ahead of him, heard the sounds of his friends in trouble, and he sped up again.

How much longer could they hold out?

How much farther until they reached them?

Every time he looked back to the rest of the company, Lattimore pumped his fist up and down at him.

Move out!

Move faster!

When Green first came into country, from a book he had read as a child, he could have imagined this race through the forests as a scout leading Major Rogers' rangers through the northern Adirondacks into French-held Quebec. But his experiences since then had taught him that these childish tales were false. They had no place here.

In combat, there was no adventure, no grand saga. It was a dirty, difficult and dangerous job.

Green would never be able to get rid of the image of the first American KIA he had seen months ago when he was a rookie. Abandoned in the jungle. The greenish gray pallor of the boy's face. The butcher-shop smell, dead flesh, fresh blood. The gaping hole in his back leaking blood and viscera. The insects in his wounds, crawling in his eyes.

No!

Green no longer believed in adventure. He did not believe in heroes. There were no heroes. Just men, boys like him really, doing their job, day after day, taking no unnecessary risks, trying to stay alive.

Green was no hero. He was rushing through these forests because he had to. Those were his orders. This was his mission. It was the only way they could reach their friends in time.

When they got there, Green, and the rest of the guys jogging behind him, would do their job, whatever had to be done to get their friends out of the shit. Some of them might be killed in the effort.

That was not an adventure. That was not heroism. That was their fuckin' job.

Mostly the terrain favored quick movement. Bamboo thickets were common along their route of march. Bamboo thickets meant little underbrush, good visibility. Bamboo thickets also made Green a good target for anyone waiting ahead.

Only twice did Green need to lead the company around danger areas, open spaces with no concealment, one about seventy meters across, the other twice that.

On both times, as soon as Green skirted around the edge of the clearing, he heard the firefight ahead of him, oriented himself on it and jogged toward it.

The company was making good time.

Green could hear they were getting close.

The sounds of the firing were becoming clear, the reports of individual weapons more distinct.

Green estimated he was about three hundred meters from their target when he thought he spotted movement to his right front.

He stopped so quickly he felt like he was one of those Saturday morning cartoon characters leaving skid marks on the ground.

He took cover and searched ahead.

What was it?

Animal?

Foliage?

Human?

Did he imagine it?

Now that he was focused, he could see nothing ahead.

He looked back toward the old man. He signaled movement with his fingers. Then he shrugged.

He could hear the firefight ahead of him. Close now.

He crept forward a few meters. He looked. He saw nothing. The forest around him slipped back into its regular pattern of lines, color, sounds and movements. Nothing seemed to be out there.

But they were close.

Slowly Green rose to a crouch and began to move forward toward the firefight. Slower now. Careful.

Someone was out there.

Green could *feel* someone out there, watching.

He signaled back to his fire team behind him. Cover me.

He continued to move forward.

There it was again!

Green could swear he caught a glimpse of movement, a shimmer of khaki in the feeble light that penetrated through the trees. Whatever it was seemed to be moving away. Seemed to be retreating ahead of him.

Green felt Lattimore move up beside him. "What is it," he hissed.

"I swear there's something in front of us. It seems to be shadowing us. Won't hold its ground. It's moving back into the trees."

"We're running out of time here," Lattimore answered, "Keep pushing toward our guys. It may be nothing. It may be an OP for the dinks. Don't know. Keep pushing forward."

Fuck, thought Green, high diddle diddle right up the middle we go.

Then he heard a burst of automatic fire in the distance. He knew they didn't have much of a choice. They had to push through whatever was ahead to get to their guys.

And, they had to be quick.

Green rose to a crouch and moved forward. After he went about a hundred meters, he saw a bright area to his right. Another open area. There was some rising ground to his left. A hill or ridge. Directly to his front between the open area and high ground was a narrow, shadowy corridor with good concealment. It seemed to lead directly toward where they needed to get.

It was too good.

Too convenient.

So, Green didn't trust it.

Green got into some cover. Signaled the rest of his team to get low.

Lattimore caught up with him.

"Something about this set-up gives me the creeps, LT," Green whispered.

Lattimore examined the terrain. It gave him the creeps too. It was too fucking neat, too fucking convenient.

Then he realized it was too quiet.

The normal jungle sounds seemed strangely hushed.

Then Lattimore thought that, if he were going to set a trap, this was the ideal place. This is where he'd set an ambush. But he could see nothing ahead. He could detect nothing moving out there.

He couldn't go to the right. The terrain was too open. They'd be sitting ducks.

He could go to the left, up over the high ground. He'd lose some time. And, if the dinks were sitting high, they could really fuck him up as he climbed.

He could move straight ahead, perhaps right into the kill zone of an ambush.

XII

Sub-Lieutenant Thanh was crouched next to the RPK machine gun overlooking the kill zone of his ambush. Suddenly he realized that he had his Makarov 9mm pistol in his right hand. He did not remember drawing it from his holster.

Then, at the far end of the kill zone, he detected movement. He laid his left hand on the machine gunner's shoulder. He felt the man's shoulder tense.

"Wait for it ... wait for it, he whispered

Thanh caught a glimpse of khaki through the feeble sunlight. Saw the moving shadow resolve itself into the shape of his scout. Saw the man jog to his position across the kill zone. He removed his hand from the machine gunner's shoulder.

"Comrade Sub-Lieutenant," the soldier reported, "The Americans are near. They are no more than thirty meters behind me."

"Good," responded Thanh, "Report to your corporal. Take a position on the hill."

The soldier gave Thanh what he considered a halfhearted salute, then moved off to the right to join his section.

"They are coming! They are coming," Thanh whispered to the RPK crew as if they had not heard the scout's report.

Soon, beyond the kill zone, Thanh could see movement, shadows.

It must be the Americans. It must be, he thought. They were moving directly toward him. Directly into his trap.

Then they stopped.

Why have they stopped? Thanh's mind screamed.

Why are they not moving forward?

Could they have detected us?

Did they see something?

Can't they hear their comrades dying in front of them?

XIII

Lattimore had his platoon leaders, NCO's and Green together behind a wide tree and some brush where no one watching them from ahead could spot them. The sounds of the firefight ahead were clearly distinct to them. They could almost hear each individual weapon as it fired.

The dinks' AK's.

And thank God, they thought, the American M16's.

"We're close," briefed Lattimore, "We're almost there. Couple a hundred meters at most."

The men around him nodded. In their eyes, Lattimore could see a mixture of fear, determination, relief.

They were "danger close.

"We got a danger area ahead of us," Lattimore continued. "There's an open area to the right and some high ground to the left. This is it on the map," Lattimore pointed.

Tracing his finger along the map, he said, "This is the ridge on our left. It runs just south of the hill where our guys are trapped. This narrow corridor right in front of us gives us good cover almost right up to their position. It's also a perfect spot for an ambush."

His leaders examined the map, looked around and forward, and nodded.

"I can see nothing up ahead, but Green here thinks we're under observation. That could mean a couple of things. One, Green's imagination is running away with him. But I don't think so. Two, the dinks sent out an OP. He went back to report to the dinks who are in contact with our patrol. They will either withdraw, try to finish our guys off, or get in a position to fight us when we try to relieve the patrol. Or, they have a nasty surprise waiting for us, and the asshole Green thinks is out there just let them know we've arrived for the party."

More nodding, fiddling with the maps.

"The terrain directly ahead of us is perfect for an ambush. It's the last obstacle before we get to our guys. If the dinks are there, they'd have placed a machine gun about seventy meters at twelve o'clock just beyond the clearing to cover the kill zone. Their main force will be deployed on the high ground to the left. I have no idea how many we could be talking about. I estimate no more than a squad, ten, eleven guys, or we'd detect them."

The men's eyes wandered from the maps to the terrain ahead, memorizing it, trying to detect any movement.

Taylor asked, "What about the 81's, LT?"

"I don't know exactly where our guys are," Lattimore said. "We may hit them ... same with recon by fire ... they could be downrange, close."

Taylor nodded his head.

Lattimore noticed Green just looked at the ground in front of him.

He seemed a bit paler than usual.

He knew what was coming.

"Here's what we're going to do," Lattimore stated. "We're going to push straight through until we make contact, or we get to our guys. Green, you and your team are on point straight ahead between that clearing and the high ground. Taylor, get your machine gun and one squad in position to overwatch Green's movement. Place your machine gun and an M79 as far to the right as you can so Green doesn't screen where the dink gun should be. If Green gets past the clear area, we all get up and follow. And we keep pushing until we get to our guys. Then up and over. Everybody got that?"

Nods all around.

"If Green hits the shit, Taylor you got to give him as much cover as you can. You got to knock out that dink gun fast."

Taylor nodded.

Green looked absolutely sick.

"Green," Lattimore said, grabbing his team leader's arm. "This is important. Close ambush. Attack the ambush! If that machine gun opens up, turn and hit that hill hard. Move up as quick as you can. No matter how many dinks are up there. If you stay in the kill zone, you're dead. You're all dead. You understand. If they hit you, you got to move left, up the hill."

Green barely nodded.

"Okay ... if Green hits the shit, I'll take the next two squads and swing around Green's left and up the hill to roll up the ambush. Jackson, you follow with the last two squads. If I break through, you follow. If I get stopped, you swing around my left and sweep the ridge. You got it?"

The lieutenant nodded, "What if I get stopped, Tom?"

"Then we are all truly fucked!"

The men actually laughed at that.

Fear and adrenaline.

That is, except Green, who was not in a fit state at that moment for any of this dark, grunt humor.

"I don't think that'll happen," Lattimore continued. "If the dinks are up there, there can't be that many or we'd've detected them. Once we roll up the dinks on the ridge, we push through to our guys on the hill ... Jackson left ... Taylor right ... I got the center. Jackson, I want your M60 with me. Any questions?"

There were none. The conference broke up and the men returned to their units.

For a very brief moment, a thought crept through Lattimore's consciousness, how many of these guys have I just killed.

Then, he shrugged it off.

It can't be helped.

He moved forward to get things going.

XIV

Green's team was ready to go.

Behind him, he could see Taylor, the second squad and the M60 ready to cover his move.

Ahead of him, the forest revealed nothing.

He saw the dark corridor he had to move through between the clearing and the high ground. His entire being was now focused on covering those hundred meters.

Through his mind, the words of a prayer he had learned as a child began to repeat themselves ... a prayer of forgiveness before dying ...

> *Oh my God ...*
> *... I am heartily sorry*
> *... for having offended thee ...*

His entire being tingled like it used to before the start of a football game... waiting for the ref to blow the whistle for the kickoff ... but this was worse ... so much worse...

... and I detest all my sins ...

Green looked back at Lattimore ... the old man gave him the signal to go ...

... because I dread the loss of heaven ...

Green's legs didn't seem to know how to stand up ... he had to think it through ... break through the clouds of fear holding him back ... pressing him to the ground...

... and the pains of hell ...

He made it to his feet ... his team rose behind him ...

... but most of all because they offend Thee, my God ...

He moved forward toward the dark corridor ... he felt like he was looking down a tunnel ... nothing right or left ... just a hundred meters down a dark tunnel ...

... Who art all good and deserving of all my love ...

He signaled his men to assume a diamond formation ... maximize fire power front, back and sides ... Dwyer left, Perez right, Little Bit center-rear with the grenade launcher ...

... I firmly resolve with the help of Thy grace ...

Green on point was about to enter the tunnel ... his eyes focused, locked on where the old man said the machine gun should be ...

... to confess my sins ...

He could see nothing, just shadows, foliage ...

... do penance ...

Run he thought ...

... amend my life ...

Move as fast as you can through the danger zone ... Green began to jog ... run straight at where the machine gun should be ... his team followed ... running...

... Amen.

XV

Sub-Lieutenant Thanh could hardly keep still.

Crouched next to his RPK machine gun, he could see the shadowy forms of the American patrol beyond his kill zone.

Why have they stopped?

Why do they not come forward?

Have they detected my trap?

Then, he saw what seemed to be movement. Some shapes stood ... began walking toward him ... shadows resolved themselves into distinct figures ... four ... only four ... will the others follow ... four is not enough ...

"Steady ... steady," he hissed to his gun crew.

Four Americans entered his kill zone ... their shapes were clear now.

"Not yet ... steady ..."

Then the Americans began to run ... run directly toward his position ...

What was this... had they seen him ... were they attacking him... why were they running, Thanh wondered

An American shouted something ... then from his right, one of his concealed riflemen on the ridge opened up on the running Americans ...

Thanh stood ... broke cover ... screamed, "Cease fire... cease fire!"

The machine gun crew thought it meant them ... they held their fire.

The running Americans seemed to hesitate ... they did not drop to cover ... the rest of Thanh's riflemen began to fire from the hill ... the Americans turned ... fired... assaulted the hill.

Thanh screamed at his machine gun crew... "Fire ... fire, you fools!"

XVI

Green was actually relieved when the dinks opened up ... the devil you know is better than the one you don't.

He turned left ... emptied a magazine into the hill ... no targets ... just fire ... move ... move ... lock the other magazine.

His team turned followed him ... fired ... ran toward the high ground ... into the trees and brush ... Dwyer ... Little Bit... straight in.

Perez crossed to Green's right.

Green was just about out of the kill zone, when Perez seemed to explode ... Perez' body slammed into him ... a hot, wet, red haze engulfing him.

Then Green felt a blow to his head.

Then nothing.

XVII

Sergeant Taylor positioned himself between his grenadier and the M60 machine gun crew on the extreme right.

He watched as Green's team rose and moved toward the narrow dark corridor between the clearing and the high ground ... he heard himself chanting go ... go ... go ...

Perez drifted right, masking the M60.

Go! Go!

Then he saw Green's team begin to run ... run right down the slot.

Son of a bitch ... that boy's got some balls, he thought.

AK fire from the hill.

Green's team seemed to hesitate.

Go you sons a bitches! Move ... get out of there!

A dink appeared to his front!

He was shouting some shit ... waving a pistol.

All hell was breaking loose from the hill.

Green's team turned, assaulted the hill.

Then the dink machine gun opened up ... right where the old man thought it would be.

"Machine gun ... front ... one hundred meters ..." Taylor yelled.

Two of Green's men went down.

"Fire!" the M60 opened up.

The shouting dink with the pistol spazzed ... fell back into the brush.

"Grenade ... follow the tracers!"

Hollow pop of the M79 ... black explosion in the brush... another M79 round following the line of red tracers ... more black smoke.

The dink machine gun went silent.

XVIII

Lattimore watched Green's team move out ... saw them jog into the kill zone ... fire from the left ... saw some crazed dink waiving a pistol ... dink machine gun, front ... two men down ... Taylor's gun opened up ... the dink flung back into the brush ... explosions ...

"Up! Up! Let's go!" Lattimore yelled, running toward the ridge. "Online to my left! Machine gun! Left! Cover front!"

XIX

The North Vietnamese riflemen on the ridge quickly realized that this battle was lost.

The Americans were attacking them on two sides ... they had interlocking machine gun fire

The riflemen did not wait for an order from their boy lieutenant ... they began to withdraw over the ridge before they were trapped.

Their only goal was to get through this day alive.

XX

Sergeant Major Trinh heard the AK fire in the distance, then the RPK opened up.

So, that righteous little shit got his wish, he thought.

Then he heard the Americans return fire, some explosions, heard the RPK go silent.

That's not right, he thought, something's wrong.

He ordered the men around him to cease fire. The only firing he could hear in the distance was from American weapons. He got the attention of his corporal, the little man with the ruined face, a veteran, a good soldier.

"Ngo! Come with me!"

The two soldiers moved out toward the weapons' fire.

Trinh and Ngo moved forward, keeping the sounds of the firefight to their right. Soon, they came to the edge of a clearing. Trinh led them along the edge of the clear area.

Soon they found the ruin of Sub-Lieutenant Thanh's grand scheme. And the ruined body of Sub-Lieutenant Thanh himself.

Sergeant Major Trinh spent no time examining Thanh's body. The boy had taken a machine gun burst in the head and chest.

He removed the map case from the sub-lieutenant's body and handed it to Corporal Ngo. Then he told the corporal to go through the Sub-Lieutenant's pockets.

From the sounds of the firefight, the Americans seemed to be concentrated on the other side of a ridge to Trinh's right. He hoped that his soldiers had escaped before the Americans could trap them.

Trinh examined the RPK. Damaged, but repairable, he judged. One member of the crew was dead, the other badly wounded. He could not be moved.

Trinh leaned down and whispered, "I am sorry, comrade," then shot him.

Then, to his front, Trinh saw a group of Americans approaching, moving quickly on his position.

"Ngo! Quickly! Take this machine gun. Return to our position. Break contact with the Americans. Return to the regiment. Get as many back as you can. I will cover you."

As Corporal Ngo retrieved the RPK and began to retrace his steps to the hill where the rest of the patrol was, Sergeant Major Trinh opened fire on the approaching Americans. He watched with some satisfaction as two went down and the others took cover.

What he did not see was the American machine gun crew on his left. Trinh briefly noticed muzzle flashes in the shadows of the forest.

He felt a hammer blow to the left side of his body that threw him back into the brush.

XXI

Doc Ambrose, the company medic, stayed with Taylor's squad when Lieutenant Lattimore led the assault on the ridgeline. Doc had seen two of Green's guys go down when the dink machine gun opened up, and he wanted to get to them as soon as he could.

Sergeant Taylor sensed how the battle on the left was going. He moved his squad forward into the corridor between the ridge and the clearing. He had the M60 stay in place to cover his movement. Doc followed with Taylor's men.

Doc reached the two casualties.

One of them was dead. He had taken a machine gun burst in his chest and side.

The other guy was on his hands and knees trying to get up. He was bleeding from his head. Doc knelt down next to him.

It was Green.

"Pat! Calm down! You're hit. Let me look at you," Doc started.

Then something hit Doc hard in the back.

XXII

Sergeant Major Trinh tried to drag himself back under cover, away from the advancing Americans.

His left arm didn't seem to work anymore. The entire left side of his chest was numb.

He managed to pull himself up into a sitting position against a tree. He was having trouble breathing. His right hand touched a metallic object on the ground next to him. He grasped it and held it up in front of his face. He was having difficulty focusing his eyes.

I am going into shock, he thought.

It was Sub-Lieutenant Thanh's pistol.

Trinh realized he had a salty, strangely metallic taste in his mouth. He laid the pistol on his lap and spat into his right hand. He saw blood, bright, red blood on his palm. He dropped his hand onto his lap. It lay over the pistol.

Lung shot, he thought. I am not leaving this place.

Trinh felt strangely comforted ... it's finished finally ... the hardships ... the incessant struggle ... the horrors ... the dead faces haunting his sleep.

He heard the Americans approaching. He gripped the pistol, tried to raise it. It was so heavy.

Father ... have I failed you ...

> *Pitié pour nous qui combattons toujours aux frontières*
> *De l'illimité et de l'avenir*
> *Pitié pour nos erreurs pitié pour nos péchés...*
> *Ayez pitié de moi.*

Pity for us who fight always on frontiers
Of the limitless and of the future
Pity for our errors pity for our sins...
Have pity on me.

XXIII

Lt. Lattimore moved down the ridgeline above and behind the dink machine gun position. He saw Taylor's people moving up on his right and realized that he had gotten in front of his own right flank.

He was about to signal Taylor, when he spotted a wounded dink leaning against a tree. The man was an NCO by his collar tabs and a dead man by the blood smeared across the left side of his chest and face.

Yet, the dink was moving, trying to raise a pistol in his right hand.

Then he said something, something Lattimore couldn't quite catch.

The pistol rose and Lattimore emptied a magazine into the dink's head.

Taylor reached his commander. He looked down at the dead dink. "You made a good dink out of him, LT."

"He said something to me," said Lattimore, still staring at the body of Sergeant Major Trinh, "He said something to me. I couldn't catch it. It didn't sound like Vietnamese."

"It was French, sir." Mike Dwyer came down the ridge just behind the Lieutenant.

"French?" said Lattimore. "I guess a lot of these dinks still know how to speak it. Do you know what he said?"

"I didn't catch all of it, sir. But I did hear him say 'pity me'."

"Pity me! Did that dumb shit think that after all this he was just going to surrender?"

Lattimore picked up the pistol from Sergeant Major Trinh's hand. He slipped it into his belt. He'd give it to Green when he saw him ... the boy earned it today.

"I think it was from some poem ..." Dwyer tried to say,

Lattimore was already moving away. He had to find Jackson and make sure he was heading toward the hill to relieve the patrol.

XXIV

Mike Dwyer found his team leader leaning against a tree at the bottom of the ridge.

Green's head was covered by a field dressing, and he was covered with drying blood.

Most of it wasn't his. The bodies of the replacement, Perez and Doc Ambrose lay nearby. Someone had thrown a poncho over them.

"How you doin', Pat?" Dwyer asked his friend.

"Head hurts like hell ... feel like I want to throw up ..."

Dwyer picked Green's helmet up off the ground and wiggled his fingers through a hole. "Looks like they killed your helmet, Pat."

"You're a fuckin' comedian, Dwyer, a real fuckin' comedian!"

"They're bringing the Medevac birds into the clearing at the bottom of the hill. Can you make it? I'll give you a hand," Dwyer said.

"Did we get here on time, Mike? Did we reach Jonesy and the guys?"

"Yeah, second platoon got to them. The dinks just di di mau'd."

"How bad?"

"Could be worse, I guess," Dwyer responded, "Jonesy and the new lieutenant are dead. Sweetie's wounded. He may be blind."

"Sweet Jesus," Green moaned, "Jonesy's dead! Doc Ambrose! Shit!"

"Yeah, boss, it's tough, but at least we're still here to bitch about it. Come on. I'll get you down to the LZ. We got to get these birds out while there's still enough light."

A Letter of Condolence

A Company, 3rd Battalion, 35th Infantry
3rd Brigade, 4th Infantry Division
APO San Francisco 96564

3 October 1968

Dear Mr. and Mrs. Ambrose,

Please accept my deepest sympathy for the loss of your son, Joseph, on 27 September 1968, in the Republic of Vietnam.

I was Joseph's company commander, and I was with him that day. If it is of any condolence to you, I can tell you that Joseph was doing his duty as a medic. He had advanced in front of friendly lines to help others who had been injured.

Having no children of my own, I cannot possibly understand the pain you must feel at the loss of your son. In many ways, the men of this company are like my children and the loss of any of them affects me deeply. I will always wonder whether I did the right thing for them on that day.

Joseph will be sorely missed by all of us. He was a dutiful soldier, a devoted medic, and a good comrade, who brought comfort and healing to many.

Again, my deepest sympathies to you and your family.

I remain,

Yours truly,

Thomas J. Lattimore
1LT IN USAR
Commanding

Tom Lattimore folded the letter, placed it in the envelope, addressed it, sealed it, and handed it to Jake Taylor, his sergeant.

"Who's next, Jake?" he asked, rubbing the bridge of his nose as if he were in some pain.

Taylor placed the completed letter in a stack with the others. "Need to take a break, Tom?" he asked.

"Yeah ... a short break would be nice," Lattimore responded, still rubbing his forehead.

Then suddenly, "No ... let's get this done ... having it hanging over my head is worse than doing it ... who's next?"

Lattimore took a fresh piece of paper from the stack on his desk.

Jake looked down at his list. "Perez, PAPA ECHO ROMEO ECHO ZULU, first name, Emilio, PFC, rifleman, first squad, first platoon; KIA," he answered.

A Letter Home

October 3, 1968

Dearest Lori,

I can't tell you enough how much I miss you and how I count the days until I see you again.

I don't want you to worry, but we've had a couple of really bad days. It's better you hear it from me than read about it in the papers or see it on TV.

We ran into a bunch of North Vietnamese a couple of days ago. We had a pretty bad time. I'm okay, but my friend, Pat Green, got hurt. It wasn't anything serious, but he had to go back to the rear. I had to help him get on the helicopter. I hope he'll be back in a couple of weeks.

Remember I told you about my squad leader, Jonesy, the guy from Tennessee. He was killed. And, a guy in my squad from LA named Sweetie Gonzalez got hurt pretty bad. He's getting sent home. Jimmy Delvecchio, a guy from out on Long Island, has the squad now. He's quiet, but he seems to be a pretty good guy, and he knows his stuff. He and Jonesy were close. Jimmy doesn't say much, but I'm sure he's pretty upset with what happened, like we all are.

The whole thing was just an awful mess, Lori. Nothing I have ever experienced could have prepared me for it. All the noise and the confusion! Friends getting hurt and killed! I pray to God that I never have to go through anything like that again. I just can't get it out of my mind.

Lori, I wish I was with you. I wish we could hold each other like we did the night before I left. I'm just so scared all the time now. I mean, this stuff always scared me, but this was so terrifying, and it came so close. These guys were my friends. Just the other night, we were all sitting around, talking, joking, telling stories. Now they're gone. Sometimes I just can't believe it.

Remember before I went into the army, and we talked about my teacher in City College who said I should study French. I told you I didn't see the point, I wanted to get on the cops. Well I don't know anymore. After all this, I don't know if I ever want to touch a weapon or see violence again.

Lori, I don't want to worry you with all this stuff. I just had to tell someone. I hope that's okay. I'm scared and I want to go home. I want to go home to you.

Okay! I've said it and now I feel a little better. Some guys get through their entire tour without having to go through what happened to us the other day. So, maybe that's it for me. I should just convince myself that it's not going to happen again and there's nothing more to worry about.

I love you! When this is over, I'm never going to leave you again! I swear! Never!

Give my love to your parents.

Tout mon amour
pour toujours,
Mickey

12

The Darkness

The bodies are lying along the edge of the clearing.

Bare, white feet protrude from under dark-green ponchos.

A chopper comes down through a hole carved out of the jungle. Purple smoke and dirt swirl up through the blades.

A medic struggles to keep the ponchos pulled down over the bare, white feet.

The sergeant climbs down from the chopper as soon as it's close to the ground. He ducks under the spinning blades and moves into the trees behind the line of bare feet.

He doesn't look at the bare, white feet.

He chambers a round in his rifle, checks the safety and throws the sling over his shoulder. He checks his load – grenades and bandoleers.

The prop wash blows back a poncho.

A bare, white leg attached to nothing. Jagged shards of white bone cut through torn flesh wrapped in a tangle of ripped, burned cloth.

The medic pulls the poncho back around the white leg then pitches it on the chopper.

The sergeant moves through the barbed wire in front of the bunker line. He slips in the mud between the concertina strands and catches his boot on a trip flare post. Pain stabs through his leg. He stops to catch his breath. He leans on his rifle to support the weight of his rucksack and equipment.

He sees a soldier hammering sandbags into a bunker with an entrenching tool.

"Hey! Where's the first platoon?" he asks.

The soldier takes in the sergeant's clean uniform and equipment.

"They got you fuckin' replacements up here fast!" he answers. "First platoon's on the other side of the LZ, past the 105's. You better get your ass over to the company CP first. It's over there by that antenna. See Sergeant Taylor, the field first. Welcome to paradise, meat!"

"Yeah, thanks," the sergeant grunts through his own pain.

The sergeant shifts his ruck on his shoulders and limps into the perimeter.

He moves past a blown-out gun pit.

A smashed, blackened mortar tube lies in a puddle of muddy brown water. Beside it, a collapsed bunker sags into the muddy earth. Black strands of commo wire run into the scorched black hole. Twisted bits of metal, torn maps and notepaper, smashed ammo crates, a ripped towel, a torn pair of pants, and a roll of toilet paper lay in the mud next to the ruined bunker.

The sergeant catches a whiff of recent fighting ... cordite, scorched metal. The faint smell of burned meat lurks in the stagnant, wet air.

He sees the first dead dink lying in a pool of muddy water next to the ruined bunker.

Another is a few yards away.

Both lie in brown, still water, limp, twisted, half-stripped, gray-white dolls, the pockets of their green fatigues turned inside out.

The ruined head of one is half submerged in the brown water, a mass of black hair, white bone, staring eyes. Red swirls float on the still water. An open, brown eye stares at the sergeant above the water. The brown water lies still in an open, black mouth.

Flies hover then swoop on the still water. Swollen, black bodies touch the red swirls floating on the brown water, then dart away.

Soon they'll tire of playing with the water. They'll find the staring, brown eye.

For now, they're content just tasting the red swirls floating on the still water.

"Hey! Whatta you doin' back out here?" a soldier calls to the sergeant from the top of a bunker, "Got tired of shamming back in the rear?"

"I came in on that last slick," the sergeant answers, "Heard you guys caught some shit last night!"

"Man! You missed one hell of a cluster-fuck!" the soldier answers "You should a seen it, man! The dinks fucked up the third platoon pretty good last night. Didn't come near us. Dinks sneaked right past 'em. One hell of a show! Must a been after the 105's. Stupid bastards came through the wire in the wrong place. Fucked up the four-deuce pretty good. Hit us right before stand-to this morning. Timed it perfect. Half hour later we would a been sittin' out waiting for 'em. Would a given 'em a world of shit. They're either the smartest bastards in the world or the luckiest. They went right by the third platoon. Those stupid bastards must a been asleep. They came in through the wire in the rain. Nobody heard a thing. Whole third herd must a been down in their bunkers tryin' to stay dry. Who the fuck can stay dry in this fuckin' monsoon? Dinks waltzed right by 'em and blew the shit out of the four-deuce. Got a gun and the FDC. Killed the platoon sergeant and an RTO. All because the third herd didn't wanna get wet. What a cluster-fuck! Some of the eleven charlies opened up on them in the perimeter and all hell broke loose. You should a seen it! A real fuckin' goat-rope! Guys shooting at anything that moved, chasing the dinks all over the place, running into each other in the dark! What a cluster-fuck! I swear I saw tracers going right through the battalion CP! The dinks almost got to it! Battalion staff weenies just about shit their trou! Bunch a dinks running around with satchel charges ... guys shootin' at anything that moved! They got some new guy in the third platoon, just come into country a month ago. Doc found him in his bunker this morning just sittin' there, dead, not a scratch on him, like he had a heart-attack or somethin'. Damnedest thing! One of those bastards tried to get out through us. Blinkey got him. Blinkey said he was just about to ask the guy for a cigarette but he didn't smell right. Stupid bastards sweat that fish sauce they eat. Blinkey said he was just about to ask for a butt when he caught the fish smell. Emptied a magazine right into the guy. Scared the shit outta Little Bit. Fuckin' dink was standing right next to him when Blinkey greased 'im. Your old hooch got fucked up. Some idiot in the eighty-one section hung an HE instead of a flare. Zero charge. Didn't know what the fuck he was doin'. Fuckin' round just got far enough out of the tube to arm and dropped right on your old hooch. Blew the shit out of it. Lucky no one was in it. What a cluster-fuck! Third platoon and the four-deuce guys chasin' those dinks all around. Tracers going through the perimeter, just one giant cluster-fuck. Right in the middle of it the battalion S3, that tall Major, comes over the horn calling for a sitrep. Thought we were takin' in-coming. 'Stick your head out of your bunker and you can see what's goin' on,' I should've told him, 'I ain't got time for this shit!' They found one dink hidin' in an ammo bunker. Couldn't get out and didn't have the balls to pull the pin on himself. Tried to give up but some guy blew 'im away. Can't blame 'im. Fuck! They killed four guys and fucked up a few more. Stupid bastards in the third platoon must a been asleep. Let the dinks walk right by 'em. When it got light, we found five bodies in the perimeter plus the guy Blinkey got and the guy the third herd blew away. We found some blood trails goin' back out the wire. Battalion wanted us to go out and get a body count. 'Fuck that!', I should've told 'em, 'I got forty-two days and a wake up. You want to go out in the bush and count bodies, be my guest. There's plenty lyin' around here!' Fuck countin' bodies! The old man took first and second squads out this morning to sweep the perimeter."

The sergeant shrugs out of his ruck and lets it drop in a dry spot. He unbuckles his web gear and drops down onto his ruck with a grunt.

"That leg still bothering you?" the soldier asked. "What the hell you doin' back up here anyway?"

The sergeant pulls some pain killers out of his breast pocket and dry swallows a couple. He stretches his bad leg out in front of him. The stitches pull tight, feels like a hot knife in his leg.

"Heard you guys caught some shit," he answers. "So, I checked myself out and caught a ride on the re-supply bird."

"Here ... take a swig of this," the soldier says passing his canteen to the sergeant.

The sergeant takes the canteen and takes a long pull ... the warm liquid burns his throat so bad it almost backs up through his nose. "What the fuck ..."

"It's some of that dink rum, the nasty black stuff," the soldier explains. "I keep it to take the edge off. Good for what ails you."

The sergeant takes a careful sip and quickly the edge is off. The pain is still there in his leg, but it seems farther away. He takes another sip and hands the canteen back.

"Hey, we got this covered," the soldier says. "Why don't you take your shit over to the old man's bunker. Get off that leg. Grab some sleep. When the rest of the guys get back from sweep, I'll tell six you're back."

"Yeah! Good idea!" the sergeant says.

The sergeant grunts back up onto his feet. The hot knife is back in his leg.

He grabs his ruck by the top of the frame to keep it out of the mud. His ammo bandoleers rattle against the grenades on his loosened gear as he walks, the ringing of hollow metal bells ... grenades against magazines.

The heat of the day is coming up.

Soon, the pools of brown water will be steaming in the sunlight.

Soon the dead will be turning black.

Clouds of fat, black flies around the bodies, crawling over the eyes.

The sergeant wishes he took the rum with him.

Have to get the bodies out of the perimeter.

Rotting bodies are bad for morale, even dinks.

Can't feel good about a lump of rotting meat.

Just bad for morale.

He wishes he had more of the rum.

The lieutenant's bunker is dark. It smells of mud, mold, body odor.

The dark stops him. He can't stand the dark, the blackness. He isn't afraid of the dark. It's something else. The smell of mud and mold in the dark.

He feels around and finds a candle and gets it lit.

Ever since that bunker caved in on him, he hates being surrounded by the dirt walls and sandbags. He can still taste the dirt in his mouth. The weight of the earth squeezing the breath out of him, pressed in the dark, dank earth until they dug him out.

The lieutenant has a cot and air mattress. His poncho liner is twisted across it.

The sergeant leans his ruck on the dirt wall.

Dark walls of dirt are all around him in the bunker. They seem to sway in the candlelight.

Logs hold the sandbags over his head. It's a good bunker, deep, damp earth all around. The rats haven't found it yet. The sandbags above him seem thick, pounded down flat.

Everything seems to sway a bit in the candlelight.

A poncho blocks the little sunlight that comes through the doorway. He can just see the deep earthen walls, black and swaying in the flickering candlelight.

He drops his web gear and sits on the edge of the lieutenant's cot.

He pops another pain killer.

He pushes the poncho liner to the side and lies back on the cot.

He keeps his rifle cradled beside him and his boots laced. Boots and rifles are hard to find in the dark.

The pain is moving farther away, fading into the darkness.

The candlelight makes the black logs sway back and forth across the ceiling.

Nothing above him but darkness, flickering logs.

The darkness closes in on him.

The taste of dirt is in his mouth.

Far away a voice. Someone calling him.

Sergeant! Wake up! Sergeant! Time for stand-to.

Dig me out! Dig me out of this fuckin' place!

Don't be fooled by the clean fatigues. They gave them to me at the aid station. More sanitary. Looks better for the lifers.

Help me out of here!

Drag those dead dinks away before everybody gets sick.

Perez' body explodes! A wet, red cloud covers him.

Flies buzzing around the eyes.

The eyes are blue.

Jonesy lying in the brown water. It flows into his open mouth.

He screams!

A colonel pinning a purple medal on the white pillow.

Flies laying their eggs in his eyes.

Big, white, soft pillow. Clean white sheets, wet with blood, soaking.

Wake up!

You okay!

Mom and Dad standing in front of the house, waving to me. They have winter coats on.

No steam coming from their mouths.

He doesn't feel the cold through his jungle fatigues.

No flies laying their eggs in his parents' eyes

It's not cold.

Fool the dream.

It's winter, but it's not cold.

I'm not back home.

It's so real.

I can see

My mother is wearing her red overcoat.

It's not cold.

Lieutenant's getting the doc.

I can see her waiting for me across the street!

Blue eyes in the darkness.

No flies buzzing around in the cold.

She opens her arms to me.

The lieutenant is looking down at him, "You awake? You okay?"

The sergeant tries to get up off the bunk. "Shit, LT; I'm on your bunk ..."

"No, lay back down! Take it easy," the lieutenant says, "Doc wants to look at your leg."

"You get those stinking dinks out of the perimeter?" the sergeant asks.

"Don't worry about that shit," the lieutenant answers. "Doc, what's it look like."

"Stitches are still in," Doc says, shining a flashlight on the sergeant's leg. "Some blood and pus seeping through. I can't take care of this up here. He's got to go back to the aid station. He's gotta stay off this leg."

"I'm OK, Doc ... I got these pills..." the sergeant protests.

"You'll pop these stitches, and it'll get infected. I got nothing for you up here," the medic tells him. "LT, he's got to go back. There's no way they released him."

"OK, Doc, get on the horn to the trains and tell them he's coming back as soon as we get a bird," the lieutenant tells him.

"I'm okay, LT, I'll be fine ..." the sergeant objects.

"And, Doc," the lieutenant continues, "No point in telling Little Doc about this. Battalion's got enough on their plate after last night."

"Sure thing, LT," the medic agrees. "I'll get a hold of the aid station and let them know he's on his way back."

"LT ..." the sergeant starts trying to get up.

"I'm sending you back, Green, just as far as the trains," Lattimore states. "You can stay with the medics in the trains. You don't want to get that leg infected. You could lose the thing. When the medics say you're okay, then you can come back, not before. Let's get you up."

The sergeant swings his legs over the side of the cot. The hot knife is back, twisting in his leg.

His head spins; he's nauseous.

"Little Bit and Dwyer are right outside," Lattimore tells him. "They'll help you down to the LZ and get you on the bird."

The sergeant pops another painkiller into his mouth and washes it down with a canteen cup of water smelling of iodine.

The lieutenant helps him to his feet and over to the doorway of the bunker. He pushes back the poncho covering the door.

Light explodes into the sergeant's eyes, stuns him.

Mick Dwyer reaches down and helps him up out of the bunker.

He steadies himself on Little Bit's shoulder.

The sun is moving down toward the tops of the trees.

Dead dinks are gone.

Guys are rebuilding the bunkers.

"Come on, Pat," Dwyer says, "The bird's in-bound. You don't want to miss your ride."

Auberge

Michael Dwyer
French 4: Mid-Term Project

St. Agnes High School
November 20th, 1964

"Auberge"
par Pierre Reverdy

Un oeil se ferme
Au fond plaquèe contre le mur
la pensèe qui ne sort pas
Des idèes s'en vont pas
On pourrait mourir
Ce que je tiens entre mes bras pourrait partir
Un rêve
L'aube peine nèe qui s'achève
Un cliquetis
Les violets en s'ouvrant l'ont abolie
Si rien n'allait venir
Il y a un champ ou l'on pourrait encore courir
Des ètoiles n'en plus finir
Et ton ombre au bout de l'avenue
Elle s'efface
On n'a rien vu
De tout ce qui passait on n'a rien retenu
Autant de paroles qui montent
Des contes qu'on n'a jamais lus
Rien
Les jours qui se pressent la sortie
Enfin la cavalcade s'est èvanouie
En bas entre les tables ou l'on jouait aux cartes.

Inn
By Pierre Revedie

An eye is closed
Below pressed flat against the wall
The thought that does not leave
Ideas skulk away step by step
Death could follow
The one whom I hold in my arms could go away
A dream
Hardly born the dawn comes to an end
A clatter
The violets opening themselves have banished it
If nothing were going to come
There is a field where one could again run
Stars without end
And your shadow at the end of the avenue
It fades
Nothing is seen
Of all that has passed nothing is kept
So many words rising
Stories that were never read
Nothing
The days rushing toward the doorway
At last the pageant has vanished
Below among the tables where cards are played

13

❦

At the End of the Day

Sergeant Jake Taylor was worried about his friend.

Since the firefight at the volcano, Lieutenant Tom Lattimore rarely left his bunker.

It wasn't that his orders and decisions didn't make sense. And it wasn't that the company wasn't operating efficiently and effectively. It was just that Tom hardly ever left his bunker anymore.

It was almost as if he were hiding from something.

And he looked like shit … pale … dark circles under his eyes … a slight tremor in his hands … and sometimes his mind seemed to wander … he had trouble staying focused on a subject.

Little Doc, the company medic, who had replaced Doc Ambrose after he was killed at the volcano, said the old man seemed fine physically … no fever … nothing to suggest any physical ailment … but Tom just hid out in that bunker of his, and Jake was getting worried.

Jake hadn't made many friends during his twelve years in the army. The army just wasn't friendly to close friendships … the constant moving about … the relentless pressure to achieve … competitiveness for promotion … and especially combat, when at any second someone close to you could be killed.

Combat certainly produced camaraderie, but not friendship. Most of these guys in Alpha Company, who were as thick as thieves now, would never see each other once they got back to the world. There, they would only remind each other of shit none of them wanted to think about.

Maybe someday, after many years had passed, and their wounds had healed, would they realize how much the loved each other ...

Jake knew his friendship with Tom Lattimore was unusual, an exception to the norm, and since he was enlisted and Tom was commissioned, contrary to army custom.

They had both arrived in the unit at the same time. Jake was an E6 at the time, so he was assigned as a squad leader in the first platoon. Tom was an "butter bar," a second lieutenant, wearing the black bar of a first lieutenant, the standard operating procedure, SOP, of the US Military Assistance Command in Vietnam, MAC-V.

Tom was assigned to command the first platoon. There, they were both mentored by the Platoon Sergeant, a crusty, long-service E7, named Sam Williams, a tall, lanky, black man, who had driven trucks with the Red Ball Express in Europe, did two tours with the infantry in Korea after the army was integrated, and was finishing off a combat tour in Nam before retiring home to his native Georgia.

"And I fuckin' dare any of dem ofay, mother-fuckin' crackers to say shit to me, I do!".

Jake's native Kentucky was not exactly known for its racial enlightenment, but he knew a good soldier and a good man when he met one, and that was Sergeant First Class Sam Williams.

Jake remembered one of the first things Williams said to Tom, "Sir! I know you're an officer and soon all the mens'll know. So, maybe you want to take that lieutenant's bar off your collar and slip it in your pocket, so them dinks don't know it too."

Green as grass, we were, Jake reminisced.

Williams taught both rookies the ropes of combat leadership, shit that Tom certainly hadn't been taught in OCS, and shit that Jake never heard of or saw in his twelve years serving in Germany, Panama and in the States. Williams was also grooming Jake, a career soldier, to take over the platoon sergeant slot when Williams finally DEROS'd back to the world.

Jake remembered one of Williams' little lectures. "Jake, you gonna meet all sorts of folk in this here army ... some you love like a brother ... some ain't worth the cost of a bullet to send 'im to hell. But I tell you this. As an NCO, you got to treat them all the same. You can't be seen pickin' favorites. And, you can't be havin' no friends. That'll just make you weak, indecisive. Think about it ... could you give a friend an order that might get 'im killed? And that's just what you'll have to do some day. I can almost guaran-fuckin-tee it."

For the last couple of days, Jake had been putting off going over the company headcount with Tom, but now it couldn't wait. Payroll was coming due, and Jake had the company pay rosters that Tom had to sign for this month's payroll. The signed rosters pretty much had to be on the first chopper out of the firebase next morning to get them back to basecamp in time for division finance to process them. This was an essential part of the "holy trinity" of the United States Army that no commander ever dared violate ... pay, mail and chow.

The sun was starting to descend below the trees. In about half an hour, the company would go to a hundred percent alert, evening stand-to.

No need for him or Tom to get involved. The men knew what to do. The squads were already beginning to unpack their claymores and trip flares to place out in front of the bunkers as soon as it got dark.

Jimmy Delvecchio, who replaced Jonesy as squad leader after he was killed at the volcano, was briefing a two-man listening post, LP, which would go about a fifty meters or so out into the jungle as soon as it got dark.

No need for him or Tom to get involved at all in the daily routine; these guys knew their business.

Jake arrived at Tom's bunker, the company command post, the CP. As usual, there was a poncho liner strung across the entry way. The two radio operators, RTO's, one for the company, the other for battalion, were both set up outside. Their AN/PRC-25 radios were lying on top of the bunker with their "long-stick" antennas up. Both operators were sitting with their backs against the side of the bunker, the radio handsets balanced on their shoulders so they could monitor any transmissions.

Jake doubted there was much going on at the moment. The next "required" situation report, sit-rep, was reporting the company at stand-to in about half an hour.

"The old man home?" Jake asked.

The question seemed to startle the RTO sitting closest to Jake. His head jerked up and the radio handset tumbled off his shoulder. His mind was probably off in the ozone somewhere, or he was taking an infantryman's open-eyed nap, Jake surmised.

"Uhh... sure thing, Sergeant Taylor ... he's down there alright," the man managed to stammer.

"Thanks," Jake responded. "And stay alert, Washington! You're not on fuckin' vacation out here!"

"Uhh... Roger that!" the man answered.

Jake yelled down into the bunker, "Lieutenant Lattimore! It's Sergeant Taylor! May I come down, sir?"

This was a new protocol between the friends. In the past, Jake would have just gone straight in. But, about a week ago, he did just that and seemed to startle Tom so badly that he leapt off his cot and banged his head on one of the logs supporting the roof. Then, Tom went off the deep end about privacy, and Jake just barging in like he owned the place and cussed up a blue streak over nothing.

This tirade took Jake completely by surprise. His friend had always been even tempered and focused. Usually nothing seemed to upset him. That was one of the reasons he was such a good combat leader. He kept his cool under pressure and rarely lost focus. Had something like this happened in the past, Tom would have just rubbed his head, had a good laugh about it and said something like, "I got to dig this fuckin' thing a little deeper or shrink about six inches."

Jake heard Tom's voice from behind the poncho liner, "Come on in, Jake!"

Again, this was new. They never used each other's first names where the men could hear.

Jake pushed the poncho aside and descended into the bunker. Tom had blocked the bunker's apertures with empty sandbags so no light could get in. He sat there on the edge of his cot, in the dark, next to a small wooden table on which a single candle, standing in an opened C-Ration cracker tin, burned. In the flickering candlelight, Tom's face seemed to hover in the darkness. His face looked yellowish in the wavering light and his eyes seemed lost in the bottom of two black pits.

"I got the payroll here, Tom..." Jake started.

"Okay," Tom interrupted, "Put it on the table and I'll sign it."

Jake hesitated for a second. No commander signed the payroll without reviewing it. He was responsible for every red cent he authorized the army to pay out. People ended up in Leavenworth over fucked-up payrolls.

"You want to go over it first. Right, Tom?" he asked.

"Uhh ... yeah ... sure ... that makes sense," Tom responded. Then he continued. "Look! I'm having one of those fuckin' headaches ... I can't even seem to focus my eyes ... would you mind reading through it while I lay back here ... I'd appreciate it."

"Yeah... sure, Tom... you just take it easy ... I'll read through this thing," Jake responded.

Of course, he had already reviewed the entire roster and knew everything on it was correct. But Tom had to approve it. And, in order to do that legitimately, he had to review and agree to every line item, every entry—name, rank, serial number and pay grade — no exceptions. Only then should he sign it.

Secondly, Jake needed to discuss their "fox-hole strength," the number of people they actually had present and ready for duty on the firebase, and to ensure they agreed that they had slotted everybody in the right spot ... especially their NCO's.

Leadership in the first platoon was an especially tough problem since that platoon had lost its new platoon leader and its most experienced squad leader up on the volcano.

That was a critical issue which Tom seemed strangely reluctant even to discuss. It was like he was hoping that it would just go away somehow.

Tom used to command the first platoon; they were still "his guys," especially Jonesy and Green, who was still back with the medics. And Tom had put the new lieutenant out there on that patrol.

As Tom's friend, Jake could understand that somewhat. But, as a professional soldier, he understood it was combat ... shit happens ... you can't blame yourself ... get over it and drive on.

So, Jake went through the payroll, line by line, making comments about personnel where necessary. "This guy's ready for E4 ... we need to add this guy to the next set of CIB orders ... this guy's been in the aid station for two weeks now ..."

Tom just responded with short answers. "Makes sense ... do it ... call back for status..."

Finally, Jake read out, "Green, Patrick A., US11815234, E4 ..."

Tom interrupted "E4 ... I thought he was a sergeant?"

"You made him an 'acting jack'," Jake answered, "So he could be a team leader."

"Oh ... yeah ... that's right ..." Tom mused, "How's he working out?"

"Tom ... he's back at the aid station," Jake reminded his friend, "He was hit up on the volcano."

"Oh ... was he ..." Tom said, "How bad?"

"Not bad," Jake said, "Slight concussion, couple of stitches ..." Jake started.

"A couple of stitches!" Tom yelled. "The medics are keeping my people in the rear for a couple of fucking stitches! How the fuck do they expect me to run ... oh shit ..." Tom grimaced and grasped his head, "This fucking headache ..."

"I don't think it's just that, Tom," Jake said after Tom settled back down. "Remember last week, I told you the air strip back where the battalion trains is located got hit with a couple of 122mm rockets?"

"Yeah ... yeah ... I think so ..." Tom responded softly rubbing his temples with both his eyes screwed shut.

"Well, Little Doc told me Green was one of the few people back there with enough sense to get under cover when the shit hit. Unfortunately, the bunker he was in collapsed. They dug him out quick enough, but something ripped his leg up ... put a nice hole in it ... not bad enough to get evacuated out to Japan ... nothing broken ... but bad enough to hurt like a mother fucker. The medics cleaned it up and sewed the hole shut, but they're keeping him on antibiotics back in the aid station until that thing heals. They say two or three weeks unless it gets infected."

"Little Doc?" Tom questioned. "Why's he involved? Shouldn't Doc Ambrose be handling shit like that?"

Tom's response surprised Jake. "Tom ... Doc Ambrose was KIA at the volcano," he reminded his friend. "Little Doc replaced him as your head medic."

"Oh ... shit ... that's right," Tom said seemingly from some distance into with he had retreated, "Some bastard shot him in the back ... he's dead ... I wonder if it was that dink sergeant I greased ... Dwyer said he was talking French ... why the fuck would a dink sergeant talk to me in French ..."

Jake had to get Tom back. "Should we finish the payroll, Tom?" he asked.

"The payroll?" Tom seemed a bit surprised at the suggestion. "Oh ... yeah ... let's get through it ... then maybe if I can get some sleep this goddamned headache will go away ... who's next?"

They managed to get through the rest of the payroll without any incident. Tom signed the forms, and Jake slid them into a manila envelope.

Tom said he was going to try to get some sleep, his head was killing him.

Jake wondered for a couple of seconds whether he should snuff out the candle before he left. It only had about an inch to burn, and it couldn't fall out of the C-Ration can, so he left it.

When Jake got out of the bunker, it was almost fully dark, End of evening nautical twilight, EENT, they called it in the army. The sun was a few degrees below the horizon, but there was just enough light that the silhouettes of the men manning the perimeter for stand-to were still visible.

Jake asked the RTO sitting outside the CP, "You report stand to up to battalion?"

"Affirmative," he responded, "Almost a half an hour ago."

Jake didn't realize how long he had been down in Tom's bunker.

"Good," he said, "Old man's asleep. Don't disturb him unless we got bad guys coming through the wire. Come get me if there's any problem. I'll be in my hooch over by the first platoon. Pass that along to your relief."

"Roger that!" the RTO responded.

As he walked over toward the perimeter where the first platoon was set up, Jake knew he had a problem. As a senior NCO, his first allegiance should be to the unit. If there was any reason that he believed his commander was unfit, he was obligated to report it.

Tom wasn't unfit, but he was right at the edge. Anything could push him over, and when that happened, he'd fold like a bad poker hand in a high stakes game.

And combat was a high stakes game.

If Tom lost it at the wrong time, a lot of these guys would pay the price for Jake's having kept his mouth shut.

But Tom was his friend.

Jake thought he understood what was happening to Tom. He was suffering from what the old-timers called "shell shock"; "combat-fatigue" was the new term. He also knew that, if that were known, it could be a career-killer.

The army didn't see combat fatigue as an injury; for them it was a character flaw. In fact, he heard it associated with cowardice.

Jake knew that was absolute bullshit.

Cowards never let themselves get close to the shit, so how the fuck could they have combat fatigue?

Combat fatigue only affected guys who did the job, faced the dangers of combat and, in Tom's case, the extraordinary strain of combat command.

Jake remembered a guy they had in the second platoon. He was a good soldier. He made it through the firefight on the mile-high firebase at the end of Tet. He did a good job, did everything that was asked of him, even at the end when they had to go hand-to-hand with the dinks to retake their own bunker line.

But, right after that, he had some sort of breakdown. He refused to leave the perimeter, go out on patrol. He just sat in a bunker, refusing to come out. Nothing they could do — threats, appeals to his manhood, telling him he was letting his buddies down — could move the guy. They finally had to send him back to the rear.

What happened to him, Jake had no idea.

But Jake did understand that the guy was no coward. He had just reached the end of his endurance. He just couldn't do anymore.

Jake swore he would not let that happen to his friend. He didn't deserve the shit the army would throw at him, not after over ten months in combat, all of it bearing the responsibility of command.

No! Jake wouldn't let that happen.

Jake decided he had to talk to someone about it, someone he could trust and reasonably approach. And, he had to do it quickly, before the shit hit the fan.

First Sergeant Morales seemed to be his best bet. He was a career man, who had seen his fair share of shit over the years. So, he understood how things worked. He seemed to like Tom, and they had worked well over the time they had served together as company commander and first sergeant.

Yeah! Morales was his best bet, Jake concluded.

He would hand carry the payroll back to basecamp and have a beer with the first sergeant while he was back there.

He was on a bunker line.

He was crouched down, under cover. He could sense the men around him in the dark.

He was back on the mile-high firebase. He didn't know how he had gotten there.

Wasn't this fight over?

They seemed to be surrounded by a fog, a cold wet mist.

Where were the dinks?

Were they still here?

Were they out there in the darkness?

He felt a wave of panic building up in his gut.

He heard something.

He couldn't quite make it out. It was coming out of the darkness, out beyond the bunkers.

Moaning. Someone was out there moaning.

Was it our guys?

Were they wounded?

Did they need help?

Fear was building in him. He wanted to scream. He suppressed it, pushed it back down into his gut.

Never show fear in front of the men ... never.

The moaning wouldn't stop.

He heard the pop of a lume round above his head. His world went from black to white. A glowing white glistening fog surrounded him. He could see the outline of the bunkers shining damply in misty smoke. He could see the outline of men, black shapes huddled next to the bunkers around him.

They weren't moving. They were crouched down, completely still, huddled against the bunkers.

Were they dead?

They didn't move.

The moaning continued out in the fields beyond the bunkers.

He had to see who it was out there.

They may be his guys. They may need his help. He had to get to them.

He stood up. He walked beyond the bunker line out into the white mist, out into the fields where a battle had been fought.

The moaning seemed louder, all around him now.

He saw a black shape lying on the ground.

It didn't move.

It seemed to moan to him.

He reached for it.

He shook its shoulder.

There was no response.

He rolled it on its back.

A bloated, swollen, rotting face ... eyes bulging out from black putrefying flesh ... round mouth ... frozen ... moaning ... dead ... but moaning

The village!

He was in the dead village!

Then the light disappeared.

It was pitch black.

He was alone in the darkness with this horror ... the moaning was all around him ... he smelled the rot ... the putrefying smell of death.

He smelled earth ... freshly, disturbed earth ... a fighting position ... a bunker ... no... a grave ... he was trapped in a grave with this rotting horror.

He screamed, "I'm not dead!"

He screamed up through the earth that covered him, "Help me ... I'm alive ..."

He was tangled in some material ... a shroud.

Where were his men ... why didn't they come for him?

Then he heard a voice ... a voice above him from beyond his grave.

"Sir, Are you okay? You need help?"

Lattimore was sitting up on his cot.

He could feel his poncho liner tangled around his body.

Someone was yelling down to him.

It was the RTO on duty, "LT, you okay down there?"

He was in his bunker. The candle had burned out. It was pitch black.

"Yeah ... Yeah ... I'm fine," he answered.

He reached out, felt around for his flashlight. He found it on the shelf where the logs supporting the roof rested against the edge of the dugout.

"I'm okay ... thanks!" he yelled as he turned on the flashlight.

He was in his bunker, his CP. He looked at his watch. It was two in the morning.

He listened.

Everything was quiet.

Tom Lattimore climbed up, out of the earthen bunker.

The night air smelled sweet, clean. He savored the fragrances of the forest that surrounded him in the darkness. He could hear the night creatures singing to each other.

His head felt clear. There was no pain.

He saw the silhouette of the RTO on duty.

"Anything going on?" he asked.

"No, sir!" the silhouette responded. "Everything's quiet. Got all my sit reps ten minutes ago. Everybody's awake."

"Good," Tom replied.

He climbed up onto the roof of the bunker and laid back. He breathed in the essence of the forest. He was lulled by the hum of the locusts.

What a beautiful place this is, he thought, an Arcadia, a paradise.

He felt its soporific ambrosia flow through his body. His muscles began to relax.

He stared up into the night sky.

He had forgotten how clear the stars appeared. The Milky Way arched over him, a luminescent cloud of stars reaching from horizon to horizon, bridging the night sky.

Streaks of light flash across the black sky, the fireflies of the heavens, performing a light show just for him.

So clear was the night, that he felt an instance of vertigo, as if he could suddenly fall into them, or that an unexpected burst of wind could sweep him away, up into these glowing heavens.

The stars didn't flicker. They just shone above him, magnificent, never changing, eternal.

He suddenly realized there was nothing between him, lying there on a sandbag bunker in the middle of a nameless forest in the mountains of Vietnam, and the eternity of the universe opening itself that night for him, for him alone.

Millions of stars, planets, endless space.

How could we possibly be alone amidst all this beauty, he wondered.

How could such a marvel, such a wondrous creation, have possibly just come into existence?

What could all his fears, his struggles, his tragedies mean in this eternal, unwavering luminescence?

RAY GLEASON is a retired army infantry officer, medieval scholar, teacher, and author of both fiction and non-fiction works.

Ray served as an infantryman for nineteen months in Vietnam with A Company, 2nd Battalion, 35th Infantry Regiment, "Cacti Blue," and as a LRRP team leader with K Company, 75th Infantry Regiment (Ranger). During his army career, Ray served in a number of command and "staff weenie" assignments, collecting the Combat Infantry Badge, Bronze Star for Valor, Air Medal, Vietnamese Gallantry Cross with Gold Palm, and a helmet-full of Army Commendations, and federal and state awards.

Upon retirement from the army, Ray enrolled at Northwestern University and earned a Masters Degree and a PhD, specializing in medieval literature and semiotics. Ray teaches on the Chicago campus of Northwestern as an Adjunct Lecturer. Go Wildcats!

Ray has authored a number of fiction and non-fiction works, including the Gaius Marius Chronicle series, the Gaius Marius Mystery series, and the non-fiction *A Grunt Speaks: A Devil's Dictionary of Vietnam Infantry Terms.*

Ray and his wife, Jan Peyser, an award-winning silver smith / jeweler, share their time between Indiana and Chicago.